RW DUDER

Desolation

Second edition

This book was professionally typeset on Reedsy. Find out more at reedsy.com

1

The Travelers

"...silence, the harsh scream of nature. She is white and pure, and yet dark and twisted in her soul. This is the heart of the storm," the calm female voice recited on the local radio station. It was a university student station that read classic poetry and novels after 8 PM on weeknights.

"Say it again, sweetheart," Mark grumbled as he leaned forward and ran the palm of his right hand across the windshield to clear some of the condensation that was building on the inside. The windshield wipers were angrily sliding back and forth at breakneck speed serving only to prevent the buildup of snow on the windshield than really helping Mark's vision.

The snow and ice had been pounding against the car since he turned onto the highway nearly twenty miles ago. This trip was gradually getting worse and the drone of the woman reading some poem on the radio wasn't helping at all. Mark Harrison wasn't new to this kind of treacherous February weather. He had seen every type of weather that the Jersey winter had to throw at him. Mark had been in state law enforcement for the better part of twenty years. At 45 he was beginning to feel like a senior on the force, since so many of the new guys and girls on the state troopers were less than thirty. The last few days he had been in Philadelphia at a convention on profiling with a speaker from the FBI. The real FBI...first time Mark had ever met anyone from the one and only, infamous, American intelligence company.

Mark's superior was insistent on him going, given he was currently the lead on an investigation that the media had dubbed the "King County Killer." Mark glanced beside him at the pile of light blue folders on the passenger seat. The folders contained evidence, witness statements and victimology for the KCK case that he had turned to the FBI and fellow law enforcement officers at the conference for guidance on. He was returning with some valid ideas and information for his superior but truth be told Mark didn't think he was any further ahead than when he left. He would keep that to himself for now. Mark was a young looking 45 but had the eyes of an experienced man. He was well built and had all his own thick dark hair which also seemed like a rarity in the police department. Mark had always been very laid back and while he took his job incredibly serious, he also tried to never let it get to him. He took things in stride. This King County killer was beginning to challenge his laid back demeanour.

Seven women over the course of two months had been killed. It began November 4 and ended with the last victim in January, nearly two months later to the day. All seven women were mid-twenties and killed outside or near their places of employment and with the exact same M.O. The women were stabbed five times each. One of the victims had been stabbed an additional sixth time which Mark had decided, after careful investigation, was an accident because she wouldn't stay submissive. After the unidentified subject stabbed them five times he would cut their throat in a clear and concise manner, straight across the jugular. The stabs he inflicted were never fierce or passionate but rather slowly executed in a distinct pattern. This killer enjoyed killing. The throat being cut was always post-mortem. With each death his kills were becoming more frequent, which according to the FBI analyst was a sign the killer was becoming more comfortable with his practice. No sexual battery and no evidence left behind. The throats were cut methodically, left to right, with a razor sharp knife which was unnecessary since they were already dead. All the victims were not only of the same approximate age and sex but they were all minorities, African American, Native American, and Asian American. All of the women had smooth, clear complexions and long dark hair. It was a fetish of some kind, or a calling card.

"In 500 meters, turn left," the robotic female navigation voice said suddenly, breaking Mark's train of thought. He slowed his SUV and looked down below the radio where his guidance monitor was. He had only been able to drive between twenty and thirty miles/hr for the last fifty miles but it had been a straight line. The only thing he could see from the highway was the occasional building or hillside barely visible but looking shadowed and angry in the increasingly pelting snow. The navigation had said nothing since he got on the highway and he had all but forgotten about it. He reached over and switched off the radio. If he hadn't been distracted thinking about his case he would have been treated to the beginning of a vocal documentary on the mating habits of bees. There were only a handful of cars that had been traveling in his direction and he had seen even less on the east bound lane across the cement median that separated the highway. He had passed only one other car going the same direction as he was in the last fifteen minutes. That car lasted less than two minutes in his rear view mirror before it disappeared into the snowy blizzard. Mark had silently wished them luck and safety on their trip.

"In 200 meters, turn left," the navigation insisted again. Mark smirked and shook his head. Why had he fallen into the latest fad and paid two hundred dollars for this piece of junk with the fake voice. Mark was traveling west on the highway which meant any left turn he could make would mean turning into the median. This was the first time he noticed the navigation blatantly misleading him since he had installed it. Maybe

it was angry that he had buyer's remorse and would probably put it in a box and hide it in his closet when he got home and forget that he had ever tried to rely on it. He picked it up and held it out in front of him so he could watch the road at the same time. The map clearly showed where he was. It seemed accurate.

"When it is safe to do so, do a U-Turn."

"Excuse me?" Mark said aloud and shook his head.

"Please connect USB. Please connect USB. Please connect USB."

"Damnit," Mark muttered. He pulled out the plug from the cigarette lighter and for a brief moment it made him want to smoke. He had quit three years ago when his doctor informed him that his shortness of breath might get worse if he didn't kick the habit. He tossed the navigator to the seat beside him on top of his files and once again leaned forward to run his hand over the inside of the windshield. It didn't matter how bad it got, he had no intention of stopping until he got home. He looked at his dashboard clock. 9:52 PM. He leaned back and stretched in his seat. He heard and felt the pleasurable pop of his back. Being cramped in the car and being tensed up over this weather made for very stiff bones. He could have stopped for a break, in fact he had passed a rest stop exit only a few miles ago, but he didn't want this to get any worse if that was possible. A car appeared, on the opposite side of the interstate heading east, going just a little faster than what Mark had been driving. Instinctively Mark tried to peer inside the car. It looked like a family but it was impossible to know for sure given the visibility.

"Maps are being updated. Maps are being updated. Maps are being updated."

Mark sighed out loud and looked at the stupid machine beside him. He thought it was just being annoying at first but now, clearly, it was not working properly. He reached over and hit the green button below the screen and it went black. It was pointless to even have it on.

As he sat back up, he glanced at the dashboard again. 9:56, it felt later than that. Driving in this weather was stressful, even if he was accustomed to it. The wind suddenly seemed to pick up and he could hear the pounding weather against his SUV. A gust that literally felt like it could tip the vehicle over made him grasp the wheel with both hands. The snow surrounded the car, beating against the windshield. Mark braked and slowed to barely 10 miles an hour. He leaned forward in his seat to try and peer through the mess in front of him.

"You have reached your destination. Destination. Destination. Destiuhhh...usb...left turn, U...destinatuhhh."

"Oh come on, what in the hell."

He glanced over at his navigation unit which must have rebooted instead of powering down. Mark intended to pick it up and make sure it stayed out of the rest of this trip when he heard a humming. He paused and listened closely. Was it the vehicle? He had only bought the SUV last year and had never had a single problem with it. He had never used it for extreme police work so no chases, no gun fights, and no misuse of any kind, other than this awful winter weather. The hum was distinctive. It almost sounded like it was part of the wind. "Geez," Mark whispered. The snow was blinding and if it got any worse he wouldn't have any choice but to try and pull over and turn on his hazard lights.

The humming was getting louder, there was no doubt. Mark glanced in his rear view mirror and then at the road ahead and then back to the mirror. There were lights moving towards him. It wasn't a set of lights or a distant car moving towards him, but it was bright. There was no break in the snow anywhere around his car and yet the brightness before him was unmistakable. The car rocked with another gust and snow and ice pelted the truck. He was barely crawling now as the hum began to intensify. He had to stop, if not for just a moment, and get his bearings. He signaled to move into the other lane, while still watching behind him and in front of him to see if perhaps a snow-plow was coming on strong. Mark winced. It came as a surprise but the humming was becoming so noticeable that it actually made him wince. The light seemed to be getting brighter and the humming was louder.

For the first time a fearful thought crossed his mind. Was something wrong with him? Was he having a heart attack? A stroke? Some sort of brain aneurysm. There couldn't be much worse of a time for any of that. Not that there was ever a good time for his body to revolt against him but he was stuck in a blizzard in the middle of...hell...he didn't know where he was exactly. He moved to where he figured the shoulder was and stopped the car, putting it in park. No sooner had he switched gears then the humming became a shriek inside his brain. It pierced his eyes and the noise and light became unbearable. Mark cried out in spite of himself and remembered looking one last time in his mirror before he clenched his eyes shut. His hands went to his head and he bent over the steering wheel as the shrieking enveloped everything around him. A brilliant flash and a wall of light passed over his SUV. His eyes were shut but he could almost feel the light wash over his car as though it were scanning the roadway. Though Mark couldn't see it, the wall of light was probably three meters wide and moving fast and then it was directly over him. Moments later, the shriek subsided to a hum and then began to fade away.

Mark looked up and could distantly see the same light that had been in front of him now moving away from him behind the SUV. A single tear rolled from his eyes from clenching them so tightly. The wind seemed to have died down but the snow hadn't let up in the least. In fact, the snow was thicker than before but the silence around the vehicle was deafening. There was nothing...he swore he couldn't even hear the storm outside anymore.

2

"Damn," Eric Green mumbled. His young wife stirred in her seat. Somehow she had managed to drift off once both kids were fast asleep in the back seat of their family van. The fact that she was able to fall asleep pissed him off. The weather was awful. They should have never left his parents' place with weather building like this. Now they were still more than three hours from home and that was on a good day. This was not a good day...or rather night. He looked at the red LED clock on the dashboard which read 9:58. Eric felt like time was crawling. He could have sworn he had looked at that clock twenty miles ago and it said the same thing. He shook his head and peered into the wasteland that used to be the highway. He could just barely see a red set of tail lights ahead of him through the blistering snow.

Eric wondered how far ahead the car actually was. There were so few cars on the road but he almost felt relief whenever he saw another one. It meant they weren't the only ones stupid enough to be out in this mess. His wife yawned and he glanced over at her. He wasn't actually pissed at her, he loved her. She was beautiful. Andrea was 33 and Eric was 35. They had met in college and never looked back. They had been married ten years but together for three more than that. Eric's life was practically idyllic. They had two beautiful children, Hannah the ever curious and sweeter than sugar seven year old and Dane their hilarious and campy five year old that kept them constantly chasing him and often laughing.

Both children were thankfully asleep, which was good because they would likely be sensing his tension right now driving in this mess. The van lurched to the side and slid on the front tires. Eric snapped to attention and gripped the wheel, pulling it back to the proper direction. Slipping like that always made his heart pound. He breathed deeply and slowed the van to a practical crawl. His wife sat up and rubbed her eyes. She had only been sleeping for a few miles. “Are you okay?” she asked, reaching across the center console and touching his arm.

Eric shrugged. “Comparatively...I suppose,” he replied, trying to smile. She looked out the windshield and then out her own window. “This is awful.”

“It’s getting worse,” he said.

“Should we pull off somewhere?” she asked.

“Where?” he said, and immediately realized he had a tone to his voice. She sensed it most certainly, but said nothing.

“There are roadside stops here somewhere aren’t there?” She opened the glove box slowly so as to not wake the children. She pulled out the neatly folded New Jersey map and slipped it open to where they were. She always knew how to properly fold a map, he mused. Most people would have the huge paper trap opened from one end of the car to the other. “Hmm,” she said, her finger running along the interstate they had taken.

“What?” he asked, leaning in closer to the steering wheel and trying to find the tail lights he had seen a few moments earlier.

“There should be one ahead a few miles, and it says 24 hours too,” she said smiling.

“Do we really want to stop and risk this getting worse?”

“The risk would be staying on the road while it gets worse,” she said, quickly slipping the map back into its original shape and putting it back into the glove box. Eric sighed and knew he was beat before they started discussing it. Truth-be-told he could use a rest anyways.

"If we can spot the turn-off we will go to the rest stop."

"It's a center lane rest stop so the entrance will be on your left."

Eric spotted the tail lights ahead of him again. The car was much closer now. Apparently the storm had slowed both of them down significantly and their van was still going fast enough to close the gap between them. The car ahead was in the right lane of the two lane highway. Eric had tried to stay closer to the median in the left lane, not so that he could go faster but just for a sense of direction being able to watch the large cement barrier that ran through the middle of this section of the highway. "There's a car," his wife said, pointing out the obvious and secretly annoying the hell out of Eric but he kept that to himself. They gained enough speed that they were going to overtake the small red Honda. The driver was clearly riding his brakes. Eric found the heavy van challenging and he could only imagine what driving that little car was like on these slick roads with visibility practically nil.

Andrea looked over as they passed by them. Two men, one probably in his fifties and the other probably her age maybe a little younger, looked back at her. The driver waved and bowed his head at the same time. Both men were wearing dark shirts and white collars.

They're priests, she thought to herself. She looked at her husband. "Priests," she said.

"Huh?" he replied, trying to see through any open patches in the snow. It was really building on the road too. "The people in the other car...two men...they're priests." "Praise the Lord," Eric muttered and then smirked.

"Funny," Andrea replied. She looked out the window again and the two priests in the car seemed to be deep in discussion. The van pulled away until Eric and Andrea could barely see the Honda's lights behind them. The snow seemed to only get heavier.

"Watch for the sign," Eric said, turning on the defroster for the front and back windows. The couple both peered through the blinding white snow. If there was anything on this normally insanely busy highway that shouldn't be there in this desolate icy wasteland it would be near impossible to see it coming. Same could be said for their van. Although, Eric did notice the priests' car in advance but that was probably more luck than anything else.

"Sign!" Andrea said suddenly and louder than he expected.

"Geezus Andi," Eric said. There was distinct movement in the back seat. Hannah or Dane were awake, maybe both. It would definitely be time for a break if the kids were up and distracting Eric.

"Sorry," she mumbled. "It was hard to see it until we were right at it."

"Speaking of which," he said suddenly. Andrea braced her hand against the dashboard as Eric braked. The van slid dangerously and he pulled to the centre of the road slightly. She wondered what he was doing until she noticed the precariously parked, old, dark blue, rusted Ford Mustang on the roadside or where the roadside would have been normally.

A young man, wearing nothing more than an old University of Pennsylvania sweatshirt, had the hood of his car up and looked at the van as it slid to a crawl right next to his car. He waved casually and Eric and Andrea peered out the driver's side window at him. There was someone in the passenger's seat of his car as well. Andrea thought it was a girl but couldn't be sure given the snow was coming in at such an angle and so heavy that they could barely see the median. Eric slowed the van to a stop and reached for the electric window button.

"Eric," Andrea started to protest. She had grown up close enough to less than desirable areas of Philadelphia and had been taught safety first and never forgot it.

"Its fine, I'm just checking on them." Andrea looked at him anxiously. "It's minus twenty out and he's barely got a jacket on."

"Hello," the young man from the Mustang yelled over the howling wind. Snow slipped in the driver's window of the van making Eric wince at the icy wind.

"Y'okay?" Eric yelled back.

The man closed the hood of his car. The woman inside the car, Eric could clearly see long blonde hair and a feminine face, leaned across to see who the man was talking to. He jogged over to the van and Eric looked in his rear view mirror. He hoped he had put enough distance between him and the priests before they came on them too quickly. "Hazard lights babe," Eric said.

Andrea reached over and hit the switch for the blinking red lights. "Daddy, snow is a'fallin," Dane said from the back seat. Andrea turned to tend to him and Hannah, who was just starting to wake up. The mustang man approached the car. He was younger than Eric had initially thought and had dirty blonde hair and was very skinny. "What a night to be stuck," Eric said, as the boy got to the window.

He looked inside the van, which kind of made Eric uncomfortable but then he was probably being cautious as well.

"Yah, no kidding," the kid replied. He wrapped his arms around himself and his teeth were chattering. Andrea could have sworn he was starting to go blue. "Got a cell?" he asked.

"I don't know if you'll find anyone to come out in this crap," Eric replied and immediately could see the kid didn't care and just wanted to try. Poor guy. "Yah I got one right here." He reached into his centre console and pulled out the dark coloured Nokia flip phone. He looked at the digital clock on the front of it. 9:43 PM. Eric pondered that for a moment. Something about that perplexed him but he didn't give it much thought. He handed the phone to the kid who gladly took it and feverishly began dialing. Eric was glad he didn't ask to get in the van because he would have to draw the line there. This was about as much risk as he was willing to take. Eric glanced at the dashboard clock as he had a moment ago. It read 9:43 PM.

"It's late," Andrea said noticing her husband checking the time.

"It's not that...I checked it earlier and I could have sworn it was a few minutes to ten."

"Well, almost, which is why we need to get on the road or get to the rest stop," she replied with the tone. He knew the tone very well. It was the exact same tone she used as a mom when she was annoyed. She didn't like that he had stopped for this guy. If he hadn't stopped she'd probably be pissed that he drove by without helping, he thought to himself. It was yet another lose-lose man/woman situation.

Eric jumped when he noticed the Mustang kid was back at the window. He rolled the window down again and took the phone from his outstretched hand. "No service," the kid replied. Eric looked at the phone. Sure enough a tiny message at the top of the screen read 'No Service.' "Best network my ass," Eric whispered.

Andrea tugged on his arm and he glanced at her. "The road side stop," she whispered and he nodded.

"Hey man, we just saw a sign for a rest stop. You and your friend want a ride there?"

He looked at Eric and then back at the car. He seemed very hesitant, too hesitant. There were no other options out here at the moment and this storm wasn't stopping or showing signs of tapering off. It was far too long before the kid finally nodded and unwrapped his hands from around his chest. He still seemed hesitant.

"Yah...yah man, thanks. Okay. Just lemme get Sheila and some stuff." Eric nodded but Sheila's friend was already gone to retrieve her. The kid got into his car and the two seemed to be arguing. Eric could tell by the body language. Andrea sighed and handed her kids a small sandwich bag of soda crackers to keep them occupied. Hannah took hers gladly and Dane took his and proceeded to try and mash a cracker into his seat belt connector.

2

After a few moments Eric was beginning to get impatient. Sheila and Mustang kid finally looked like they were grabbing their things from the back seat of the car. Eric looked in his rear view mirror again and wondered where the priests were. If anything happened to them what chance do the rest of us have, he thought with a sly smile. His wife would be disgusted with his sacrilegious thoughts, however true they might be. He noticed what appeared to be the sky behind them looking brighter. It was likely just the snow building up because it certainly hadn't let up any. The windshield wipers were pumping like a super strength work out just to clear the crap off the window and hold off the build up. Eric suddenly felt a lump in his throat as he peered behind him. Was that a snow-plow? It was too bright to be the priests' little car. Was the sudden brightness behind the car standing still or coming towards them? "Shit," he muttered.

"Eric Green," his wife scolded.

Eric ignored her and threw the van into drive. "Daddy said a no-no naughty word," Dane called out from the back. Hannah smiled with her mouth full of soda cracker. Some of it spilled out onto her bright purple jacket.

"There's something on the road behind us and it might be coming towards us," Eric replied.

Andrea looked in the side mirror and then turned around to look over her shoulder.

"Mommy, see food," Hannah remarked, gaping open her mouth allowing more crackers to spill out.

"What is that?" she asked her husband, ignoring her daughter.

"Something I don't want wiping us off the road." Eric noticed that mustang kid and Sheila were both out of the car and looking behind them at the bright sky. It was getting brighter there was no doubt about it. Eric moved the van slowly forward and the crunch of the already building snow could be heard through the bottom of the car. He pulled the car over behind the Mustang as far as he could but it certainly didn't make him feel any safer. Anything coming through this mess would never see them especially if it was already barreling down the interstate and plows kept to the shoulder as it was. Eric parked the van and opened the driver's door. "Get behind the wheel," he instructed his wife. For once she didn't argue. She slid across the center console and into the driver's seat.

The snow slapped Eric's face hard. He zipped up his jacket and his breath iced out in front of him immediately. He was sure the radio had said the low tonight was going to be 10 degrees Fahrenheit but this felt like 0 or lower, easy. Wind-chill was an understatement. It felt like snow and ice were coming from every direction. It was like all the nasty winter elements had met in this spot to wage the war to end all wars. The sky was getting brighter; it almost seemed to part the snow. Eric tapped the van's window and held up his hand to his wife telling her to wait one minute. She nodded and he jogged toward the trunk of the Mustang which was still open.

The guy was feverishly stuffing things into a duffel bag and Sheila was standing beside the passenger door staring into the heart of the storm where the brightness enveloped the entire sky. Eric reached him and put his hand on the guy's shoulder. He jumped and whirled around and Eric noticed he had sweat on his face. Sweat? Ten degrees and the guy was in nothing more than an old University hoodie? "We gotta go. I think that's a plow coming."

"I'll just walk to the stop, take my girl," he yelled back over the howl of the storm. Eric glanced in the trunk. Spare tire, old books, a tool box, a wrench outside the tool box and a jack. The duffel bag was sitting inside the trunk and he hadn't zipped it up yet. Sitting on top was what looked like some sort of weapon...a gun to be exact. Eric had never seen a real gun in his life outside of on a cop's belt, or something of the like, but he wasn't stupid. The guy followed Eric's gaze and grabbed the duffel bag and zipped it up, tossing it over his shoulder and slamming the trunk closed.

"Between me and myself mister," he replied. Eric was sure he could hear a plow coming. It was a dull hum, probably the sound of the massive metal shovel scraping the highway. He wondered why they would bother plowing when it would snow-over in seconds and why in the hell was this plow coming up their side of the road. "Sheila, get in the van," Mustang boy yelled. The girl didn't respond. "Sheila, I'm talkin' to you." Eric began to realize this was not the best situation to be in. His head was starting to pound probably because of the cold. "What the hell is that noise?" the guy yelled to no one in particular.

"I think it's the plow," Eric yelled back. The light moved towards them but still no headlights or spinning orange light to warn of the oncoming danger. Eric stumbled over and braced himself on the trunk of the car. The guy yelled at Sheila again who still refused to move and was staring right into the snow and the bright light. He looked over at Eric.

"Hey man," he yelled at him. Eric looked up, his eyes aching and the humming pounding at his ears now. The guy motioned with his hand across his nose. Eric reached up and put his bare hand under his own nose and took it away. Blood. It looked thick and dark and brutally red against all this white. A spot dropped to the snow drenched highway and to Eric it looked like a huge pool of red against everything else.

"Geez," Eric muttered under his breath. The light hit them. It was nothing he could describe except that the humming sounded like a power converter flying overhead and the light was like a thick spotlight from an airplane passing over. Eric cried out from the pain shooting through his head. Both hands were now propped on the back of the Mustang and he had no idea where the guy or Sheila was. He could only pray that they weren't heading to the van with that gun. The guy did say he was going to walk; maybe he wasn't a threat to him or his family.

Back in the van, Andrea's head was throbbing and the kids were crying. At least one of them was crying she was sure of it. She tried to turn to face them but the humming was worse and she was sure something was passing over them. My God, was it an airplane? In this mess? She had barely enough time to think anything else before there was complete silence. And then the silence was broken by the unmistakable sound of her daughter crying. Andrea was about to turn around when the back sliding door of the van flew open. A burst of cold air and snow breathed into the van and someone jumped in. "Eric?" she said, trying to look into her mirror.

"Drive," said the voice, which was unmistakably younger than Eric's. She looked over her shoulder only long enough to see the young man from the Mustang. He had a duffel bag and was clearly out of breath. "Drive dammit," he screamed.

"My husband," she protested.

"Lady, you wanna save your kid, I suggest flooring it now. We're like a half mile from that rest stop so he can walk."

Andrea had no choice. She was scared and didn't know what was going on. Against her common sense, she put the car in drive and pulled away. She tried to look in the mirror again but saw nothing but the snow flying behind the car and a dark back seat. She could make out the shadow of the intruder but other than that nothing. Hannah was still crying but there was nothing from Dane. Perhaps he was in awe of the lights and noise although whatever that noise was it was hardly anything to be in awe of. There was one last sign proclaiming the next exit was to the rest stop. It featured every possible icon of a rest stop haven. Food, washrooms, entertainment and lodging although someone had nailed a piece of wood across the lodging as though that were no longer a feature. Andrea breathed deeply. She would drop the guy off and go back for Eric. Once they got to the stop, Andrea would offer generously to go get his girlfriend or sister or whoever she was.

Hostage? The thought crossed her mind and then she pushed it aside.

She maneuvered the van into the exit lane and put on her signal light which was mostly a waste of time. Who was she signalling?

Hannah was sobbing now, deep and serious to her. "It's alright baby, Mommy's here," Andrea said. "...sir...sir is my son okay back there?"

"What?" he asked. He was distracted, she could tell. He seemed scared, out of breath. Had he done something to Eric during that light passing over?

"My son, is he okay?"

"Your daughter? Yah she's fine. Just a little snot nosed aren't ya kid?"

"Yes, that's Hannah but my son in the car seat, is he alright? He's just not usually this quiet."

"Lady there ain't no other kid back here."

The words felt colder than the snow around them. As she pulled around the bend in the off ramp she could just barely make out lights that looked like a parking lot and maybe even the distant glow of a window. It almost made her feel better. She leaned up and looked in the mirror again. She reached down and turned on the inner light that hung over the middle of the car. The light came on and the guy who was perched in the back seat cringed at it. Hannah was there. She could see the top of her head and the pony tail which was perfectly pulled to one side just as she had been the last time Andrea had looked at her. There was no one else in the van that she could see. She adjusted the mirror downward where she knew she could see Dane and the car seat. The spot was empty. The man was sitting just to the left of where Dane should be.

She swallowed hard. "Where in the hell is my son?" she screamed. That made Hannah start crying again.

The guy reached up and rubbed his temples beneath his thick mop of blonde hair which was wet from the snow melting on it. "Lady, seriously, are you insane?" Andrea slammed on the brakes. It was about the stupidest thing she could have done, given how slippery off ramps were even in the lightest of snow. The van lurched to the right and began to fish tail across the road. Hannah screamed louder and the guy was jostled forward. Andrea could not concentrate enough to get the van back under control and they began to slide sideways. The car spun once just in time to find the open part of the parking lot which was graciously empty. One more spin and the van came to a stop cockeyed across an eighteen wheeler parking spot. She reached for her seat belt and frantically pulled it off. Turning around in her seat she practically threw herself into the back. "Where is Dane? Where is my son?" she screamed.

The Mustang man threw his hands up, his duffel bag parked over his shoulder like an army cadet going on a camping trip. Ironically, the duffel bag was camouflage but no one would mistake the skinny, mop haired kid as military, but rather following some sort of fashion trend that often included camo pants and a hat to match. But this kid was wearing blue jeans and a hoodie in the worst winter storm of the year. "Lady relax, relax," he hollered. Hannah was literally screaming now at the top of her lungs, tears streaming down her face and a pile of half eaten soda crackers in her lap. The guy, against his better judgment reached up and grabbed Andrea Green's shoulders. Her face was throbbing with anger and fear. "Did your husband take him?" he tried saying but he knew that was ridiculous. The woman's husband had not been toting some kid when he approached the Mustang and you'd have to be brain dead to pull a kid from his car seat and take him out in this mess.

"He's gone, he's gone," she moaned in the most eerie voice he had ever heard.

"Lady...lady...what's your name, what's your name?" he asked trying to get her attention.

"Dane...Dane is gone."

He had no choice. God knows he wasn't opposed to hitting women. He had shown Sheila the back of his hand many times and even his forehead in what turned out to be a rather poor decision to head-butt her during a drunken fight. He didn't want to hit this lady but she was clearly hysterical and he suspected that there was only one way to get through to someone like that. The next sound was the slap of his palm hitting her face. It stopped her, stopped her in her tracks. Andrea was lucky enough to never have had anyone hit her, man or woman, under any circumstances until this moment.

Her hand went to her cheek which was already red from the slap. It wasn't hard but hard enough to get the point across. Sometimes women needed a reminder of who was in charge, the guy thought to himself. The adults in the car were silent but Hannah never stopped to take a breath in her screaming frenzy. If he really wanted to be a douche bag he'd smack the kid too but he'd leave that for an emergency situation.

"Ann...Andrea," she whispered.

"Huh?" he asked, almost as shocked as she was.

"My name...is Andrea."

"Okay. Okay good. Andrea. My name is Josh. Josh Barton."

The two were silent for several minutes until Josh couldn't take the crying anymore from the hysterical little girl. "Please, stop her from crying,"

Andrea reached over and stroked Hannah's face. "It's alright baby. It's going to be okay."

Hannah still sobbed but the simple touch from her mother calmed her significantly.

"Sir...Josh...where is my son?" Andrea asked. Her eyes were less frenzied and it made Josh feel a little less harried himself. The wind was rocking the van and it sounded like the snow and ice were desperate to get in. Since Andrea had stopped the van in the precarious spinning park job, the front windshield was already blanketed. Josh thought that it was beginning to feel dark and claustrophobic.

"I got in your van and your kid was crying and you were screaming but there wasn't no other kid in this van," he replied. He was trying to speak calmly. There were three solid knocks on the driver's side window and it made Josh and Andrea jump. Andrea whirled around and stared out the window. The man standing there was bundled tightly in a winter jacket with a fur lining and a large hood. He looked like a well dressed snow monster. His face looked somehow familiar to Andrea. He was tall and slim, well over six feet, and older. His eyes were kind and looked like he had seen his share of battles of various kinds. He had a thin brown mustache that didn't really suit him either.

His muffled voice came through the window but the wind prevented any of it from making sense. Andrea reached over hesitantly and lowered the window a crack. The icy cold air seeped in. "Everything okay?" the man repeated. Andrea stuttered and could feel tears welling in her eyes.

"My s...my son...is missing. He was in the car and now he is gone and my husband is out there...he's out there, my Eric..." Andrea stuttered.

The man nodded compassionately. "Why don't you come out miss and come inside where we can straighten this out."

She had already allowed this young stranger...Josh as he was now known...into her van and now her son was missing and she wasn't going to be stupid enough to let herself get into any more trouble. The man obviously sensed her hesitation and unzipped his coat down to his chest. He pointed inside his coat and suddenly Andrea knew exactly where she had seen him. He was one of the priests from the car they had passed. How had he gotten here ahead of them? No one had passed them while they were on the side of the road with Josh and Sheila. Josh and Sheila? Referring to them as that, even in her head, made it sound like they were family friends. *You and Eric doing anything Tuesday? Oh, just playing bridge with Josh and Sheila.*

She unlocked the door and the priest opened it for her. He offered his hand to her and Andrea took it. Andrea could hardly hold back her tears and the cold wind made it worse. Josh looked at the two of them and shook his head. He had sensed Andrea's hesitation in opening the door in the first place for the man. "Are you kidding? A priest is even less reason to open the door," Josh said, mostly to himself, and smirked.

The wind howled around them as they got out of the van. Andrea reached across where Josh had been sitting and unbuckled Hannah and scooped her into her arms. Hannah's crying had subsided and she seemed more in awe of everything going on. Andrea expertly zipped up Hannah's coat and held her close allowing her to bury her face into her mother's shoulder. Josh closed the sliding door and the four of them made their way across the parking lot, struggling against the fierce wind with the snow stinging their faces.

3

"*What a friend we have in Jesus, all our sins and griefs to bear*," he sang quietly, almost to himself. His mother had sung him that song a thousand times. Sometimes when his mind got cloudy and confused it was the only thing that made him see clearly. Well, not the only thing but a close second. He made his way down the highway going far too fast. He wasn't doing the 65 miles that the highway allowed by any means or he and his passenger would likely be in a ditch frozen solid... especially his passenger. He glanced over at his lovely co-traveler. She said nothing. He wondered how long it had been since she spoke. "You're very quiet," he said. Nothing. No response. The storm that was becoming disastrous didn't seem to bother her. "Does my singing bother you?" he asked. He turned the heat on one more click higher just to make sure the car stayed defrosted. It was getting a little chilly after all. He pushed his thin rimmed glasses up on his nose and glanced in the mirror.

"I used to be in a choir you know," he stated matter-of-factually. The girl didn't lift her head from the window. She was enjoying the view or lack thereof. "I can tell Peter, you have a lovely voice," Peter said in a high pitched mocking tone. "Eh, whatever. We can drive in silence, I'm used to it." They drove a few more miles. Peter Oswald was an insurance agent. He had been in insurance for eighteen of his thirty-eight years. He had seen every corner of the United States but especially every corner of New Jersey, New York and Pennsylvania. His main office was out of Pittsburgh. He had driven the highways in every type of weather imaginable and this was no exception.

Peter's mother lived in Washington DC, and he had a brother down in South Dakota whom he never saw. He had never been married because, according to him, his career and his hobbies were all he needed. Both allowed him to meet plenty of people. "Would you care for some music?" he asked. Still nothing. He leaned forward and looked at the young girl beside him. Maura? Maureen? He couldn't remember exactly what she said her name was. At a rest stop near Rochester she had been hitchhiking at the off ramp. Peter figured the company would be nice and she even offered to pay for gas. She was going to Ithaca and Peter was going there as well so it worked famously.

The girl was pretty and in her early twenties and looked exhausted when Peter picked her up. They had only stopped once after that for a quick washroom break, coffee and some small talk. She wasn't much of a talker and Peter was beginning to wonder if she would be much company at all. He would do his best to get to know her on the trip or at least take a stab at it. Her eyes were closed and her head was resting against the window. The window was probably freezing cold but she looked peaceful. He nodded and turned his attention back to the road. "Rest well Mauraaa...whatever your name is," he whispered and turned on the radio. The station he usually had on in this area was nothing but static. He should have asked for a car with satellite radio...at least then he could listen to some proper business news.

Finally, Peter was able to tune into a talk radio station. The announcer was chuckling at something witty he had just said. He had no idea whether anyone else in radio land found what he said amusing and didn't care. That made Peter smile. "Government says we are no longer in a recession but investments are down, profits are down, retail and sales are down...who is it over for?" the man exclaimed.

"Amen brotherrr," Peter said in a fake southern accent.

"You know what is up? Insurance! Everyone wants to protect themselves from everything out there."

Peter's spirits rose and he jumped boisterously in his seat. "Oh, speak the truth my brother," he hollered and looked over at his silent companion and immediately realized he was being loud. He giggled and quieted down but she didn't stir.

"Out of all the people in the world who are making money it's the insurance agents. Like Peter Oswald, he's completely raping the insurance world," Deke Aikens from Q103.3 out of Detroit somewhere said feverishly.

"What?" Peter said snapping back to his reality, hearing his name.

"Yah Oswald, cleaning up, taking advantage of old ladies and young ladies. Different advantages but same ideas...take everything from them eh Pete?"

"Hey screw you pal," Peter said, yelling into the radio.

"Peter, you're talking to your radio. Does that seem normal to you?" Deke responded.

"Uh hello...you spoke to me first," Peter replied.

"How much money did you make on this trip? How many policies did you get for perfectly young healthy people that you scared into signing on the dotted line?"

"People die every day at any age," Peter defended. His sudden change in emotion was causing the car to swerve dangerously from one side of the highway to the other. The ice under the tires threatened to send the car flying across its slick surface. "Like that young girl with you there Peter? Is she in danger of dying? Does she need insurance?"

"Indubitably!" Peter hollered.

Deke chuckled again, a low and provoking chuckle. "Well...siggggn 'er up ol' Oswald."

Peter slammed his hands against the steering wheel. The car lurched towards the median. The snow was pelting the car from all sides and Peter hardly noticed. "It's too late for that now you stupid shit," Peter screamed. That was all that was required for the car to slip from his control. Black ice caught the front tires and the car was spinning hellishly. Peter hollered and instead of grabbing the wheel, his hands flew to his head. The car spun and a loud high pitched hum assaulted his senses. It invaded his brain. He couldn't even look over at Mary. Mary that was her name! Wasn't it? Why wasn't she awake? She hadn't even stirred. Her seat belt wasn't that tight. Peter groaned as they spun and the relentless humming continued. Where was that median? Why wasn't the car smashing into the cement? There was a ditch on the other side of the road...that wouldn't be so bad and the snow would have made a significant pillow of resistance to stop the spinning.

Peter couldn't even hear the radio anymore and he could feel the headlights flashing all around him...or was it something else. The humming sound, like electric voltage, was burning into his brain and the flashing lights and spinning car overwhelmed him. Peter vomited. It hit the steering wheel and splashed back at him making him gag even more.

The light subsided as did the humming and the right side of the car crunched into the cement median. This finally stopped the spinning. The car slid violently along the cement and finally lurched to a stop. There was dead silence everywhere around them except for the angry wind and, with it, more snow. The car was now completely stopped and the snow was already burying it.

Peter could see and hear his own breath. The car heater had stopped and the ice was building in seconds. He moved his head around just slightly. Nothing felt out of place. His head was spinning but nothing was broken he didn't think. He carefully looked over at his passenger. Mary...Maureen...whatever the hell her name was, she was clearly not in good shape. She was slumped over and her seat belt was now awkwardly pinning her against the door. There was no getting out that side. "Well girl this is the end of the line for us apparently." He looked out his own window and across the highway. He could see how bad the roads were from where he was. He shouldn't have been going that fast. He was always so cocky. That was because he had such amazing insurance coverage he thought and then grinned.

He peered out into the wasteland that was formerly one of the busiest highways in New Jersey. There was a sign in front of where the car had come to a stop. He could read it...maybe. He reached up and cleaned the condensation off his glasses. He couldn't see the sign. Against his better judgment he rolled down the window. The icy wind would make anyone cringe and yet it felt good against his face. It made him thankful that, when all was said and done, he was okay even if Mary Maureen was not. He looked into the driving snow but still couldn't read the sign. Fortunately whoever came up with road signs created the brilliance of those infamous icons. Food, shelter, gas...it was a rest stop. That was good enough for him. Peter pulled on his door handle and miraculously it was fine. The door opened as though nothing had happened. Before getting out he reached into the backseat and grabbed his jacket.

He liked this jacket because it looked good over a tie.

He jumped from the car and closed the door. He had left the window open and leaned back in. "Darling, I'll be back for you. Don't go away now." With that he turned away from the car and walked across the highway. He didn't figure there was any need to look both ways in this case. It was strange to think he was standing in the middle of the highway. He shielded his face from the driving snow and walked over to the sign and looked up at it. It was a rest stop all right and the sign clearly read 1 Mile. He could handle that on a normal day but would he make it in this? "No other choice," he whispered to himself. He covered his head with his hood and stuck his hands in his pocket. With one more glance at his car he headed in the direction of the rest stop.

4

This was just ridiculous, Mark thought. This was the nastiest trip he had ever had on this road or any other for that matter. He turned the heat down slightly once the windshield finally cleared up again. He would have to repeat this ritual with the heat in a few minutes. When he looked ahead of him he could distantly see a light...maybe two lights. They weren't red so he doubted they were tail lights. It wasn't bright enough to be that awful thing that had passed over him earlier. The windshield wipers were still working overtime and each time they proceeded to the down position he spotted the distant lights. He vaguely wondered if he had actually found whatever it was that had gone over top of him earlier. These lights weren't nearly as bright though and as he approached them he realized they were blinking. Years of state trooper experience made him realize that this was a road block. It looked like they had closed the highway and yet there had been no official car that he had seen. Maybe they were just setting up, but in his opinion he would have closed the road hours ago. This entire highway was practically impassable. Still he knew where he was and he knew where he needed to go and Mark would play his employment card to be let through in order to get home. He knew what he could handle and more importantly what his truck could handle. It was four-wheel-drive, with every possible amenity for a reason and this was one of them.

He approached what turned out to be exactly what he had expected, a road block. It was a long orange barrier with two flashing lights on top. The median had stopped in this section of the highway and there was a space where they could easily put barriers across both sides of the road. Normally, their barriers had *State Trooper* across the top in white reflector tape but this one was just orange. This wasn't particularly alarming given they did often borrow barriers from various city works departments when necessary. The part that did strike Mark as strange was that there was no one around the barrier. There was no car, no truck, and no official vehicle of any kind anywhere to be seen. Mark stopped inches from the barrier and turned on his high-beams which were useless. The bright lights only reflected the increasing snow blowing in every direction. It seemed to be even heavier in the direction he was heading.

He rolled down the window and leaned out, peering into the dark white hole that the snow was making ahead of him. Maybe they closed the road now because it was even worse ahead although he couldn't imagine that. He leaned on his horn twice. The sharp noise cut through the air but seemed to make no difference. Mark opened the door and got out. The wind hit him hard and he stumbled backwards. He held his hand up to shield his face and could swear he saw someone crossing the road towards him. It was probably just a sign or his eyes playing tricks. The closer he looked the more he could see that there was definitely something moving beyond the barrier towards him. He would likely regret yelling out at some sort of inanimate object. "H...Hello?" Mark cried. It probably wasn't even loud enough given the howling wind. "Hello, anyone there?" Mark yelled again, louder this time. He braced himself against the front of the car still holding his hand up.

A dark shadow moved towards him. There was no doubt now that someone was out there with him. The orange lights on the barrier did nothing for his vision. Instead it only turned the heavy white flakes into orange colored crystals as they came down. Shuffling, coming from the snow, moving slowly through the storm was the shrouded image of a person. “This is Mark Harrison, Trooper Mark Harrison!” he called out.

“Mr. Harrison,” came the reply from the storm. It was a man’s voice, older, mid 50’s perhaps but it was hard to tell. The shadow moved closer and the flashing lights finally revealed the man. He was wearing a bright yellow winter jacket. The hood covered his entire head. He was wearing thick dark leather gloves and what looked like heavy cargo pants. The yellow coat man was not covered in snow so Mark doubted he walked any distance. Maybe there was a vehicle off to the side but he saw no sign of that.

“Sir?” Mark replied. The man maneuvered around the barrier and walked to where Mark was. He was an older man as Mark suspected. He had a grey mustache and thick eyebrows. Other than that there were no particularly striking features about him outside of his bright yellow jacket.

“Hello Mr. Harrison,” the man said with an unusual hint of calm to his voice.

“Are you with the state troopers?” Mark asked, still having to raise his voice over the storm.

“Mr. Harrison, I’m going to have to ask you to get back in your vehicle and head back to the rest stop,” yellow coat man replied, ignoring Mark.

“Sorry?”

“The rest stop. You need to be at the rest stop. It’s a few miles back, you’ll have to do a U-Turn but I can assure you it will not be a problem out here.”

“I’ll be fine Mr...,” Mark asked, digging for an introduction.

“The rest stop is where you’ll need to go back to Mr. Harrison,” the man replied. He stood a few feet from Mark and ice was starting to build on his mustache. Mark’s face stung from the cold. It felt like it had dropped ten degrees since he got out of the truck. This man in the yellow jacket didn't seem to be bothered by the cold all that much.

Mark shook his head. "Sir, I'm with the New Jersey State Police and I'm going to need you to identify yourself."

"Oh Mr. Harrison, I'm afraid your status matters very little here," the man replied and Mark could see him smile. It was not a warm smile,

Mark thought about this a moment.

"Matters little here?" Mark questioned. "What does that mean exactly?"

"Here!" the man exclaimed raising his arms and turning around in a circle demonstrating that he meant here in the middle of nowhere, in the worst storm in years.

"I need to pass. I can get through this strip of road. I know it well," Mark replied.

"No sir. You need to return to the rest stop. There is nothing beyond these barriers."

Mark sighed exasperatingly. "Sir, identify yourself please."

"Mr. Harrison, there are people at the rest stop that will need you. You cannot pass through this barrier. I assure you it is extremely dangerous. I'm not even sure you would get anywhere."

Mark cursed and thought about where his cell phone was. He had it a few hours ago and then he had put it in his suitcase. It was nearly dead and he didn't have his car charger. "What's the problem?"

The man smiled and chuckled again, his breath coming out in thick fog. "The road ends here Mr. Harrison. You cannot go through and passing by me will not end well for you." Was that a warning or a threat? Mark wasn't sure and he was exhausted. He didn't feel like fighting with this stranger.

"If I go back to that rest stop, I'll be contacting my office," Mark replied.

"I doubt that Mr. Harrison," yellow coat man replied, waving his hand at him. He was turning to walk away.

4

Mark was tired and cold and more annoyed than angry. Maybe returning to the rest stop wasn't a bad idea. He had seen the sign for it just before that light had gone over his car. For the time being he was prepared to back down and go find it. Certainly his retreat to the car was not to be confused with weakness; he had no intention of letting this man get the better of him. He got back inside and turned the key in the ignition and it started with little protest. Mark looked up after starting the car and saw that the yellow coat man had stopped walking away and stood in front of the car. Mark turned on the headlights again. The lights flooded the man and all the snow driving down around him. Mark rolled down his window and leaned out. "I assure you sir that this will be a problem for you."

The man smiled and waved his hand as Mark put the car into reverse to turn around. He wished suddenly that he had not only brought the car charger for his phone but also brought his bubble light for the windshield, which would make the ride back at least safer. He could drive around the barrier and ignore the man but felt like that could be more dangerous. Maybe the man was being honest and there was some sort of accident or an impassable piece of highway. The circumstances still left Mark with an uneasy feeling in his mind.

After turning around in the snow he made his way carefully back up the other side of the road. He could see the barrier's lights in his rear-view mirror only momentarily before they disappeared in the storm. He could also make out the shadow of the man standing where he had been when Mark left. There was a distinct buzz from the back seat of the SUV. It was low but Mark heard it immediately. It was his cell. He was sure of it. He tried to reach behind him but his hand found nothing. He stopped the SUV long enough to look into the back. His cell was sitting in the center of the seat vibrating against the leather interior. He was sure he had packed it and yet there it was. Maybe this would solve the issue and he could turn back to the barrier once he called the local trooper detachment.

He grabbed the phone and looked at the small screen which displayed incoming callers. ***UNKNOWN NAME*** It looked like Asian letters of some kind. Mark, perhaps unfortunately so, had never been worldly. He had spent his adult life in law enforcement and had never learned anything besides a little bit of French and even less Spanish. Maybe the cold was wreaking havoc on his phone. It was after all a Panasonic and that was...Japanese? He thought so. He hit the green call button. "Hello," he growled into the phone as he headed back the way he had just come. The snow was coming straight at him which he could have sworn was the same as when he had been going east. The storm was simply everywhere.

The phone hissed back at him. "Hello?" he said again. The connection was clearly poor. "Best network my ass," Mark grumbled mostly to himself. There seemed to be a hissing noise from the phone. Mark held it away from his ear a few inches.

There was a distinct voice on the other end but it was indiscernible. Mark didn't think he heard anything at first. "*Fubuki no naka ni tojikomotte iruno*," said the whisper.

"Who is this?" he said. The SUV slid slightly and Mark pulled it back under control. "Hello?" he demanded. There was just silence. He looked at his cell screen again. The call had ended. He shook his head and tossed the phone onto the passenger seat. He felt like he was ignoring his instincts and that something was terribly wrong beyond this storm. It was only another mile before he saw the rest stop sign on the roadside. He turned his car into the lane and moved towards the exit ramp. Finally, he could see lights in the distance. Probably a parking lot, he thought. He looked at the console clock which read 9:43. What in the hell, he thought? The clock was wrong, clearly wrong. When had he looked at it last? It should be well after ten. He was into the parking lot now. There were three vehicles in the lot that he could see.

One mid-2000 blue Ford was parked directly in front of the large stone building. He only knew it was blue from the uncovered area around the wheels. The car was piled with snow, probably more than two feet on all sides of it. It had been there awhile.

There was a van parked ridiculously askew near the far end of the parking lot opposite from where he had come in. It looked familiar he thought, making a mental note of it. Another red car, which was far less covered in snow, was parked near the front of the building as well but several feet away from the buried Ford. It was building up some ice on it but it hadn't been there long.

Mark pulled into a row of spaces behind the red car. He put the SUV into park and turned his car off. Icy air seeped in the moment the ignition went off. Mark rubbed his hands together and got out of the vehicle. He clicked the automatic lock on the key chain and the headlights blinked verifying all was safe from the horde of car thieves out tonight. Mark stuck his hands in his coat pockets and made his way through the snow towards the glow of the rest stop's windows.

"Hey!" a voice called through the snow. More insanity to ignore, Mark thought. "Hey man," the voice yelled again. Mark looked over his shoulder and was treated to another face full of blinding snow and cold wind. There was a thin looking man in a very small winter jacket making his way across the parking lot. He could have come from the stupidly parked van but it looked dark and no one was inside when he pulled in. Mark paused and turned to face the man. The new stranger picked up his pace and jogged up to Mark. He had no hat on and had thin rimmed glasses. His face was red and almost blue in other places. His ears were bright red, the color of blood, they were so cold.

"Y'okay?" Mark said.

"My car...," the man was out of breath and looked terrible. "I had a car accident and had to walk..." Mark motioned for the man to follow him and they walked to the overhang at the front of the rest stop. Both men banged out their coats and stomped their feet before Mark opened the swinging glass door. The middle foyer was no warmer than it was outside but at least it was relief from the snowfall. The two men stomped off the rest of the snow as best as they could. The stranger was far more covered than Mark was. He took a deep breath and smiled at Mark. He offered his hand which looked almost as red as his ears. Mark grasped it and shivered at how cold his hand actually was.

"Peter Oswald," the man said. He was breathing heavy. His lungs were probably practically frozen.

"Mark Harrison," he replied. Here was a guy who actually wanted to introduce himself, unlike yellow coat man and the cell phone caller.

"I had a car accident," Oswald said again, his voice raspy from the cold. "My car spun out on some ice and I saw the sign for the rest stop so I walked up the highway."

"How far back was that?" Mark asked.

"Sign said a mile."

"In this mess? You're a brave man."

"Walk to safety, die in the car, no option there," Peter replied and chuckled morbidly.

Mark nodded and opened the next set of doors into the rest stop.

5

It opened in the mid-eighties as the third rest stop along a huge expansion of highway. It was 57,000 square feet and was the largest rest stop anywhere along the highway from beginning to end. It was far more than just your average truck stop. It catered to practically every kind of traveller. Through two sets of double glass doors, with signs and stickers such as "VISA", "INTERAC" and the ever popular "NO SHIRT NO SHOES NO SERVICE" pasted on them. The stop featured three different types of food choices.

Inside on the far left was a small coffee shop. They served hot coffee, mocha, tea and any sort of hot beverage you could imagine. Their coffee could have been barely drinkable, given they were the only choice for many miles, but instead most people actually enjoyed it. In better weather, regular travelers even made this coffee shop a destination stop during their trip to enjoy the coffee, fill a thermos and continue on. They also served fresh baked donuts that were made in the small kitchen in the back. They prided themselves on fresh donuts so much that they sold off a bag of day-olds for two bucks just to make sure they were gone in 24 hours. The coffee shop was far from modern. Their old slat lettered menu had the coffee prices and the various other amenities listed. Coffee refills, it proclaimed, were free with drink in china cups. Not many travellers stuck around unless they had no other choice like on this particular night.

Next to the coffee shop was the bakery. It was the third largest space in the stop and had a fully equipped kitchen where all baking was done on site, which was impressive for a rest stop. Hot bread, buns and various types of sweet baked goods were extremely popular with travelers. The rest stop cakes were a well known treat for weary travelers along the highway.

Finally there was Big Mike's Eatery. This was the heart of the rest stop. Mike Otterman had put everything he owned into the rest stop ten years earlier. He had worked on a manufacturing line for over thirty years and was ready to retire. However, at 51 he just couldn't afford to do that and wanted something different. His wife died two years before that from breast cancer, she was only 48. He took his savings, everything they owned and her meager life insurance and bought the rest stop for nearly a million dollars. He was scared to death that it would ruin him. A man at his age should never take on such a responsibility and such an enormous risk let alone a million dollar property. The paperwork on the place looked good. It had turned a profit for the five years prior to Mike taking over and a decent profit too. The leases alone on the coffee shop, the bakery and the convenience store would pay his mortgage and he hoped to use the eatery as his own spot. Mike (Big Mike to his friends) loved to cook and he was damn good at it too. He had taken classes in his twenties but never followed it through as a career. Instead, he married and had two beautiful daughters and a lovely wife and never looked back but he was enamored at the idea of being able to cook professionally.

So everything fell into place and Big Mike Otterman started his second career at 51 years old. Ten years later and things had gone better than he could have ever expected. Not only had he turned a profit every year since then but profits had doubled the first year and stayed consistent since then making him very comfortable. People liked Big Mike. Not just those that worked in the rest stop, though they were like family to him, but anyone who came by the rest stop. Big Mike was never just cooped up in the kitchen. He made sure to come out on the floor and survey his rest stop and greet people. At Christmas he dressed as Santa for the children and at Halloween he was always a clown. He made decent balloon animals so it made sense. Now at 61 Big Mike felt like he had found what he loved to do. He worked nearly twelve hour shifts, usually around two in the afternoon until well after one in the morning. He didn't require a lot of sleep and he loved to be at the rest stop.

As you entered the double doors there was a large open concept convenience store on the left. You could get soda, snacks, cigarettes, lottery, cheesy romance novels and a few other terrible paperbacks that never sell anywhere else but in rest stops where choice is extremely limited. There was a large magazine rack against the wall with every possible magazine for every possible interest which was also a popular browsing point for tourists. This was where travelers discovered there were actually bi-weekly or monthly magazines on cats, woodworking, skiing and professional wrestling (which is ironically the furthest thing from professional.) Near the magazines was a rack with every map, for every area, in every direction for hundreds of miles. New Jersey was still the best seller. The store also carried a very small selection of T-Shirts that had terrible pictures on them like beavers, ridiculous looking moose, and even a red shirt with a bright yellow horse on it smiling and holding the New Jersey flag.

To the right of the front door was a long hallway. At the end of the hallway was a smaller secondary exit leading to the side parking lot. Also down this hallway were the men's and women's washrooms. If you stopped at the mouth of the hallway and turned to your left it would lead you to the large eating area with various booths and tables easily seating 75+ people if the need arose, which it wouldn't tonight. In the far corner of the eating area was a modern jukebox with CD's rather than records. It took a dollar rather than a quarter and that was for two songs. It wasn't used much but it was on Big Mike's Eatery's side of the stop and he liked it. He would often throw in a dollar to listen to some *Journey* or *REO Speedwagon* when it was really slow.

On the other side directly in front of the convenience store was a small entertainment arcade. There were three pinball machines, one was Gilligan's Island, one was Indiana Jones and the other was some sort of retro-arcade table that featured Pac-man look a-likes and Galaga knock offs. Then there were two actual arcade machines that had hunting and beat 'em up action to enjoy. And of course there was the necessary "prize machines." You know the classic "win a stuffed animal" by dropping the claw in the right way and another electronic machine where you had to stack bricks to win prizes. Big Mike was always impressed with how many people actually won prizes in both but he still made a profit and it made him happy that people had a good time.

Mark Harrison and Peter Oswald entered the rest stop. It was quiet, very quiet. Even through the thick stone walls the wind still howled but the air in the rest stop was decidedly warmer than outside. The heat was working very well. As quiet as things were the stop was not empty. There were people inside. Somehow, seeing other people made Mark feel better about the situation. No one seemed to be speaking but it was comforting to finally see some other people out in this mess. Peter spotted the sign pointing to the restrooms. "Uhh...washroom, talk to you again," Peter said. Mark waved casually and Peter hobbled towards the washroom still trying to shake off the icy chill.

Mark walked further into the rest stop and surveyed everything. From where he stood he could see the convenience store clearly. There was a young man, maybe mid-twenties, leaned over the counter reading a hardcover book. It might have been a text book. He looked bored and, as if to confirm this, he yawned deeply as Mark watched. The guy looked up at the clock that advertised cigarettes on it and Mark followed his gaze. The clock was sitting at just before quarter to ten. The young man turned his attention back to his book and didn't notice Mark at all. The clock which was analog read the same as Mark's dashboard had earlier. It also had a minute hand that was stopped and not moving. Perhaps it was a weird coincidence?

The cupboard behind the guy reading his textbook was closed but Mark knew that inside that cupboard were the cigarettes. He didn't know why it was such a strong desire but tonight he really wanted one. He hadn't wanted one this bad in a long time. He ignored the craving and walked a few more steps into the main area which was made up mostly of the seating with the three restaurants in front of him. A coffee would be like manna in the desert right now. Mark had a habit of surveying his surroundings quickly and efficiently which he had been doing since the moment he walked in.

To the right there was a woman sitting at a table. She had a man with her, a priest actually, Mark thought noticing the collar. The priest was touching her shoulder and speaking to her. The woman was crying and clearly upset. Beside her, playing with a small hand sewn doll, was a little girl...six maybe, Mark thought. On his left was the bank of arcade machines and there was another young man slightly younger than the convenience store guy. He was pacing back and forth and running his hands through his mop of greasy blonde hair. He was clearly annoyed.

Mark looked ahead at the eating stations. The coffee shop was dark and had a metal grate pulled down over the front of it. There were no signs but COFFEE CORNER was clearly closed. The next booth was "Buns N' Stuff" the neon sign above the booth said. Only unfortunately the first 'n' and the second 'u' was out so if it were dark in here it would read "Bu s N' St ff." Why did that matter, Mark thought? The sign on the counter at "Bu s N' St ff" read "CLOSED" and a small cardboard clock below that proclaimed "WILL RETURN AT:" and the clock was set to read "8:00 AM." No luck with baked goods tonight. He looked to his right at the biggest spot. This one was still open. No one was being served but lots of lights were still on and there was someone in the back kitchen area moving around. They likely served coffee or something similar. Maybe he would even grab something to eat. The roof above him had an enormous glass paneled section like a sun roof that covered nearly the entire mid-section of the stop. It was covered in snow and he could see the wind still whipping around out there. It made him shiver. He wondered where his new friend was. He had been in the washroom for awhile now. He hoped he was alright.

He walked towards the eatery marked clearly and brightly as "BIG MIKE'S." An eatery with big in the name would certainly serve some good solid greasy travel food and strong coffee. The coffee would help calm him down and warm him up and the greasy food...well that would be great for the moment but he would regret it later on. The woman who was crying did not notice Mark whatsoever as he walked by them. The priest glanced over at him and nodded. Mark returned the nod politely. The little girl also took her attention away from her doll to watch Mark walk past but then returned to stroking the doll's hair with her hand. There was a pile of winter jackets and clothing on the table beside them.

Mark got to the counter and peered around the back. There was definitely someone back there but no one made an appearance. There was no bell on the counter to announce his arrival. He glanced up at the menu. It was as he expected. Steak Sandwiches, Big Mike's Burger Xtreme (three 6 oz patties, bacon, cheese, Big Mike's special sauce), Onion Rings, fries, gravy, soda...the menu did not list coffee or warm drinks of any kind. "Hello?" he said quietly. He looked over his shoulder to see if he had disturbed the small group at the table but they hadn't changed their positions at all. Mark cleared his throat. "Hello?" he repeated louder.

"Just a sec," said a young female voice. Mark was satisfied with that. A few seconds passed before a young and very attractive brunette girl came from the back. She was carrying straw and napkin dispensers. She put them on the counter in front of her and walked over to Mark. She was young...very young, early twenties, Mark guessed. She had long hair that was tied back in a tight pony tail, the typical display of a diner server. She was wearing a black top and a mostly clean light blue apron. Mark couldn't help but notice she had a very nice figure. "Evenin'," she said and smiled. She had perfect teeth and a nice smile but was clearly tired.

"Hi," Mark said and gave her a weary smile. "Tell me you have coffee," he asked.

She smiled again. "Normally we don't but anyone coming in tonight definitely wants coffee. What would you like in it?"

"Two cream and two sugars would be fine," Mark replied.

"Done," she said and turned back to the kitchen. She was only gone a few moments before coming back with a Styrofoam cup of coffee.

"How much?" Mark asked reaching for his wallet.

"On the house," she replied. "It's almost gone anyways and we don't usually sell coffee on account of the Coffee Corner." Mark nodded and took the cup. He lifted the cup in thanks and turned back to the seating section behind him. He certainly wanted to sit away from whatever drama was unfolding with the priest and the woman. He walked to the back wall and sat in a two-seater booth next to the jukebox that was powered on but not playing anything.

Mark sipped the coffee. It was okay. It was actually about the same he'd get at nine in the morning at the trooper dispatch office. It would do the trick for certain. He looked up in time to see the traveler he had found in the parking lot. He was walking towards the eatery as well and he was no longer alone. He had another man with him. He was shorter than Peter Oswald by about a foot and he was very skinny. Both Peter and this other man had barely 200 pounds between them. Mark wondered if this other person was a friend of Peter's that he had come across or had been meeting somewhere. They almost looked like they belonged together. Peter spotted Mark and waved. Mark nodded back. The other man did not acknowledge Mark. In fact, he seemed to keep his eyes glued solidly to the ground.

Peter and his new friend went to the counter where the girl served them what looked like soup from a large slow cooker. They both paid separately and turned away from the counter. Mark was a solitary guy. He would take being alone over company any time but he didn't feel it was polite to not invite them over and shoot the shit for awhile. Mark waved at Peter and they made their way towards him. Mark moved from his two-seater booth to a four chaired table nearby and the two men sat across from him.

"Friend of yours?" Mark asked.

Peter cleared his throat. He looked better than he did when Mark had seen him outside moments ago. "Actually we just ran into each other in the washroom, just another weary traveler."

"Mark Harrison," he offered his hand to the new man. The man stared into his soup but did not take Mark's hand. He looked cautiously up from the steaming soup and nodded. He glanced at Peter and then spoke.

"Stephen. Stephen Camp," he said and then returned to his soup.

"So where are you guys from?" Mark asked. He wasn't a talker and it was awkward for him that he had to start the conversation.

"Pittsburgh for me, born and raised. I've been in insurance for years. I was hoping to get home tonight," Peter sighed, sipping his soup.

Mark and Peter both looked at Stephen waiting for his response. He said nothing.

"I'm from Hoboeken," Mark said ignoring the new guy's silence. "I'm a Jersey State Trooper."

Peter stopped eating and set his spoon down. "Really?" he said, smiling a big toothy grin.

"Yes sir, going on twenty years." Mark took another swig of his coffee which was starting to cool off now which was disappointing.

Peter leaned forward anxiously and smiled again. "Fascinating. I've always respected what you guys do and what you put up with. There are some crazy bastards out there," Peter said nodding and then realized his language and looked ashamed. "I'm sorry. Pardon my language."

Mark half smiled. "I've heard worse than that believe me."

"Andover." Mark and Peter looked at Stephen who had just spoken. "I'm from Andover...b...but I was born in...Brigatine," he stuttered.

Mark nodded. "What do you do Steve?"

"It...It's Stephen, please officer."

"Mark," Mark confirmed.

"...Mark. I work for a private medical company. I'm a ph...ph... physicist."

"Hmm, I see a dirty joke on the make here," Peter said, smiling his big grin. "A cop, a physicist and an insurance salesman walk into a bar..." Mark smiled. It was rather amusing but the feeling passed quickly. What followed brought an icy chill back into Mark's veins. The woman sitting with the priest screamed a horrifying echoing scream that even made the convenience store kid put down his book.

Mark, Peter and Stephen all turned to look at the table. The little girl was now clutching her doll to her chest and the priest was looking towards the front doors of the rest stop. The woman had stood from her chair but was not moving. She stood in place with her hands clasped over her mouth. Another person had entered the rest stop. He was slightly over six feet, with dirty brown hair and wearing a heavy plaid coat. He had a truckers hat on that had something written on it but he took the hat off when he walked into the eating area.

He only stood a few feet from the screaming woman. He was shuffling his feet and looking from the woman to the priest. "Better check this out," Mark said and stood up. He tossed his nearly empty coffee cup into the nearby trash receptacle and walked towards the small crowd. Peter and Stephen stayed where they were. As Mark got closer he could hear the priest talking very quietly to the distraught woman. He was trying to calm her.

"Andrea, he'll be fine. We'll try again when the storm lets up. He probably is on his way here." The words of encouragement didn't seem to help her any. As Mark got to the table he could see the little girl had tears in her eyes but was calm for the time being.

"Hello. My name is Officer Mark Harrison with the New Jersey State Police, is there a problem?"

He wondered who would address him first. His least likely thought was the woman but she did. In fact, she left her spot and rushed over beside him and grabbed his arm making Mark step back from surprise. "Officer, my husband...he was in the snow and he didn't get in the van and my son is missing, my son is gone. He wasn't in the van and now no one knows where he is," she sputtered. She seemed near hysteria. The pacing greasy guy was close to them now and Mark could see his face clearer. His eyes were watery and puffy and the way he was fidgeting Mark figured he was probably shaky on his feet. He wouldn't bet his life on it but he'd bet dollars to donuts that the kid was high or coming down from something. The woman whirled around to face the greasy kid. "This jackass...he kidnapped me."

The kid's eyes widened and he held his hands out in front of him. "I never did that. I just thought we needed to get to safety."

"You left my husband and my baby and you left your girlfriend," the woman screamed. Her voice was echoing through the rest stop.

"Your girlfriend is missing too?" Mark asked the kid. He nodded but said nothing else. "Okay ma'am...calm down. Look at me." Mark took her shoulders and turned her to face him. He was easily a foot taller so he had to look down at her. "Can everyone here tell me your name please and tell me what is going on."

5

The priest cleared his throat and stood up. He was an older man, older than Mark. He was in good shape and probably looked younger than he was. "Patrick John. Father Patrick John but Patrick is fine. I got here...maybe an hour ago. I was riding with my colleague Father White. He had forgotten his prayer book in the car. We were going to pray for protection in this storm. However, I don't really know where he's gone."

"What do you mean?" Mark asked.

Patrick shrugged. "He didn't come back from the car. I went outside looking for him but he's nowhere to be found. But I saw Mrs. Green's van take a spin on the ice so I got her, little Hannah and this gentlemen inside and we've been searching for our companions ever since."

Mark tried to wrap his head around the situation. "So Father Patrick, you're missing your colleague and Mrs...Green was it?"

"Andrea," she sobbed. Patrick put an arm around her.

"Andrea...your husband is missing and so is your son?" She nodded. Mark looked at the young man who was still standing in shock behind them all. "And your girlfriend is missing?"

He nodded and looked at Mark. "Sheila. She was standing near Mrs. Green's husband. They mighta got hit," he replied. This sent Andrea into another temper frenzy actually lunging past Patrick and towards the guy. He stepped back and Patrick grabbed her.

"What's your name kid?" Mark asked.

He seemed hesitant. He was still high or coming down fast and nasty. Meth maybe? He finally spoke up. "Josh Barton."

Mark turned to the newest addition in the room. Plaid jacket guy had said nothing but he certainly looked concerned for everyone.

"And you?" Mark asked. So far everyone was co-operating.

"My name is Ethan Datsun sir. I drive a truck."

"I didn't see a truck out there?"

"I...I went to see if I could find their friends and mine."

"You're missing someone too?" Mark asked, almost with a hint of disbelief to his voice. Ethan nodded.

"I was traveling with my boss. We were going up to get a load in Philadelphia because it had to be in Atlantic City by tomorrow morning so we thought we'd share driving. We stopped here to gas up and then I came in to use the pisser," Ethan cleared his throat and corrected himself, "...washroom...and when I got back to the truck there wasn't nobody there."

"So we have four missing people and a child?"

Patrick and Ethan both nodded. Josh and Andrea said nothing. Mark could sense someone behind him and looked over his shoulder. It was the waitress and she was watching with concern on her face. She met Mark's gaze and smiled half-heartedly. "I'm Heather," she said pointing to the small gold plaque above her right breast. "Heather Morton. I work here."

Mark's head was beginning to ache. "Heather do you have a phone here I can use?"

Heather nodded and walked back towards the eatery counter. She leaned over and grabbed something underneath the counter. Mark noticed that Josh was checking out the girl's ass and smirked. The kid might be high and distraught but not enough to miss some tail. She returned moments later with the cordless phone. It was far from a new model, it looked like it was from the early 2000's given its size. Mark hit the talk button and turned away from the crowd that was gathering so he could call his dispatch and get some help out here. There was nothing. He looked at the face of the phone and hit talk again. No dial tone, no static, no strange voices like his cell phone...there was just nothing.

"Something wrong?" Father Patrick whispered, approaching Mark slowly.

Mark lowered his own voice. "Phone is dead. Like completely dead."

5

"Shit," Father Patrick said under his breath and glanced at Andrea who was still hysterical. Mark looked at the priest and he shrugged.

"Sorry. I have lots of time for penance later."

Mark looked at each of the traveler's faces. Andrea, the hysterical mother and wife, Josh, the strung out tail chaser, Heather, the object of Josh's lustful attraction and current employee of Big Mike's Eatery, Ethan, the truck driver and attempted hero to find the missing persons, Peter and Stephen behind him and Father Patrick.

He turned to the Priest and lowered his voice to a bare whisper. "Father, I think it's going to be a long night."

6

Father Patrick John loved nothing more than Sunday brunch with his congregation. He had worked very hard for the past thirty years, since getting out of the seminary, to build his own church and take care of his flock. Now it felt like his time to move on to something else. He truly believed the Lord was speaking to him and telling him that he was needed elsewhere. That didn't make him feel any better about leaving the church he had worked so hard to build. He hadn't officially told anyone in the congregation about his plans to leave. Rumors were already circulating and people suspected his intentions.

However, the congregation and church board intended on letting Father John find his replacement so that made him feel like at least he had a hand in who he was leaving his beloved church to. He needed to find just the right person. He respected men of the cloth and there was nothing Father John disliked more than the priest stereotypes. His mother and father both raised him as a devout Catholic and he had spent two years after high school traveling around the world because his father insisted it was "good for him." And it was. Europe, Italy, all the way through Russia (USSR at the time), and eventually made his way into Egypt and the Holy Land which affected him the most.

He had spent his entire life hearing about the biblical heroes and the Holy Land. They had become icons to him of respect and dedication to their beliefs. By the time Patrick had returned to the states he knew what the Lord wanted of him and he entered the seminary a year later. Patrick John was an honest, good, hardworking man. He wasn't perfect; he knew that and accepted his quirks and bad habits. Regardless, no one would ever speak an ill word about the man because he truly tried to live righteously and had never been within a hundred feet of any scandal involving the Church or his personal life.

As he spent time with other ministers and missionaries and folks within the Catholic Church he started to form a short list of the men he would consider to succeed him in his parish. One name in particular would come up on a regular basis with many different people and that was Noah White. An inspirational and clearly devoted man but to say that Father White's reputation preceded him was an understatement. He was still young at 27 but was getting acclaim already after graduating from seminary and doing incredible work with a group called "Street Smarts." Street Smarts would bus to urban areas like Philadelphia, New York and Washington and work with street people helping them find work and change their lives. In only four years since Father White had graduated he had become the youngest leader ever elected to the head of Street Smarts. The same words always accompanied Noah White's name...honorable, full of compassion and conviction, Lord inspired, lovely.

By the time Patrick spoke to Noah on the phone he felt like he knew him. Noah White had recently taken a temporary position at St. Andrew's in North County, New York while their permanent minister had fallen ill. His contract there was three months and when that was done he would be open to other ideas. Patrick thought his ministry in Atlantic City would be ideal for him but nothing would be decided until he got to know Noah. The two began weekly telephone conversations. What started as a pseudo-interview became a friendship between the two men. They called each other for advice and guidance and sometimes just to chat. They both loved baseball, their congregations and God...and not in that order. Every telephone conversation, no matter how brief, ended in prayer.

So it was with great reverence and excitement when Noah's three month term expired. Patrick offered to drive to North County and spend some time with Noah and his congregation. Then the two of them could drive back to Atlantic City together to meet Patrick's congregation. Patrick headed out Monday morning. The wind had picked up but it wasn't snowing and the forecast called for sunny skies from here to New York State. The trip was a solid seven hours with a stop for lunch but the weather looked fine. When it was time to come back the sun was high and they had no reason to think they would run into any bad weather. Unfortunately, it was somewhere a few miles outside of Philadelphia that the snow began to fall. Both men contemplated the idea of getting rooms in the city but decided it would be better to make it home that night to be well rested for the men's breakfast in the morning and the congregation dinner in the evening.

By the time they were on the east side of Philly, it was nightfall and the snow was coming in quickly. The highway was almost barren and the temperature was dropping. The snow got thicker and heavier until they were practically crawling on the highway. Patrick peered into his rear view mirror but could see nothing more than his own red brake lights on the curtain of snow around them. It had been nearly a half hour since they had seen another car. He took a deep breath and gave a silent prayer for safety.

"Are you okay?" Noah asked.

He turned to his friend and nodded. "I'm just a little nervous driving in this mess." Patrick focused on the highway and Noah sat silently looking out his window into the white canvas around them. "It was probably foolish to leave North County at all with the storm coming. This could get much worse before it gets better." Eerie words of premonition from the priest. There was silence between the men asnPatrick focused his attention on driving.

"What...what do you know about possession?" Noah asked, breaking the silence in the car.

"Sorry?" Patrick said. He was surprised at the question as it was very sudden. "Possession? Like demon possession?" He glanced at Noah who seemed almost ashamed at mentioning it. Patrick had to slow twice to allow the car to ride carefully through drifts of snow. He cleared his throat. "It isn't something the church talks a lot about anymore."

"I know. I mean, I asked another priest and he told me someone like me shouldn't even be discussing such things."

"Well, I think some might see you as too young to be looking into demonic possession but I know you better than that and I know you're curious about all aspects of the church. The thing is...in today's modern era, I believe, as does the church, that demonic possession is very, very rare."

"But possible?" Noah asked, almost hopefully.

"What's going on?" Patrick asked curiously.

Noah sighed as though he were hesitant to say more. Since the day they started speaking Patrick had never known Noah to be hesitant about talking about things, especially matters of spirituality. Then again, they had never talked about demons or possessions before. I think perhaps once there was a joke said about *The Exorcist* film between them that they both chuckled about at the time.

Noah finally spoke, but cautiously Patrick noted. "A man in my congregation would come in very sporadically, always sit in the back and he would always leave before my closing prayer. I finally followed him to his car to introduce myself and perhaps get his commitment to see me for confession. His name was William Callow." Noah seemed to hesitate more. Patrick had to maneuver through another gust of blowing snow. He glanced at Noah and nodded as if encouraging him to continue. "He asked to speak with me privately and obviously I granted him a meeting. He wanted to ask me about demons and the possibility of one bringing attention to themselves from the other world. I literally was speechless. I didn't know what to say to him which I was ashamed of. I wanted to help him."

"What was the situation he needed help with?"

"Well he insisted that it wasn't him that had the issue but rather a...a colleague. He said he had messed with some dark power and now this colleague believed he had brought something...out," Noah tried to explain.

"If you want my honest opinion..." Patrick paused and looked in his mirrors again. There appeared to be some light moving up behind them. Another vehicle he figured. He hoped that they weren't driving like a maniac on a night like tonight. That would put all of them in danger.

"I do," Noah said snapping Patrick back to reality.

"You do what?"

"...want your opinion," Noah said.

"Right. Well I don't think demons can be summoned or brought out of some dark place. I think very few of these situations and experiences are truly demonic possession outside of metaphoric personal demons. I would have explained to this man that, while his friend shouldn't be messing with things he doesn't understand, he should come to confession, confess his sins and stay away from whatever he was getting into."

Noah looked at his friend and mentor in near disbelief. "That's exactly what I told him!"

Patrick chuckled and the car slid slightly but he turned into the slide and pulled it back in the right direction. "You don't trust yourself to give good advice." Patrick didn't look but sensed his friend shrug. "The fear of the Lord is the instruction of wisdom; and before honor is humility."

"Proverbs," Noah replied and Patrick smiled.

"On the other side of things...I think...sometimes...there are more things in heaven and earth, than are dreamt of in your philosophy," Patrick quoted, glancing at his friend.

Noah seemed to look quizzical. "Is that Biblical?" he asked.

Patrick smiled and leaned close to the windshield to make sure he was still in his own lane. "No, Hamlet...Shakespeare."

The light behind them was closing in. Patrick signaled and pulled into the left lane of the three lane highway in order to give him options for sliding if necessary. "What's up?" Noah asked.

"Someone is coming up behind us I think. I see headlights."

It was only moments after he had said this before a van moved up behind their car. Patrick slowed his own vehicle and the van pulled up beside them. A blonde haired, pretty, tired looking young woman peered through the blizzard at their car. Patrick smiled and nodded and lifted his hand to wave. The woman turned and said something to the driver. He had to imagine that she could see his collar from where she was. Maybe seeing him would make her feel better about this nasty weather. It looked to him like there was a little girl in the back and perhaps someone else, although he could only see the girl.

"So you don't believe a person can conjure up a demon?" Noah asked. Patrick glanced at his companion and smiled. He knew that Noah would never be able to ask any other priest these types of questions. Some would not be offended or upset but would most likely tell him not to bother with such things. The rest would be upset that a young minister, fresh from seminary, was asking about such things which were becoming more and more taboo within the church.

"No," Patrick replied definitively. He sensed that Noah was looking for more. The van was pulling ahead of them and Patrick let them gain some distance. He didn't figure that driving parallel to the van was a good idea for either of them. "Conjuring is bringing an already existent element of the supernatural to the forefront. I have never seen anything that has led me to believe a person can bring something out of the darkness into reality. You cannot create an evil power."

Noah seemed to appear thoughtful as they drove silently the next several miles. Patrick was happy to just focus on the road which was getting worse by the minute. Finally, Patrick broke the silence, "this is getting awful."

"There's a truck stop ahead," Noah replied.

"Will it be open?"

"Are you kidding? Those places don't close for anything," Noah said smiling.

"Willing to stop?" Patrick asked hopefully.

"Absolutely, we could use the break and this is getting dangerous."

Noah watched carefully for the exit and Patrick pushed the car through the worsening blizzard. They didn't see the van that had passed them but Patrick wondered if they too would be at the stop. Patrick drove the car onto the exit ramp. The glow from the windows in the rest stop was reassuring and inviting to both men. There were plenty of lights on but literally only two vehicles in the enormous and normally packed parking lot. The family van was not one of them. Patrick found a spot and pulled in. Both men got out of the car and ran into the stop as quickly as possible with the snow whirling around them in small cone shaped funnels.

They walked through both sets of doors and stomped themselves off, the snow falling to the large maroon colored mats. The young man at the convenience store looked over at them. He was leaning on the counter with his hand firmly planted under his chin chewing gum, looking extremely bored. It appeared from where the two men stood that the stop was completely empty other than the young man. There was a clatter of what sounded like pots from the eatery in the corner so someone else was here.

6

Patrick brushed off his coat and walked over to the convenience area. The boy barely glanced at him. "Good evening," he said. The boy looked up.

"Hey."

"Patrick," he said, offering his hand to the young man. This barely warranted a glance but the boy happened to notice the collar underneath the jacket and immediately straightened up. He stumbled over his words before shaking the priest's hand.

"Paul," he managed.

"Good to meet you Paul. Can you tell me where we are on the highway?"

"East. Uh..I mean you're about 35 miles east of Philly."

"Damn," Patrick muttered. They weren't all that far from Atlantic City on a good day. This was not a good day. He noticed Paul look at him with distrust hearing the priest curse. "Sorry. Bad habit. Eatery open?"

"Yah, Heather's workin'" Paul replied. He was losing interest in the minister already. He reached below the counter and pulled out what looked like a vampire novel of some kind. Patrick considered talking to Paul about why he was reading about vampires but decided against it.

He walked back to where Noah stood and they decided to see about getting a bite to eat. They approached the counter underneath the sign that read "BIG MIKE'S" and waited only a few moments before a pretty girl appeared with a warm smile. Heather served them quickly and before long both men were sitting in a booth near the back of the stop enjoying their coffee and sandwiches. It was quiet in the stop and gave the men time to talk some more.

"I think we should pray for the safety of travelers, our safety, and for the souls of the others in this stop as well," Patrick said. Noah agreed and reached for his prayer book. He checked his inside pocket but it wasn't there.

"Everything okay?" Patrick asked.

"My prayer book, I must have left it in the car. I'm going to run out and grab it," he said standing.

"You can pray without it," Patrick teased the younger priest. Noah grinned.

"I'd prefer to have it, I'll be right back." Patrick assured him it was no problem and Noah headed outside. That was the last time Father Patrick John and Father Noah White would ever see each other.

7

There isn't anything quite as grating as the sound of an alarm clock. How is it that all alarm clocks sound the same when they are going off? They all have this dull braying tone that digs into the core of one's brain. *EHHH EHHH EHHH EHHH* . It's probably one of the worst noises known to man.

Is anything more natural, more health affirming, more fantastic than the world of sleep? Is sleep like stepping into the world of the hereafter? If a difference can be found with every human being on the earth there is literally one constant in every single person, they sleep. Your favorite celebrity, the richest man alive, Hitler, The President of The United States....at one time or another they all slept. "*For in that sleep of death what dreams may come, When we have shuffled off this mortal coil, Must give us pause—there's the respect—That makes calamity of so long life.*" That's Hamlet by the way...Shakespeare. The same William Shakespeare that Paul had just finished striking out with an incredible curve ball in Yankee Stadium. Shakespeare swore and threw his bat against the ground which was clearly a velvet shag carpet. "Damn," he muttered. "That's the last ice cream I've ever driven in," he said.

Paul laughed and sat down on a cushion in his kitchen. The kitchen was bright yellow with a red trim and even the appliances were yellow with black buttons on them. It looked as though the appliances had never been used. That was silly though, his Mom baked in here all the time and so did Audrey Hepburn sometimes...Paul thought. The cushion Paul was sitting on had a lion's head to lean back on, not a real one of course, a stuffed one. Shakespeare was gone but Tom Cruise was leaning into the fridge looking for bologna.

"It's on the second shelf..." Paul said leaning back on his cushion.

"Beside the cheese," said Paul's stuffed lion head cushion.

"Shuddup both of ya," Cruise replied. "I'm looking for lemons for the desert."

"Dessert has two S's," Paul said matter-of-factly.

"Not dessert, desert, we have a football game there tomorrow, moron," Cruise yelled slamming the fridge door. "And for crying out loud turn off that alarm," he added.

"What alarm," Paul asked?

EHHH EHHH EHHH EHHH Paul opened one eye and cursed under his breath. He was wearing only boxers and his comforter was twisted up at his feet. The room wasn't cold though, the heat was turned up and the room temperature was just right. He hated sleeping in more clothing than he had to, even in the dead of winter. He also hated going to work...especially in the dead of winter. Paul Janson was 25 years old, just turned two months prior. He was a good looking kid with dark hair, blue eyes and a decently kept body. He had been athletic in high school right up until the end when he suddenly got hit with extreme laziness. He barely passed his final courses, didn't bother applying for any colleges, and told all his more productive friends and classmates he was taking the proverbial "year off." This meant getting a job at the local paper factory with his dad. He did this for two years and then moved on to a retail management job at the Atlantic City boardwalk. This was great for the summer, especially for all the women he got to meet.

The store he worked in was a sunglasses/accessories store and the lovely ladies would make their way in to check out the goods so Paul could check out their goods. Before and after work and sometimes during, Paul got the chance to enjoy the scenery and meet some friends. High School had been only relatively successful in the dating department for Paul. He had dated Jenna Bartel in ninth grade but then they broke up right before tenth grade. Jenna had been his first and he had been hers...or so she said. After that he played a lot of sports and only dated once or twice during tenth grade. Then he met Angela Woods in the eleventh grade and they dated almost right through Senior Year until she dumped him for some exchange student from Quebec. Seriously Quebec!? That's not even an exchange, that's like a field trip. And much to Paul's disappointment he understood, through the grapevine, that Monsieur Pattrelle was giving HIS Angela the ride of her life. Ironic since Angela wouldn't even let Paul go to second base with her.

Then came his post high-school dating dry spell with only one blind date, a set up from a friend of his that lasted three dates. But then came the summer at the boardwalk. That summer he successfully courted three different girls (if you could ever call what Paul Janson did "courting.") He was lucky enough that none of the girls he met on the boardwalk wanted to be serious. Courtney James (they called her Corky), man she showed Paul things that he wouldn't ever forget.

Then Janet Russell, who was a little plump but the melons on her... .wow...still she wasn't as popular as say...Courtney, so he kind of kept their three week fling on the down low. It ended rather abruptly when she told him she missed her period. It turned out she missed her period all the time and it was a false alarm.

And finally the twilight of that summer featured Samantha Welling...a backside you could bounce a quarter off of (Paul didn't actually know what that meant.) She was wild and crazy but she was also from out west and only visiting for the summer.

When the summer fun ended, Paul's Dad told him to get a full time job or get the hell out. He was 25, still living at home and not paying any rent worth mentioning. He tried the local factories and some better high end retail jobs but nothing panned out and finally his Mom set him up with an interview at the highway rest stop. It reminded Paul of being at the dead end of his life. Like he had inadvertently turned down a road that said "NO EXIT" and at the very end was this rest stop.

Paul looked groggily over at this iridescent alarm clock that he had been given as a stocking stuffer years ago. Apparently his parents never heard of video games or candy in a stocking. The clock stared back at him 1:45...EHHH EHHH EHHH EHHH....He reached over and slapped it off. Paul planted his face back into the pillow and sighed. His head popped up again and he looked at the clock. 1:4...6 "Shit!" he exclaimed and dove out of bed. He was due at work for the 3-11 shift and it was almost an hour drive as it was. He dove out of his room which hadn't changed much since high school. Hell, he still has a poster of Aerosmith's BIG ONES on his wall.

He managed to cut his half hour preparedness time to a more acceptable 20 minutes and was on his way out the door by 2:10. As long as the roads were clear he might make it on time. The only good thing about working on the interstate was being able to use it to get to work. As good as that was, it was still 3:04 when Paul pulled into the rest stop which was bustling with tourists and travelers. Paul had no idea that within hours the rest stop would be a desolate proverbial ghost town. The sky had started to cloud over and Paul figured it would snow tonight but he had no idea just how bad.

He had been trying to chat up Heather Morton who worked at Big Mike's Eatery across the stop from him. She was a cute little brunette thing that he thought liked him and he felt the same and then some. Only problem was she actually worked pretty hard so it was hard to find time to talk to her.

Paul slipped off his sunglasses, an unfortunate keepsake of his previous employment, and looked up at the overcast sky and the thick cumulus clouds rolling in. Snowflakes began to drift towards him and he cursed again and locked his car door. He strolled into the rest stop where the voices washed over him. He stomped his feet once on the mat and turned left into his little convenience alcove that he hated to his very core. This was his life. Bonnie, the morning girl, was standing impatiently at the counter with her purse out. He was only five minutes late and clearly that was an issue for her.

"Welcome to work, Paul," she said sarcastically emphasizing his name. Bonnie was in her mid-forties, had a couple of kids and a husband who was a truck driver or something. He didn't know and he didn't care because she rarely pretended to like him and they never had to work together.

"Weather's gettin' bad," Paul said, opening the small square swinging door to their cash wrap area. They had a small black piano stool behind there and some old newspapers and magazines underneath the register along with paperwork and communication books from the boss. Bonnie wasted no time exiting the swinging door and walking away from the booth.

"Drive safe!" Paul called out, mostly sarcastically. He thought Bonnie might even flip him off but she didn't. In fact, she ignored him and left. First sale is cigarettes, almost always is, along with the second, third, fourth....then a soda, chocolate bar, newspaper, magazines, more cigarettes, lottery tickets...damn...not a winner, another lottery ticket... hey 5 bucks! Cigarettes, change for the the arcade, a small paperback novel called "A Heart's Discontent" with a poorly drawn muscle bound man and some big titted 19th Century dame. By 7 PM the sales slow down and Paul's patience and energy slopes further and further until his head is on the counter and he's flipping through an old issue of Time magazine with the President of The United States on the cover making some eloquent speech.

Paul didn't even notice when Heather Morton approached him with a paper plate and a plain hamburger and some fries on it. She almost always brought him a snack, much like this, when they worked an evening shift together. "Hungry?" she said. Sexy voice, Paul thought. He smiled but quickly hid his reaction to remain coy and aloof. Never show too much interest, he thought.

"Oh hey cutie," Paul said. He was chomping on a piece of gum rather unattractively. Heather didn't notice, lucky for him. She set the plate down on the counter where the glass cases of scratch tickets were housed. Paul should have restocked them by now but he felt lazy today...well everyday... but he figured with the weather getting worse that he would have plenty of time to do the menial tasks before he left at eleven.

"It's getting pretty slow in here," Heather commented, as Paul put down whatever it was he was flipping through.

"Weather's gonna be bad," Paul replied, smiling at her as he pulled the plate towards him and took a fry. Nice and hot just the way he liked it, he thought, and the fries were good too...he smiled at his own joke. He thought he was very smooth. "Maybe when it clears out we can sit down and play some cards?"

"Sure," Heather said, smiling. She had nice teeth, and a perfect body. She winked at him and headed back to the diner. A couple of hours later and Paul was barely keeping his eyes open. It was so ridiculously slow and the weather was beating against the large glass windows like an angry lover demanding to be let in. Paul looked at the small digital clock in the corner of the computerized cash register...8:58...it read. It felt to Paul like he had been here nothing short of ten hours. It had been almost two hours since Heather had brought him the hamburger. It was good but Paul didn't feel much like eating so most of it was buried covertly in the small plastic waste basket under the desk.

For the moment, the rest stop was completely empty except for him and Heather, although he hadn't seen her in some time. She was likely counting inventory or making something else in the back of the diner. He wished suddenly that it was his old flame 'Corky' working at the diner because she would be more than happy to play some kinky games in the kitchen or even in the washrooms. He didn't figure Heather was that kind of girl but it didn't stop the young man from closing his eyes and fantasizing. Paul sighed and pulled out book two of the vampire series he was gradually making his way through. It was another five minutes at least before he heard the swinging glass doors open. He didn't look up to see what crazy traveler was making their way in this time. It wasn't until someone was standing right in front of him that he looked up.

"Good evening," said the voice. He sounded friendly enough.

"Hey," Paul replied. He looked up casually and, immediately, he caught a lump in his throat. Five minutes ago he was imagining having Heather Morton's rather pert body on one of these rest stop tables, and reading a particularly gruesome story about a vampire murdering people to find one man, and the man standing before him was clearly...a priest. Some say God has a sense of humor but Paul thought it was more of a practical joke than anything.

"Patrick," the middle aged Priest replied, smiling. He outstretched his hand in greeting and Paul shoved the piece of paper he was using as a book mark into pages 42 and 43, and stuck the book below the counter. Paul managed to wipe his sweaty palms on his cargoes before shaking the priest's hand.

"Paul," he said nodding.

"Good to meet you Paul. Can you tell me where we are on the highway?"

"East. Uh..I mean you're about 35 miles east of Philly." Paul just wanted to be alone again. Men of cloth made him nervous. Churches made him nervous. Anything that had to do with religion made Paul nervous. He wasn't a bad guy, he didn't think so anyways. He just really liked to enjoy life. That included many things that, he knew well enough, would cause him many hours in confession if he was catholic, which he wasn't. He wasn't anything really. His parents had been Baptists at some point but it never rubbed off on him, and it never stuck with them, that was for sure.

"Damn," Patrick muttered. Paul looked at the priest curiously. "Sorry. Bad habit. Eatery open?"

"Yah, Heather's workin'." Once the man of God had cursed Paul felt like he really wasn't peering into his soul or anything and was getting rather bored of him. Paul sat back down and pulled out his novel. The priest nodded and looked like he was going to say something else but didn't. He turned and walked away and Paul was glad of that. He noticed the priest...Patrick...join another man at the diner counter. Perhaps another priest but he was wearing a heavy dark winter jacket so he couldn't make out any sort of collar.

Twenty minutes passed before the front doors of the stop opened yet again. Paul didn't look up but he thought to himself that no matter how bad the weather was there were always people coming in and it annoyed him. Customer service his ass! He did glance up eventually and saw two men that had entered. They were wearing heavy winter coats and what looked like steel-toed construction boots. Probably truckers, which meant if the weather didn't let up they'd be here for a long while. Eventually Paul saw one of the two priests get up from the booth where they had settled. Paul noticed that indeed the other man had a collar under his jacket. The second man was much younger, almost looked like he was Paul's age. I bet he missed out on a lot, Paul thought smirking. He returned his attention to his book. The younger priest, Noah, went outside into the insane weather. Shortly after that the older priest headed towards the rest-rooms while his partner was still outside.

7

On top of this boring-ass evening, Paul thought, he was definitely getting some sort of migraine. He felt a humming inside his head and it was getting worse. He set his book down and rubbed his index fingers against his temples. Man, this was coming on fast and furious and wasn't going to let up. He looked out past his convenience store and into the dining area. The lights seemed to be dimming and then glowing brighter along with the thump in his head. They couldn't be losing electricity; Big Mike had a very good generator out back. He sighed and clenched his eyes tightly. He wasn't sure where anyone else was. Heather was likely in the back of the diner and the younger priest had just walked outside for some unknown reason. It must have been something pretty important given the beast of a storm that was looking to freeze everyone to death out there. Paul was just suffering alone at his booth. Suddenly, his head pounded and he winced. The humming inside his brain was excruciating. He could swear the snow and wind outside got worse as the pounding in his head did. He thought he saw bright lights pouring in the front of the stop and through the roof top window before his headache suddenly slipped away. It was gone, just like that. It didn't melt away like headaches usually did; it was there and then it was gone. Any of the previous pain he had was gone and everything seemed normal. Normal not counting the weather outside which was still pounding against the windows. The only thing he noticed was the rest stop seemed just eerily quiet.

Eventually the older priest came from the rest room and looked a little disheveled. He was rubbing the back of his head and shaking it a little. He started to walk towards Paul who was still recovering from his strange burst of headache so he didn't have time to be annoyed. "Hey...Paul...do you have any...umm like ibuprofen or acetaminophen. Apparently I got a killer headache coming on." Paul looked at the man and for the first time actually smiled genuinely. "Yah, me too Father."

"Well you get me a small bottle and we can share it."

"Agreed," Paul said, and walked to the far wall where there were some minor first-aid items.

8

Heather was always early for work. It wasn't that she adored her job so much that she just had to be early, she was always punctual. Heather was twenty three and she came from a nice family where both parents loved her dearly and worked very hard to give her a good life. Her Dad was a hard working blue collar guy that worked in a car parts factory in Hoboken for the better part of thirty years. She was their only child and they worshiped her. Mrs. Morton worked numerous jobs over the years to help keep them afloat. She was a multi talented woman. Seamstress, cook, hair stylist, secretary...there was very little Mrs. Diane Morton couldn't do, especially for her family.

Most of all Mr. and Mrs. Morton encouraged Heather to follow her dreams. Heather knew at less than six years old that she had a talent for art. She could draw just about anything using paint, crayons, marker, chalk or whatever she could find. The biggest difference between Heather Morton drawing at six and other children drawing at six was that her east coast skyline at dusk actually looked like a skyline at dusk. She was nine when Barry Morton used up their savings to enroll Heather in the best private school in New York with a top notch art program. It wasn't just that she was good at it, Heather loved art. It didn't matter what kind of art either, she would do just about anything, but painting was her passion.

Everyone, including her own art teachers, insisted that art was not a lucrative career. However, she managed to sell a painting to a local restaurant for one hundred dollars. Her Dad had let her keep every penny and she had bought a new easel and a set of paint brushes that she had wanted. Her love for painting had never waned and now, as she worked her way through university at the off ramp in 'Big Mike's Diner', she took every spare moment to draw.

Mostly she loved nature. In the warmer months she would find the best possible views from various locations in the area to draw the most breathtaking spectacles. She even got some freelance work from Pennsylvania's Tourism Board drawing local spots that had to be visited. Overall though nothing was paying the bills when it came to art but she worked very hard. She knew what she needed to do and how hard she had to work even if it was a server/counter girl at Big Mike's. She certainly didn't have time for a boyfriend of any kind and had only dated here and there since high school. Truthfully, she had only had one serious boyfriend that had lasted about seven months. He was nearly thirty and a Prof's assistant in the English department. They met when she was 22 and broke up a few months later. He was a nice guy but wanted more than Heather was willing to commit to at this point in her life. He had proposed, she'd turned him down apologetically but their relationship couldn't survive her denial and his pride was irreparably damaged at her rejection. Still, he had been her first true love and the only man she had even been with.

It was 2:23 PM when Heather pulled her parents old Dodge Caravan into the truck stop parking lot. The weather had been decent and the sun was fighting to break through the thickening gray clouds. She killed the engine and the Bee Gee's tune silenced from the 'Oldies Radio' station her Dad enjoyed. *The best of the 60's and 70's right here on Classic 94.3 FM.*

She checked to make sure she had her small red handbag with her name tag safely clipped to the strap, and got out. She didn't bother locking the van, she rarely did. The locks on the old van hardly worked anyways and the whole family just made sure they took anything important with them when they left. They had a second car now and this old junker was just being used until it gave up the ghost, so to speak.

Heather wrapped her fur-lined, brown, faux suede winter jacket around her and hurried to the front foyer of the stop. The glass doors swished as she pushed them open and the warm air inside pushed against the cold air from outside. There were a few travelers milling about inside, a family by the arcade machines and a man buying cigarettes from Bonnie at the convenience kiosk. Bonnie was a very friendly lady. She had three children, all under the age of ten, and her husband had left her for her sister six months ago leaving her to care for her beautiful boys. Heather babysat on a few occasions when Bonnie just couldn't get out of an evening shift at the rest stop. She waved at Bonnie as she came in and Bonnie smiled and waved back.

Heather went to the blue door to the right of Big Mike's Diner and to the left of the bakery. The door was marked with a neat gold sign that clearly stated "EMPLOYEE'S ONLY." However, the door was never locked. Fortunately, the sign seemed to deter random travelers from entering the hallway. Heather opened the door and it shut solidly behind her. It was a short cement hallway about twenty feet long with a red door at the end with FIRE EXIT on it that lead to the back of the rest stop where the garbage bins were. On the right side of the hall was another red door marked B G MI ES DIN R...which translated to Big Mike's Diner when you added the missing letters. On the left, further down from Big Mike's door but before the fire exit, was the side entrance to the bakery. The hallway smelled like cement. It wasn't a bad thing really, just something Heather always noticed.

She turned the handle to Big Mike's and entered the side door which led to the kitchen. The kitchen was large, especially considering there was really only a handful of staff. Big Mike almost always did the cooking himself. Then there was Heather and three other girls that worked the counter and did some minor cooking or sandwich making if need be. At any given time the most she had ever seen working at once was three of them. There would be someone on the grill, usually Mike, and two girls up front on a Saturday night in the summer.

This afternoon Shelly Richards was working the counter and Mike was around somewhere, Heather suspected. Shelly was a nice girl, only a little older than Heather, but they didn't really chum around or even speak more than to be cordial to one another. Heather always thought Shelly didn't really like her and something about her didn't seem right. Heather prided herself on trying not to judge people but she just had this gut feeling that Shelly wasn't on the up and up. She had made mental notes to count her own cash register before starting and really watch that no one else was using her till just in case.

Heather walked to the back of the kitchen where there were two rooms along the back wall. One room was Mike's office where he did paperwork and sometimes took naps. The other room was like a staff room of sorts with a small television, a ridiculously old floral couch, and a quickly made wardrobe/closet for their coats, boots, and personal items. She walked into the staff room and noticed the TV was on and tuned in to a talk show with some psychic blathering away about the afterlife and contacting the dead.

She opened the wardrobe, grabbed a hanger and put her coat into the closet. It was empty except for another small winter jacket, a hat and a scarf, presumably Shelly's. Heather made her way to the couch, sat down and opened up her purse to look for her lip balm. Nothing made her lips drier than this cold bitter weather. She was applying her coke flavored lip balm in her compact mirror when a shadow fell over the door. "Hey Mr. Otterman," Heather said, smiling but without looking up. I mean, after all, Shelly wouldn't even cast a shadow in the door.

8

Big Mike Otterman lived up to his name. He was the sweetest man, in his early sixties, balding but with a hint of graying hair on either side of his head. He had a glowing red face, reminding everyone of St. Nick, and Big Mike Otterman got his name from his girth. It wasn't that he was enormously overweight or had a fat belly that shook like...well you know how it goes. Big Mike had likely been athletic in his younger years, probably a football player. Now he clocked in at well over 250 pounds but he had big muscular arms for a man his age, and while Heather had never been close enough to the man to actually know this, she suspected hugging him would be like hugging a giant stuffed animal. He was like a burly, masculine grandfather and that was okay with her.

At the same time she always thought he looked like he could be pretty damn tough in a tight spot. In their down time he gloated about his daughters and reminisced about his late wife. His daughters were his pride and joy and that made Heather think of her own Dad. She hoped she would make him as proud as Big Mike Otterman was about his daughters. "Miss Morton, early as usual." Mike had a supervisory tone about him but that was when he was in a good mood.

"A little early. Probably a busy day ahead," Heather replied, closing her compact and smiling at her boss.

"Dunno 'bout that, storm is comin in," he said. He walked towards her and handed her an envelope.

"What's this?" she asked.

"Well, with the weather the way it's been and people comin' in here to get away from it, I've just done really well the last month so I'm givin' all of yous a little extra."

Heather nodded and looked up at him. "Thank you, Mr. Otterman."

He nodded back and smiled at her. "Just keep it between us cuz I ain't givin everyone the same. You work your ass off here for me," Big Mike cleared his throat. "What I mean is you work real hard Heather."

Heather stood and placed the envelope carefully in her purse. "I really do appreciate that."

He waved his hand at her modestly. "I gotta go out and get some supplies. Truck that was supposed to come got laid up on account of some bad weather down south; you'll be okay after Shelly leaves for an hour or so?"

"I'll do my best," she replied.

At that point Shelly poked her head around the large stainless steel appliances. "You coming to cover me?" she asked, clearly referring to Heather. Heather looked at her watch; it wasn't even twenty minutes till when Heather was supposed to start. She noticed Mike roll his eyes and head towards his office.

"Relieve her, I'll pay you the extra time," he said quietly but loud enough that Shelly likely heard him. Heather nodded and as she left the staff area she grabbed her light blue smock they wore. She suspected it would be a decent day as things had gone alright so far. As polite as she tried to be with the small bonus, she couldn't help but wonder how much was in there. They had gotten three hundred dollars apiece for a Christmas bonus and quite frankly three hundred more dollars, hell even one hundred more dollars, would help a lot with her student loans and expenses.

Four hours later, it was nearly seven o'clock and Heather realized the place had been all but empty for nearly an hour. As Big Mike had predicted the weather was taking a turn. Being in the dead of winter, it had been dark since shortly after five and the snow was almost all you could see outside the huge glass windows at the side of the rest stop. She had finished wiping down the appliances, mopped the floor, and now she was just reading a novel in the back area. Big Mike had called nearly two hours ago. He was already an hour later than he thought he would be and wanted to let her know he would be even longer. The weather was bad and the supplies he needed weren't quite as easy to acquire as he had hoped. She had assured him that holding down the fort was a piece of cake tonight and the only people in the place at the moment were her and Paul, the young guy who worked the convenience store.

Paul...hmm...what about Paul? He was cute. She thought he even had the ability to look sexy from time to time. But there was no doubt he was a slacker. Everyone in the stop knew that Paul worked at doing as little as possible. But it had been so long since she liked a guy and she liked that Paul checked her out as much as he possibly could. Heather wasn't the type of girl to use her looks to get what she wanted but at the same time it still felt pretty good catching a guy eyeing her up, especially when he looked like Paul. Chances are she wouldn't dream of going out with him, or doing anything with him. It was harmless flirtation, she figured. She went to work preparing him a little snack as she often did on slow nights. Hamburger and fries was what she always made and he seemed to enjoy.

She brought it over and they made small talk for a few minutes. He didn't seem interested in talking to her tonight, which made her feel a little annoyed, but he did suggest they play cards later if it stayed dead like this. Yah, strip poker is what you'd like she thought and smiled to herself. The night ticked on and she did as much as she could around the place. Big Mike still wasn't back and hadn't called since before seven. Finally, a little after nine the huge glass doors were pushed open and two men stomped in letting the snow fall off them.

They looked practically frozen and she hoped that they wanted something more than the free coffee she had set up. Big Mike always suggested setting up the coffee pot if it was nasty out and the bakery and coffee place were closed. The one man cut out and went and talked to Paul briefly, maybe he was buying cigarettes or looking for directions. Eventually they both made their way towards Heather. She noticed, once they had their jackets undone, that they were wearing black suits and had distinct collars around their necks. They were both priests, she thought. They both asked for coffee and sandwiches which took Heather no time at all to make. At least it killed a few minutes. Then they retreated to a booth on the other side of the eating area.

A few minutes later, the younger priest got up and pulled his coat around him. She assumed they were leaving but the other man did not join him. One of them left the rest stop and the other man retreated down the hallway where the washroom was a few minutes later. She shrugged and went back into the kitchen to make sure the phones weren't out. She was actually a little concerned about Big Mike and where he might be at this point. Heather and he had punctuality in common.

She looked at the clock....9:45PM. She lifted the phone and heard the dial tone. Satisifed it was working, she hung up the phone and turned away from it. Oddly, Heather swore she could still hear it buzzing. She turned back and looked at the phone to make sure she had hung it up properly. It was. There was a humming from somewhere, maybe the fridge/freezer combo. That would suck if Mike brought back supplies to a broken freezer. She walked closer to it but the humming was not coming from the stainless steel appliance. Heather instinctively closed her eyes for a moment. She felt a little light headed and thought that it came on awfully quickly. Maybe she had some aspirin in her purse, and if not she was certain that Paul had some at the convenience store.

The humming was louder now and instead of thinking it was something in the restaurant she was beginning to think she was just getting a whopper of a headache. She walked back to the staff room and had no sooner hit the door when she lifted her hands to steady herself against the door frame. She cursed quietly under her breath and clenched her eyes tight. The buzzing was unmistakable and brutally loud. "Geez," she said, tilting her head back. Ten seconds, maybe twelve at the most, and it was like it had never even happened. She unclenched her eyes and everything was back to normal. No humming, no noise, no pain, nothing. She felt perfectly fine. "Well that was...different," she said aloud but quietly. It must be from studying so much and sleeping so little as of late. Maybe it was time to see her doctor because normal people didn't have striking headaches with buzzing like that. As she thought about this, she could literally hear the wind beating against the walls of the rest stop. This was going to be a long, quiet, brutally deserted evening.

9

Big Mike slammed the back door of his large cube van that was half filled with boxes. It was mostly canned goods at this point but he still needed bread and some hamburger meat. He checked his watch. 6:30. It was more than two hours past what he had hoped this trip would take. He had to drive to the nearest warehouse store to find the bulk quantities of what he needed. He had to do this all the time before he got hooked up with a supplier that usually brought him everything directly. However, the weather was getting nasty down that way and his truck of supplies was delayed. He couldn't risk not knowing when they would get here so he figured he'd go load up now.

The roads were already a little slick when he left his rest stop and it took him longer to get to the warehouse store than he anticipated. Once he got there, they weren't nearly prepared to give him what he needed so he had to wait for his order. He grabbed something to eat, a double cheeseburger, fries and a shake and then returned to his truck to discover that they had only gotten half of his order ready. This was going to simply take way longer than he hoped and now, to top everything off, bad weather was moving in and it was going to move in fast and nasty. He could see a massive dark cloud indicating a huge squall approaching.

Mike shook his head and walked around to the front of his van. He was at a loading dock where business owners did their order pickups.

9

A young man was moving boxes, filling multiple orders and hopefully working on Mike's as well. "Storm is coming, how close are we fella?" Mike asked.

The kid stopped for a moment and wiped his forehead with his work-gloved hand. "Not sure Mr. Otterman, we're trying, what can you do without tonight?"

"Not without the bread but the meat I could live without."

The kid nodded and disappeared back into the warehouse. Mike looked straight up at the snow coming down. He always thought snow falling looked almost peaceful. However, with the wind throwing that snow around, this storm was shaping up to be anything but peaceful. He shivered despite himself and turned back to the open loading dock. He would duck inside for a bit and get warm; maybe they would have some coffee for him as well.

It was easily another hour before everything was loaded into Mike's van. This would at least keep him until the truck of supplies could get through with his regular order. Mike was sitting in a hard blue office chair drinking terrible coffee from a white foam cup. To Mike coffee was coffee, it didn't matter how bad it was. The two young men who had worked diligently filling Mike's order came in from outside. They were literally covered in snow, head to toe and shivering to their core. They stomped on the cement leaving melted snow to make a dark wet stain around both men.

"Son of a bitch!" one of the guys exclaimed, and then seeing Mike, he quieted down and went red...or he was already red from the freezing cold, Mike wasn't sure which.

Mike smiled and fired his foam cup into the trash can nearby. "No worries son, I've heard far worse I can assure you. What's it doin' out there now?"

"You don't wanna know Mr. Otterman," the other man replied. He pulled a yellow and black snow cap from his head and slammed it against his jeans. "It's a shit-storm out there."

"Well then I guess I better get out there and get back to the stop," he replied.

"Drive safe," they called, and he waved over his shoulder at the men.

Big Mike pushed the back door of the warehouse open and immediately the heavy steel was ripped from his hands and swung out. The world before him had changed dramatically in the hour that he had been drinking coffee and watching the workers fill orders. It was pitch dark now, not unusual for this hour, in this area, at this time of year, but the darkness was the least of his problems. The snow had built up to a major force that prevented him from seeing more than six feet in front of him.

The wind had started to build four foot drifts against the building and they were rapidly getting higher. Big Mike had to steady himself and pull his jacket around him. He managed to catch his balance and close the door behind him as he made his way to his van. This wouldn't seem like a trek of any kind, given he had pulled the van nearly right up to the loading dock, but the parking bay was not sheltered. The small loading dock was the perfect place for the wind to whip the snow into a frenzy.

There was a howling noise from beyond the dock and Mike started to push his way to his van. He thought he could see the truck but eyes played tricks in weather like this. He could feel ice forming on his cheeks and shook his head in disgust. East coast winters were as unpredictable as a woman, one minute sunshine and warmth and the next...bitter cold and icy winds. Mike looked towards the back of the warehouse hoping to shield his eyes. The back of the warehouse faced nothing more than a rock wall. Between this rock and the back wall of the warehouse was a thousand feet of parking lot and usually a picnic table for the staff to smoke at. The picnic table was likely still there although it would be buried securely under the snow until April, or more like May with the way this was keeping up.

The warehouse was far from isolated; it sat in a very busy area of the city. If you ventured around the front of the store there was a huge expanse of parking lot and two more chain stores nearby, one was electronics and the other a clothing store. Mike looked towards the huge jutting rock wall which was 100 feet high easily. Somewhere above the rock was the highway but you had to drive around to get onto it. He glanced into the snow and then back in the direction of his van. Something had caught his attention. He stopped and shielded his eyes. There was something in the snow...or someone? This was the worst place to be wandering around out back of a bulk warehouse. Surely no one would come out here, even to smoke in this mess.

He narrowed his eyes and looked closer. It was nothing. He shoved his hands into his jacket pocket and dug around until he found his wool hat. He pulled it out and immediately pulled it over his generously sized head. It didn't really cover his ears well but he still felt better with it on. He took another dozen steps. The snow under his feet made a crunching sound. He stopped again. He didn't want to stop because Lord knows he just wanted to be in his van and trying to make his way back to the rest stop. If he couldn't get back there tonight he would have a lot of frozen bread loaves and mayonnaise.

"H...Hello?" he called into the blinding snow. It was likely nothing but he could have sworn he saw something or someone only a few feet from him. There was no doubt now, he could see there was the shape of a person standing there. "Everything alright?" Big Mike called. He shielded his eyes again and the snow was driving towards him at supernatural speed.

Mike had to make sure that everything was alright or it would haunt him. He cleared his throat and walked further into the storm. As he got closer he could make out the figure of the person. They weren't moving; in fact they were standing perfectly still letting the snow build around them. From where he stood it looked like the snow was avoiding the person entirely. In fact, it looked like they were wearing a dress. This person was clearly a woman and she was wearing what looked like a long flowing white dress of some kind.

The sheer oddity of this situation was not lost on Mike and all he could think of was finding out what was going on. "Miss? Are you alright? I can take you inside." She didn't move or turn around and more than anything Mike was worried for this woman. He approached her and a gust of wind picked up, throwing tiny snow pellets into Mike's face. He could see she had incredibly long dark hair. Her hair was black...maybe a dark brown and it was stark against the white snow and the white dress she was wearing. Actually the dress looked more like a bed sheet as he got closer. Mike wasn't one to use profanity but the situation was incredibly strange. "What in the hell?" he whispered.

The figure finally started to move. It was only the smallest of movements at first and Mike leaned in, watching her closely. She was turning, her head first and then her body. Mike was caught in some sort of frozen hypnosis. Her movements were robotic. He could hardly feel the icy weather building around him anymore. Her hair flew distinctively away from her face and she turned around entirely now. Mike stared at the beautiful woman before him. She was tall, although not as tall as he was. Her skin was pale but not as white as the snow around her or the dress she wore. She had beautiful dark eyes and distinctively Asian features. The most noticeable thing of all was her deep red lips. She was wearing blood red lipstick that was so stunning against the backdrop of everything white.

"Miss, what are you doing?" Mike asked, once he found his words again. She did nothing. She had stopped again, facing Mike and was staring at him completely unresponsive. He realized that the dress she wore was more like a nightgown and yet she didn't seem to be showing the least bit of problem with the cold or the snow coming down. He felt like he couldn't move. He wanted to help this woman but everything about this situation seemed so wrong. At the same time nothing truly out of the ordinary stood out to him. The woman tilted her head only slightly before finally speaking. Mike understood nothing.

"*Arashi no naka, aitsu o otte iku. Aitsu no chi ga hoshii. Kono watashi no arashi no nakade fukushu shite yaru.*"

Her voice was easy to hear, even above the wind. In fact, it was almost as though the wind stopped howling long enough for the woman to speak. Her voice was erratic, raspy and angry. Perhaps the cold was having an effect on her but no matter how her voice sounded Mike understood none of it. What she spoke was lovely, poetic even, but he understood nothing and was beginning to feel the ice creep into his boots and around his feet. He didn't have arthritis but his old bones sure hurt in this weather.

"I don't understand you. Come inside, you'll die of pneumonia out here...you'll die..."

It was as though the words meant something to her. It was the first time she truly heard or recognized that Big Mike Otterman was in front of her. Her eyes widened and he could see that they were black. Not just her pupils but the whites of her eyes blacked over like oil seeping into an ocean. Her clear, smooth, pale skin began to squirm and Mike could see blue veins running up the sides of her temples. His feet finally found movement again and he stepped back from the woman. It took a few seconds before Big Mike realized the woman was clearly floating several feet above the ground.

"What in the blue hell," Big Mike hollered, and he took another step back tripping over the snow building around him and falling hard onto his substantial backside. He felt pain as he hit the ground. His hands were not gloved and the ice bit at his bare palms. The woman continued to rise above him, whispering in a breathy tone, "*Arashi no naka, aitsu o otte iku.*" The woman's completely black eyes watched

Mike with frightening intensity. Mike tried moving away from her but she was advancing rapidly. Just then, there was a humming noise that he thought maybe was a nearby car or even the power lines around him. The woman rose above him and her face began to transform into a hideous figure. The humming noise buzzed around him and he took his hands off the icy ground and grasped his head. To make matters more bizarre, there was a distinct light around the woman now. She turned her head and looked in the direction of the humming noise. There was no way to tell where the light was coming from and Mike didn't care because the combination of the frigid cold, the insane driving buzz around them, and now this light from beside, behind or inside her convinced him that this was the end for Big Mike Otterman.

He held his head, sitting on his ass behind the warehouse bulk store, and he knew in his very being that this was the end. He was having a stroke, delirium or a heart attack, or all three. The woman was directly over top of Mike now and the light was blinding. Mike's eyes were clenched instinctively trying to block the noise that would soon explode his brain and then it would be over...he hoped. It took all his strength to open his eyes and look at where the woman had been only moments before. The woman was gone and instead looming before him was a pillar of light unlike anything he had ever seen. The pillar was drawing in snow like a storm cloud, a vicious funnel of light and ice, and it was slowly moving further and further away from him.

From the pillar came a voice which was now just a raspy monstrous scream. "*Fukushuu o shite yaru! Oboetenasai!*" Mike's eyes widened and he screamed into the storm. His scream seemed to last forever but when he stopped and opened his eyes, taking his hands from his head, everything was over. Not for Mike Otterman, not yet anyway. He was still very much alive. The snow hadn't let up, not for a moment. He looked into the sky and thought how lovely it looked coming in at that angle. She was gone. The light had somehow taken her away.

9

"Mr. Otterman?" said a voice. Mike didn't move. "Mr. Otterman," it repeated.

"Hey...hello?" he called back over his shoulder. The two young men that had prepared Mike's order rushed out into the snow and over to Mike. They stood on either side of him and helped him to his feet. Mike stood for a moment to make sure he was steady and waved the men off. He brushed off as much snow as possible.

"Are you alright?"

"Yes, yes I think so...I don't know. Got a little disoriented is all."

"We'll walk you to your van?"

"I'm old but I'm not that old yet son. I can get there," Mike replied. He stopped when he reached the driver's side door. He felt relief at just seeing his old rust bucket. He paused and turned to where the two men were heading back into the warehouse. "Hey!" he called. Both men stopped and turned to him. "You guys see that light...like an airplane or something?"

They looked at each other and immediately Mike regretted asking. They already helped the crazy old man off the ground in a snow storm. He might as well continue his descent into madness and tell them a lovely Asian woman turned into a beast while yelling a foreign language at him. Let's not forget the blinding head ache. They both shrugged and he waved at them. He opened his driver's side door and felt absolute relief when he turned the key and the old beast turned over...snow be damned. Big Mike took a deep breath and threw the van into gear. He was never more determined to get back to his rest stop, have some coffee and sit in his office looking at the increase in sales. This was a night to remember that he would rather not.

10

Lyle Lovett was singing about the lady being his wife. It wouldn't have been Ethan's choice of traveling music. Of course, it was expected that a truck driver who was originally from Tennessee and who always wore a camouflage truckers cap would love country and western music, but he didn't...Lyle Lovett or otherwise. He was in fact a 70's and 80's fan all the way. Give him REO Speedwagon, Journey, maybe even some Bee Gee's any day of the week. However, he wasn't going to question the choice in music even if he was the one behind the wheel. The man sitting in the passenger seat hadn't said much since they started their trip and they still had six or seven hours to go, and then the trip back. It wasn't that they didn't talk, they talked once in awhile, but they didn't usually make runs like this together.

Ethan Datsun was thirty-two years old, in good shape and a good looking guy or so women told him. He was single and he was on the road a lot so he just hadn't found the time to date anyone seriously. He had gotten a college degree in auto mechanics and worked at that quite successfully for nearly eight years. It was just after he started doing some mechanic work for Roston Trucking that Harvey Roston himself suggested Ethan drive truck part time. It was good money, good travel, and a smooth job. Ethan agreed to try it and it wasn't long before he was licensed (at Roston's expense) and he was doing short day runs in the area and enjoying it quite a bit.

Ethan was a loner and he liked it that way. He loved his audiobooks, so it was a dream come true to drive, get paid and listen to books while he did it. The money was good, very good, especially because he was good at the job and fast at getting the loads where they needed to go. So it wasn't long before he put mechanics behind him and started driving full time. No family to speak of and nothing tying him down meant he could do any runs that "Harv" needed him to do. It was unusual however, that Ethan would have to do a straight run to central Jersey and back to the coast in less than 24 hours. He was already pushing over time, having done a run to Michigan yesterday. He tried to turn it down but Harvey insisted he wanted him to do it and then offered to go with him to give him some company and help with the driving. 60-40 split when it came to driving, he promised.

Ethan didn't necessarily care for the company, especially with his boss that he really only had a handful of conversations with, but the co-driving was actually appealing. They were two hours into their trip, country music in check and no conversation to speak of. The song ended and Harv turned down the radio. The snow was really starting to come in now and Ethan, despite being the excellent driver he was, had slowed down quite a bit. It was starting to get dark; they hadn't been able to leave earlier as they were waiting for their truck to get back to the lot from a run to Montreal, Quebec. "Might be a nasty stretch here getting outta Philly," Harv said.

"Yeah, it definitely could be." Ethan looked at the digital clock on the truck's massive front panel. It read just after 9 PM. He would likely drive at least 4 hours before they'd trade and hopefully he could catch some sleep. Some people had trouble sleeping in trucks but Ethan was completely relaxed being a passenger or a driver. He could be wide awake driving and be fast asleep as a passenger.

There was a sudden gust of wind that rocked the rig back and forth but Ethan kept it straight like a professional. One of the first things to get used to when driving a rig was the thousands of pounds on the back end of the truck that was susceptible to the smallest changes in weather, wind or road conditions. This was about the worst possible conditions for a rig but the right driver could handle themselves properly. Ethan had never driven with Harv behind the wheel and he wasn't sure he trusted him yet to brave the icy roads and minimal visibility. The truck barreled through the growing snow storm sending enormous clouds of frozen precipitation into the air around them. There were very few cars on the road, and even less in the last fifteen minutes, so Ethan wasn't concerned about causing anyone behind them undue stress with the rig-made squall he was creating. It wasn't long though before he had to slow the truck down to less than 30 Miles to really keep control of it. The enormous headlights on the beast really only showed just how much snow was falling. There were several road signs before Ethan noticed a big green one that said "ROAD SIDE STOP—-EAT, GAS, STAY..." Only stay had been struck out with what looked like black spray paint. "I know it's only been a couple hours but you want to stop for some coffee and a snack maybe?" Ethan suggested. He expected his boss to protest saying they had too far to go and a deadline to be there.

"Absolutely," Harv replied, nodding. He sounded almost relieved at the suggestion. Ethan thought maybe the weather was making them both a little jumpy. No one enjoyed driving in this crap, no matter what you were driving. Ethan moved the massive truck into the proper lane and started his preparations to gear down and move into the stop. Another blast of wind made the trailer rock and groan but Ethan didn't hesitate as he signaled onto the off ramp. Ethan glanced at the clock again, 9:24 it read. He wouldn't mind a little break whatsoever and there would still be plenty of time once this blew over a little bit.

Maneuvering the rig onto the off ramp took a little strategy but there was truck parking to the right of the main parking lot. Waves of snow were building but the 18 wheeler made short work of them. Ethan switched off the ignition, and they both checked their belongings before opening the huge truck doors which groaned in protest. The snow and wind hit them and Ethan heard Harv mutter a curse word as he jumped down onto the snow packed pavement. They slammed their doors one after another and both met at the front of the truck to move inside.

The warm air felt incredible when they swung open the doors. Ethan held the front door for his boss to go in. They stomped their feet to clear the snow and moved into the rest stop. It was as quiet and dead as Ethan had expected. The radio piped throughout the place blaring out yet another country song. A young girl was on the far side at Big Mike's Diner, wiping the counter tops. A young man in the convenience store was reading a book but he looked half asleep. The only other patrons were two men sitting off in a corner with their heads together talking. Ethan noticed both men wore collars but thought nothing of it.

"Need smokes," Harv grumbled, and schlepped off in the direction of the bored looking young man. Ethan nodded and walked further into the eating area. He noticed now there was another man sitting at the furthest table on his right, by himself. He had a laptop open in front of him and the power adapter ran down beside him and was plugged into the wall. He had the most intense eyes. He was very scrawny, even Ethan could see that from where he was. He was likely around Ethan's age but had thick almost horn rimmed glasses that were pushed tightly up on his face. He wasn't looking around and was clearly very involved in whatever was going on at his computer.

The priests hadn't made any indication that they even noticed this other man.

Ethan walked to one of the tables closest to the front door and sat down to wait for Harv, who joined him shortly after. Just as Harv returned with his cigarettes, one of the two priests walked past them. Ethan thought maybe he was heading back out on the road but a few moments later the second priest went down the hallway to the left.

Harv looked tired and they weren't even a quarter through their trip. "Gonna step out for a cig," he said to Ethan. Ethan looked at him and smiled. "What?" Harv asked.

"You need one that bad to brave that crap?" Ethan asked, nodding towards the snowy mess outside.

"You know it," he replied and smirked. Ethan waited a few moments and then decided to visit the washroom. He casually glanced at the computer geek again before making his way down the hallway where the washrooms were. The hallway was nondescript, had a water fountain and two doors leading to the men's and ladies' washrooms. There was also another door that led to a small janitorial closet and a third door that led to a back hallway that linked together the rest of the hallways behind the various eating establishments. There was no one else in the hall but as he reached to push open the "Men's" door the older priest came out. The two exchanged apologies for the near miss and they went their separate ways.

As a trucker Ethan had seen every manner of public washroom you can imagine, from spotless and swanky to crouching on the roadside behind the protection of his 18-wheeler. This particular washroom was somewhere in the middle. It was decently well kept with a schedule hanging of when it was last inspected. There was a vending machine on the wall with everything from Halls lozenges to no-name condoms. He had seen enough ladies of the night frequenting trucker stops to know that a condom machine wasn't a bad idea. He had never gotten so lonely that he took advantage of that particular service but he was only a man and it had crossed his mind. He was single, young, and morbid curiosity often made him wonder what it would be like. These women that had approached him, or he had seen with other truckers, weren't exactly street walkers with thick make-up and six inch heels but usually attractive middle-aged women looking for quick cash.

In the corner, near the washroom sinks, there was a coin operated fortune telling machine. There was a disturbing cartoon image of a genie of some kind with an enormous hat on him, reminding Ethan of Johnny Carson's Carnac the Magnificent. There were cheap LED red lights circling clockwise around the machine. Ethan shook his head and walked past it before it belted out a digitized voice that said "Do you want your future?" in some sort of bad Transylvanian accent. There were five sinks, all manually operated, none of those crazy hands free stations that were all over the city to protect everyone from the diseases that lurked on faucets. On the other wall were four stalls, surrounded in blue steel, with the last stall being extra large for wheelchair access or for those people that slip in there because it makes them feel like they have their own personal bathroom. There was also a row of six urinals. They were all well maintained, with those blue bricks in them keeping things minty fresh and giving men everywhere something to aim at. Ethan walked to the middle of the urinals and unzipped. There was a buzzing noise that made him look up at the fluorescent lights above him. They seemed functional but the buzzing started suddenly and he thought maybe one of them was on their way to going out. He finished his business and walked to the sink closest to the urinal.

He looked in the mirror, turning his head to each side and examining himself. The buzzing was worse and he glanced at the lights behind him but nothing was going out. He turned on the water and ran his hands under the cool liquid. Soap came next into his palms and he worked it around before running them under the water again. "Geez," he whispered suddenly. He clenched his eyes shut and shook his head. It was like an immediate migraine shooting through his temples. The buzzing he had attributed to the lights was getting worse and when he opened his eyes and glanced in the mirror his eyes looked red and blood shot already. There was a tear trickling down his left cheek from clenching his eyes so tightly.

The buzzing turned to a high pitched whine that actually made Ethan cry out and bend over the sink grasping his head and then, seconds later, silence. “Geez,” Ethan repeated, with his head still over the sink and his eyes closed, but his migraine was gone. No migraine that Ethan had ever had behaved quite like that. He stood up straight and realized the water was still running full stream. He reached down and turned the faucet off. His eyes didn’t look as red as they had a moment ago, perhaps he was just over analyzing what had just happened. It wasn’t just that his migraine was suddenly gone, the buzzing stopped and there was no dull after-ache or any indication that anything had happened. He looked into the mirror and noticed there was a small trickle of deep red blood coming from his right nostril. Ethan shook his head and ran the back of his hand across his face, wiping off the blood. Other than that oddity he felt perfectly fine now.

He wasn’t one to look a gift horse in the mouth; a migraine that wouldn’t quit was awful so he’d take this reprieve. He turned from the sink and walked to the two blow dryers by the fortune telling genie and pressed the big silver button. Hot air pumped loudly from the machine and he ran his hands under it until they were mostly dry. He glanced at the vending machine and among other things there was the familiar logo for brand name aspirin. His head ache was gone, as fast as it had come, but he wasn’t going to take any chances. He fished in his pocket and pulled a few quarters out and dropped them into the old style push slot. It clocked in and he hit the button for aspirin. The machine burped and sputtered and dispensed his purchase into the plastic slot below. Ethan held out what he had spent his dollar on. It was a condom. The package was solid red and had ‘RIBBED’ written across the top. He shook his head and couldn’t help but chuckle. He shoved the condom into his pocket and exited the washroom.

The main area of the rest stop was no different than when he had left for the washroom, only there were even less people. The priests who had been conversing so intently were no longer in their booth. One of the priests however, the older of the two, was at the convenience counter purchasing something. The man with the laptop was still at his table but the laptop was gone and he was scribbling something on a notepad. The young lady who had been washing tables was back behind her counter now and had a glass of water in her hand. It looked like she was taking some pills...maybe she had a headache as well.

The priest finished his purchase and was putting a bottle of something in his jacket pocket. He walked back towards the tables where Ethan was standing. Harv was nowhere to be seen. Ethan turned and tried to glance out the front doors where the snow showed no sign of letting up. "Looking for someone son?" the priest asked.

"Uh..yah my boss...he went outside for a cigarette and I figured he'd be back by now." The priest nodded and put a stick of sugarless gum in his mouth.

"Nasty habit, you can brave just about anything for it."

Ethan looked at him rather curiously. The priest nodded. "Been a quitter since '96," and then offered Ethan some gum. Ethan smiled politely but shook his head. "My friend went to get his prayer book out there, maybe they're talking."

"Maybe," Ethan said, but something didn't feel right. "I'm just going to check on him, Father." The men nodded at each other and headed in opposite directions again. Ethan opened the inner door and he could hear the howling, horrible wind and he could see the snow piling up against the door. Ethan looked out the front door, cupping his hands around his eyes. He could see nothing, not even a foot in front of his face as the old expression goes. Ethan pushed the door open further and the frigid blast made him take a step back. The howling wind was brutal, and if the parking lot lights were on you couldn't even tell. Ethan cleared his throat and yelled, "Harvey!"

The response was only whistling and howling. "Harv!" he called again. Nothing. Ethan closed the door and realized his face was almost frozen. It felt like minus 20 out, even worse than when they had gotten here just twenty minutes earlier. He turned back to go inside and was startled by the priest who was standing at the inside door.

"Sorry," he said smiling, seeing he had startled Ethan. Ethan was beginning to feel like the priest's smile was condescending. "Any luck?"

Ethan shook his head and walked back inside past him. He heard the outer door open behind him as the priest went outside. His funeral, Ethan thought, no one should be out in that. He walked towards the eatery where the girl was now wiping down the counter and humming to herself. "Hi," he said. She smiled and put down her cleaning cloth. She had a beautiful smile and was very attractive. She was probably ten years younger than Ethan, which made him feel old, but didn't stop his mind from wandering.

"Hey yourself, what can I get you?"

"Maybe some fries...if it's not too much trouble."

"Comin' right up," she said, winking at him. She turned and disappeared into the back to throw some fries into the deep fryer. She returned two minutes later and punched numbers into the register. "4.30, hun." Ethan nodded and reached into his jeans to pull out a fiver he had in his front pocket. He pulled it out and along with it the condom he had inadvertently purchased. The condom flipped out with his cash and landed on the counter. She looked at it curiously and once the concept sank in she looked at Ethan with her eyebrows raised.

Ethan wondered how red he was turning. He looked at her and tried to smile. "I was trying to buy aspirin from the washroom vending machine and got this instead. She actually giggled and nodded.

"Yah sometimes that gets messed up like that...you still kept it?" she asked.

He was getting more embarrassed. Then he realized she was still smiling, she was joking with him. "Hey a buck is a buck," he replied, and she laughed. She took the five from him and when she was getting his change he scooped the condom back into his pocket. There was a banging from the front foyer and Ethan turned to look as the girl was getting his fries. The geeky guy at the table was still scribbling on a pad and paid no attention to anyone. The priest was coming back in from outside. His shirt was covered in snow and all through his hair. He wasn't alone, but it wasn't Harv and it wasn't the other priest he had been with. Instead, it was a woman and a little girl. The woman was clearly distraught. She was sobbing and the little girl was clutching an old doll of some kind. There was another younger man behind them. He had the hood from his sweatshirt pulled up and it was covered in snow. He was pounding his shoes on the weather mat at the front door.

The priest took the woman to a table closest to them and was kneeling in front of her trying to console her. The little girl tucked herself up beside her mother but said nothing. The young man was looking around but doing not much else. Ethan ate his fries for a few minutes and noticed that the girl from the eatery had joined the priest and the woman. The woman was out and out sobbing now. Ethan started to feel like he should try and help too. Where in the hell was Harv? He'd probably gone out to the truck to warm up and sleep. Nice of him to let Ethan know. Ethan pushed his half eaten fries away and sauntered towards the small group of people.

He listened to the commotion. The priest was trying to calm the woman, telling her it would be okay and they would figure something out. The girl, Heather, he had overheard her say her name was, had her arm around the woman. She looked at the priest. "We should go out and look for her husband."

"I only have a small car and its getting really bad out there. I'm not sure we could make it back up the highway."

"I have a truck," Ethan blurted.

All of them, including the distraught mother, looked at Ethan. He cleared his throat. "I came in a large truck. I could unhook the trailer and if I gear down and really put the pedal to it I can probably force it through the snow."

The priest nodded and looked at Ethan. "Well if you're willing. I mean, this woman says her husband and son are stranded out there."

Ethan licked his lips out of nervousness and nodded. "My boss is out in the truck I think; I'll head out and let you know." He turned and walked towards the front door.

"'Excuse me son," the priest called. Ethan stopped and turned.

"Ethan, Ethan Datsun."

"Ethan...I'm Father Patrick, it's a pleasure. Listen, my co-traveler went out to get his prayer book like I mentioned. Could you just check out there and make sure he's alright?"

"Sure Father, I'll do that." Ethan opened the front door to face the monstrous storm and glanced back into the rest stop. Heather, Father Patrick, the mother and daughter were still together, the hoodie kid that had come with them was checking out the video game machines and he couldn't see the geeky guy from his vantage point but everyone was there; now to find the rest of the weary travelers. He nodded and took a deep breath before heading out into the winter blast.

11

By the time Ethan returned from looking for anyone outside on the highway, Mark and Peter Oswald had joined the rest stop crew. Mark was with Father Patrick weighing the situation and options. Mark was tired. This was too much work for such a brutal night and a long trip. He turned to face Father Patrick John and his voice was just a whisper. "Father, I think it's going to be a long night." The two of them stepped to the side away from the rest of the group.

"Do you believe in prayer officer?"

"Sure...absolutely, just doesn't usually work for me."

"Well perhaps I can pray enough for both of us and everyone else here."

There was a banging outside as the wind ripped something away and blew it against the building. The snow was piling up at the windows and it was clearly getting unpassable and none of them could have expected it to get any worse. Ethan joined the two men in their huddle.

"What are we planning here?" Ethan asked.

"How many people are still out there...missing?" Mark asked.

"Andrea's husband and son, Barton's girlfriend, my partner Father White, Ethan's boss...who were you traveling with?" Patrick asked Mark.

"No one, I was alone and so were Peter Oswald and the other guy...the doctor."

"Physicist," said a quiet voice from behind the three men huddling. They turned to face the somber, awkward looking man. "I am a doctor but not that kind of doctor. I am Dr. Camp and I think the best thing we can do is all stay here until this storm passes."

"I'm not sure I can do that Dr. Camp. I feel obliged to ensure the people are okay out there," said Mark, and Father Patrick nodded.

"I got my truck about a mile up the road, I mean if anyone was out there I sure as hell didn't see them but then I didn't see much of anything. I expected Harv...my boss to be in the truck but he wasn't," Ethan added.

"So let's lay down a plan," Patrick said. No sooner had he said that, there was a bang through the front door that silenced everyone in the stop. The doors were thrown open and a burly man powered his way through. His head was wrapped in a scarf and his coat was pulled up around his head. It was Big Mike. Paul, who still hadn't left his counter, spotted his boss and the book he was reading instantly disappeared. He jumped the counter and rushed to his boss's side.

"Mr. Otterman, you're back! I didn't think you'd make it back tonight."

"Wasn't gonna leave you here running the place Janson." Mike pulled his scarf off and opened his coat. "What in the hell is this, a welcoming committee," he said, nodding towards the group of travelers and Heather.

"I dunno, something about people missing," Paul said, uninterested. The two of them walked over to the whole group. The huddling men had returned to stand with everyone else.

"Problem here?" Mike said in his loud booming voice.

"And you are?" Mark said, stepping up.

"Mike Otterman, I own this place."

"Officer Mark Harrison, New Jersey State Police and while I was just a traveler, I am now considering this an emergency situation, we have people missing out in this storm." "Missing? Like stranded?" Mike asked.

"Presumably," Patrick replied.

"Missing like gone," Dr. Camp said, mostly under his breath.

"I just came from north of here and didn't see a soul for the last... thirty miles. I don't even know how in the hell I got back here. I'm tired and pissed off and I have had one hell of a night and I'm thinking I'd like to close the rest stop."

A sudden and deep laugh came from Dr. Camp that made several of them look at him curiously. He went straight faced and cleared his throat shrinking back into the background.

"I'll do what I can to help you Officer Harrison..." Mike said.

"Mark."

"...right Mark. But I'd like to be closed and gone by 11."

"And how do you think any of us are going to get out of here in this?" Heather asked her boss. Mike looked at her and shrugged.

"Better to try now then wait until this gets worse," he replied.

"How could this get worse," Patrick said.

"Find my husband," Andrea suddenly screamed, and they all turned their attention back to her.

"Sorry Mr. Otterman, I appreciate your position but no one is leaving here until I clear this situation. The road to the east is blocked off, probably an accident, and the road is likely closed anyways," Mark explained.

Josh Barton spoke up for the first time in awhile. "I came from the east; there ain't no road block, or accident."

Mark looked at the young man. He still had reservations about him, there was something going on. "You came from the eastbound lane?"

"'That's what I said," he said with a distinct tone. Mark's brow crinkled at the guy's attitude. Josh noticed and took a proverbial step back. "I did, yah man, and I didn't see any accident."

"Did you see any officers or any road blocks?"

"Nope nothing like that."

Sitting back beside Dr. Camp was Peter Oswald. He had said nothing since the gang all got themselves together. "I came from that direction as well and I can assure you there were no officers." He looked casually at Dr. Camp who just glared at him.

"Should there have been officers Mark?" Patrick asked.

"I was going in that direction and I was stopped by a road block. A man, an older man in a yellow coat, told me to turn around and that there was an accident. I assumed he was State Police, he knew my name."

"I gotta piss," Josh said, and walked away from the crowd.

"Don't go outside," Mark commanded, to which Josh just waved his hand over his shoulder.

Josh was in the washroom at the urinal when the door opened behind him. He glanced over his shoulder. It was the tall thin guy that had said his name was Peter. Peter stood in front of the mirror while Josh finished his business and the two men were standing in front of the sinks. Josh was washing his hands when he noticed Peter's shoes. They were patent leather, probably expensive, but he had a dark red stain on them even after coming through the snow.

"Dude you got shit on your shoe."

Peter looked down and smiled. He was staring at it like it was a fond memory.

"Maybe I'm getting my rag huh?" he said, and laughed an unnerving laugh.

"Yah...okay dude, that's messed up." Josh turned to the hand dryer. Peter looked at him and noticed when Josh raised his hands that he had something tucked into his waist band. He peered closer and was certain now that it was the butt of a gun. Interesting. The kid glanced at him again and left the washroom. Peter looked in the mirror and smiled, showing a full set of white teeth.

"That's messed up," he said, doing his best impression of the young man that had just left. "I'll mess you up you gun carrying cowboy," he growled. He laughed in a high pitched tone and cleared his throat before winking at himself in the mirror and turning to leave the rest room. The group of travelers were still standing in the middle of the eating section talking. The distraught wife, Andrea, was now pleading with Mark to find her husband and son without exception. Patrick and Mark and Ethan then stepped aside once again to put their heads together. Peter walked over to the geeky little doctor who was sitting by himself. Out of all the pretentious bastards in this little shit-hole, he only felt comfortable sitting around the mostly quiet geek. Birds of a feather?

"The cowboys gonna launch a rescue?" Peter whispered to Camp. Camp said nothing. He looked at the floor without as much as flinching when Peter spoke to him.

The men parted again. Mark cleared his throat. "Let's do a vehicle check. My SUV is outside, along with Andrea's van, Father Patrick's car and Ethan's truck. So what does that leave us. I assume, Mr. Otterman, your vehicle is here?"

Mike nodded. I drove my cube van down but I have a pickup around back. It's a 4x4, not that it will help in this."

Mark nodded. He turned to face Heather and Paul. "You both have vehicles?"

Both employees nodded. "Parking lot, far left," Heather said.

"Same," Paul replied.

"Dr. Oswald is it?" Mark said, turning to face Peter and the Doctor. Oswald nodded and pushed his glasses up. "You drove here?"

"I was dropped off," Oswald whispered.

"Dropped off?" Big Mike said, smirking. "Who in the hell would drop you off here?"

"Is there a point to this?" Paul said, getting bored.

Mark faced Paul and looked sternly at the young man.

"We have people missing in a storm that has us stranded here. If there are people stuck out there in their vehicles, I need to figure out who is out there and what vehicles before I go calling this in," Mark replied.

"Well I came in with mommy and daughter so my car is out there on the highway, and so is my woman," Josh said. He ran his hands through his hair and sighed. He was getting tired and kind of feeling like he needed a joint or a fix of some kind. This was getting lame.

"Right, and your car is out there Mr. Oswald, on the highway somewhere?" Mark asked, turning to face Peter. Peter was turning red unintentionally. He cleared his throat and looked around at the faces looking at him. Why were they all looking at him? Their eyes were red and accusatory. He closed his eyes and when he opened them they still stared. Stupid sluts and their whore masters. What the hell were they looking at? He could cut out their eyes with his pocket knife and then they couldn't stare at anything. Bitch. He wanted to scream and this stupid dumb ass cop was standing here looking at him. Bitch. He cleared his throat again and regained his composure.

"Yes, I hit the barrier on the curve. But it's far...and I was alone...its way down there...two maybe three miles."

"You walked three miles in this?" Mark questioned. Peter swallowed and nodded. "Alright, can I get a phone so I can call this in? Even if no one can get out in this, we can at least get the ball rolling." Mike looked at Heather and motioned for her to get the phone. She nodded in understanding and retreated to the eatery to get it. "Mr. Otterman?"

"Please...Mike...or Big Mike," he replied, smiling.

"Alright Mike...do you have anything better than a four wheel drive vehicle. I mean, my truck has four wheel drive too but I just don't think that's going to cut it. Maybe a snowmobile or something?"

"Yessir, I have a snow-cat in the back shed. Bought it cheap from

MountainSide Skiing south'a' here. Got a helluva deal and the funny thing is I never use the stupid thing."

"That would do just fine. Could we take it up the highway to find the abandoned cars?"

Peter jumped forward. "Car. Just this young fellows car, he's missing people...mine is a write off."

"Then we need to get to it, I mean, if its impeding the road it could be dangerous," Mark replied.

Hannah Green had curled up on one of the booth chairs and seemed to be asleep. Andrea had stopped sobbing and was staring at the tiled floor. Most likely she heard nothing that anyone was discussing.

Heather returned with a black cordless phone in her hand. "We have a small problem," she said, coming up behind Mark and Mike. Both men looked at her. Heather clicked the talk button on the phone which beeped once and then went dead. Mike took the phone and put it to his ear. "The phone is dead. All three phones, and the pay phone in the back, all dead. No dial tone, nothing."

"Shit," Big Mike said.

Paul turned and easily jumped over one of the seats and slipped over to the bank of pay phones beside his convenience area. Everyone watched as he picked up each handset and put it back down. There were five phones and Paul checked all five of them. He turned and faced the crowd and shook his head. Mike called across the room, "try in the store." Paul nodded and jogged to his sanctuary to try the phone there.

"The lines might be down," Mark said. He pulled out his cell phone which already had been acting up even before the storm got worse. He flipped it out and the bars marking signal showed zero. The battery was more than half full but the phone showed useless. "Anyone else?" Mark asked, shaking his cell phone in the air. Ethan and Josh both dug into their coat pockets and pulled out similar looking cell phones but a few moments of investigation turned up obvious results of nothing.

Paul returned to the group. "Nothing, phone is dead and so is my cell."

"This storm has knocked out everything," Father Patrick said speaking up for the first time in awhile. He had been silently praying outside the group.

"That's alright. We still need to try and get out to Josh's car and see if anyone is still there. Can we take the snow-cat?" Mark asked Mike. Mike nodded.

"I dunno how much gas is in her but if anything can get through this it'll be that beast."

"Fine, you and I will go out and see what we can find and we'll take it from there," Mark said, nodding.

Father Patrick stepped forward and leaned in close to Mark. "I don't want to be negative here but is it a good idea that you leave everyone here. I mean, you're sort of in charge right now and you're really the only one capable of being in charge in an emergency situation. Let me go, or Ethan here," Patrick said.

"You think that's necessary?" Mark asked. The two men looked at each other and Patrick nodded. Ethan overheard the conversation and nodded as well.

"I'll go...with Mr. Otterman. You guys need to be here I think," Ethan said. Mark thought for a few moments, trying to formulate his plan carefully, and then nodded in agreement.

"Fine, you guys both go. Mike, do you have a CB radio here or anything?" Mike shook his head.

"Hey!" Paul said. He held up his hand and then jogged back to the convenience store again. He returned with a red and blue package that was marked with a green price sticker that said "19.99$" Inside the package were two red and orange walkie-talkies with red tipped antennas. WALK AND TALK was written across the top of the package in bright yellow lettering. He handed them off to Mark who looked at them curiously. “These are toys?”

“Yes but they have a mile range and they’ll do the trick under the circumstances,” Paul replied.

“He’s right,” Mike said, grabbing the package and pulling them open. “Get some batteries Paul.”

12

The snow-cat was a monstrous machine that used to groom ski trails. Big Mike Otterman's snow-cat was a Bombardier BR100+, 2007 model. It was small but well built. He had gotten an absolute steal for the thing at 5K when a local ski resort sold it to him in order to upgrade. Actually, he had outbid another businessman in order to get it. He thought having the snow-cat could come in handy someday, and also thought it was kind of bad-ass having it.

Mike Otterman and Ethan Datsun, two men with plenty of experience working in the outdoors and had seen their share of weather, thought they were well prepared to face what was beyond the rest stop. The two men went through the back of the eatery to the big metal fire exit doors. Both of them had their hoods wrapped around them. Ethan had a blue scarf snaked around his neck covering his mouth. "Ready?" Mike asked. Ethan nodded. Mark stood behind them.

"Josh's car is a dark blue Ford Mustang, old model. He said it was on the side of the road but don't take any chances as to where it might actually be. And keep your eyes open for Oswald's car. He says it's a rental and he doesn't even know the make or model but still...watch for it. But most of all watch for people, in unknown condition if you know what I mean."

Mike and Ethan nodded. "If they're injured they could be on the side of the road or in the snow," Ethan said, and Mark nodded in agreement.

12

Mike took a deep breath and hit the push bar on the fire doors. The doors swung open and the weather assaulted them. The snow was still coming down and the wind howled into the back hallway. Mark stepped back from the door feeling the icy chill. It had to be 20 below now, or worse, and there was zero visibility outside the back door.

"Should we wait this out?" Mark hollered over the wind.

Mike shook his head. "It's not getting any better and those missing people could be in trouble out there." Ethan and Big Mike turned and walked out into the snowfall. The shed that housed the snow-cat was no more than 200 feet from the back of the building but it still wasn't an easy walk. Mark pulled the double doors closed behind them and there was already a pile of snow on the cement floor.

It was impossible to tell which way the snow and wind were coming from, making it equally as impossible for Ethan and Mike to turn their face away from the storm. The storm was surrounding them. Ethan stayed close behind Mike since he knew his way better than anyone. This wasn't even what Big Mike had driven back in, this was worse, far worse. It crossed Mike's mind briefly that he wasn't sure he had ever seen a storm like this, not in Jersey, not anywhere. The wind howled as if in response to what he was thinking and he had to steady himself to not topple into the snow.

He figured they must almost be at the shed when he spotted something. He tried to open his eyes wider but his eyelashes were already freezing shut and he could feel the ice on his face. He stopped walking and he felt Ethan hit the back of him and stop as well. "Everything alright?" Ethan yelled over the howling squall. Big Mike said nothing. In fact, Big Mike heard nothing. Ethan's yell was drowned out by the noise of the storm.

Big Mike felt his stomach drop because if he saw what he thought he saw then everything was definitely not alright. He had almost completely put the incident at the warehouse out of his mind, having subconsciously chalked up the situation to some weird headache or some bad hamburger beef or something. He hadn't thought of his mysterious vision since the moment it happened and now if his eyes weren't playing tricks and they weren't...she was here, again.

Against his better judgment he yelled, "H...hello?" Ethan couldn't hear Mike anymore than Mike had heard him. He just assumed Mike needed a moment to catch his breath. Big Mike finally took a few more steps forward but then stopped again. It was as though the snow was shadowing her, she was there, standing not twenty feet from where they were. Her long white dress seemed as though it was made from snow and her skin was only a shade away from the color of the driving weather. It seemed as though the snow fell around her but not on her, like she was inside a bubble of some kind, but unlike at the warehouse where she seemed to ignore Mike, she was staring directly at them. She stared at Mike and he could once again see her blood red lips. "Who are you!" Mike yelled. Ethan heard him say something this time but couldn't hear what.

He tried to move to Mike's side but Mike put out his hand and pushed Ethan back. Ethan had no idea what was happening but Mike clearly wanted Ethan behind him so Ethan stepped back and waited. "What are you?!" Mike yelled. The woman said nothing and did nothing. She was simply staring at him blankly. Her eyes were black, with only a hint of white around the outsides. He could see nothing else in the storm besides her. He could feel something when he looked at her. Certainly he felt afraid, and curious, and even a little bit angry at the thought that maybe he was having some kind of stroke or breakdown. Most of all he felt dread. Whatever this was, whatever she was, wasn't safe and he had the unmistakable feeling that she was even less safe than this weather and the worsening of it. Mike turned away from her, almost ninety degrees, moved to his left and began to hustle through the snow. Enough was enough and ignoring her was his only option.

He hoped Ethan was following and keeping pace. Big Mike looked over his shoulder and saw that he was.

When he looked up again the shed was there, right in front of them. He literally slid on his heels to stop at the enormous double metal doors to his garage where he kept his tools, extra freezers, gasoline tanks for his generator, his vehicles and his snow-cat. He fumbled with his key ring and found the large silver key. He took one more glance towards where he had seen his snow bound woman but there was nothing, or rather he saw nothing more than the storm. The lock snapped open remarkably easy and he swung open the door just enough for him and Ethan to slide in. The lights were rigged with a motion sensor so two sets of flood lights spread across the room as Ethan and Mike hurried inside and pulled the doors closed behind them.

The howl of the wind died off only slightly once they were inside the room. Ethan took a deep breath and felt ice in his throat. It was still frigidly cold in the garage but not having the snow and ice and wind beating on his face was still a big improvement. Mike moved across the garage and grabbed a small white stick hanging on the wall. He glanced at it and dropped it back into place. "Geezus."

"What's wrong?"

"Thermometer says minus 42...that can't be right. It hasn't been that cold in New Jersey...ever, I'm sure of it" Mike said, looking at Ethan for confirmation. Ethan shrugged and a shiver went up his back.

"Did you get disoriented out there?" Ethan asked.

Big Mike looked uncomfortable and stomped out his boots. "Something like that." The snow-cat was directly in the center of the room and loomed over them. There was something distinctly ominous about it being there. Mike moved to the driver's side and pulled open the door. Ethan moved to the passenger side and both men maneuvered into the machine. Ethan rubbed his hands together and blew into them. Frost blew out of his mouth and did nothing more than make him feel colder.

Mike turned the key and the cat spat and sputtered. He turned it again and the dials and lights came to life and the machine rumbled.

He nodded in approval. "Gas?" Ethan called over the noise. Mike checked the gauges on the dashboard in front of them.

"Enough...not a lot, but enough," he responded. "Get the doors?"

Ethan jumped down and pushed the garage door open and moments later they were moving like a tank into the snow. The wipers on the enormous front windows pumped furiously. The large spotlights on top of the cat tried to push through the snow but it really was doing nothing more than showing exactly how much snow was falling. Regardless of this, the cat seemed to move through the snow effortlessly with Mike at the helm.

Ethan pulled the walkie-talkie from his coat pocket and turned on the switch. "Hello, Ethan to Mark...ya there?"

Inside the rest stop the walkie-talkie buzzed and had a lot of static but Ethan's voice did come through. Mark was talking to Heather about getting some food together for everyone so Father Patrick grabbed the walkie-talkie. "Ethan...it's Father Patrick, I hear you."

"Mike and I are moving around the building. We can't see much of anything."

"Is it safe to continue?" Patrick said.

There was a pause before Ethan spoke again. "He says he can handle it. I don't know if these walkies are gonna last much longer.

"Well there is a little ....back....can....you," Patrick's voice cracked in the walkie.

"Repeat that?" Ethan said.

There was no other response from Father Patrick, proving Ethan's point about these useless toys. It was worth a try he supposed. Mike moved the cat around the building and leaned in closer to try and see through the mess. The last thing he wanted to do was hit the vehicles already in the parking lot. He moved to the far right hoping that no one parked that far over and it seemed to be working. “I can’t see a damn thing. Should we do this,” Ethan questioned, looking at Big Mike. Mike was clearly determined.

“I know this land and this road better than anyone else. I can do this,” he replied.

14

Peter Oswald slammed into the washroom and the door closed behind him. "DAMMIT!" he yelled. "SON OF A BITCH," he screamed. He slammed his hands down on the sink counter. He looked into the mirror. His perfectly styled hair looked disheveled for the first time, as did his clothing. "Screw them, screw all of them. You're so stupid. Why did you just leave that car and leave her there," he said to himself in the mirror.

There was a noise and Peter paused and said nothing else. There was the noise again. Someone was in the washroom with him. "Hello?" Peter said, in a happier tone. Someone sniffed, it was distinct. "Oh... hellooo," Peter said turning away from the sinks. He looked at the bank of stalls behind him with chipped blue paint on them. There was a click of one of the locks sliding across and the stall door opened. Josh Barton stumbled out and leaned against the door. His eyes were red and he looked half asleep. His black traveling bag was on the ground behind him near the toilet.

"Man, who are you talking to?" he said quietly.

Peter felt a lump in his throat. "I was just...letting off some steam."

Josh looked at him and smiled. His eyes were more than just red, they were blood shot. His collared green shirt had one sleeve cuff undone and rolled up. Suddenly the situation settled in and Peter understood. Josh Barton had been shooting something in his arm. He was a drug addict. How perfect was this?

"You havin' a party in there young fella?" Peter asked, smirking. Josh ambled over to the sinks and Peter leaned back against a wall.

Josh ran some water into the sink and splashed it on his face.

"Don't judge me."

"Judge you? Oh no my friend not at all. I think you should do whatever makes you happy. We're stuck here, why shouldn't you have some fun," Peter replied.

Josh turned off the water and turned to face him. "Who are you?"

"Peter Oswald, I sell insurance."

"Uh huh, whatever."

"So your gal is out there?" Peter asked.

"I dunno, she was. I don't really give a damn. Stupid bitch is always screwing stuff up."

"What else you got in your goody bag," Peter said. He moved quickly and snatched the bag off the stall floor. Josh tried to stop him and continued trying to grasp at it but his extra-curricular activity made him slow and his reflexes non-existent. Peter smirked again and unzipped the bag. There was a pair of shoes, a sweatshirt, and a small white envelope. Peter looked inside the envelope and then at Josh. "Well, look at this. You know what this is I think?" Josh had given up trying to stop him. The drugs were taking their effect and he didn't care and didn't have the ability to protest. "Diacetylmorphine is what I think this is."

"What the hell you talkin' about, its heroin."

"That's what I said," Peter said. He put the envelope back into the duffel bag and moved the sweatshirt aside and saw something that truly caught his eye. There was a brown handle that looked distinctive and lead to the barrel of a semi-automatic handgun, the same one he had seen tucked in Barton's waist earlier. Peter's eyes widened and he pulled the gun out by the handle and dropped the duffel bag on the floor of the washroom. "Ohhh this is nice!"

"Put that back!" Josh said, getting a sudden burst of energy. He stepped forward and Peter put the weapon out in front of him aiming down the barrel and pointing it at Josh's chest. Josh wasn't tripping enough to not stop and raise his hands slightly. Peter tilted the gun and looked at the side.

"Safety's on cowboy," Peter said, and winked at Josh.

The washroom door opened but Josh didn't move. Peter looked over at the door. Stephen Camp stood in the doorway quietly and awkwardly, as usual. Peter smiled and Stephen stepped into the washroom, letting the door close behind him. The three men said nothing and Josh still stood with his hands raised. Peter lowered the weapon and reached behind him and tucked the gun into the back of his pants. He pulled out his shirt and let it drop down over his waist to hide the weapon.

"Dude, that's mine!" Josh said, dropping his hands. Peter put his hand out and pushed the young man backwards slightly.

"Who are you going to tell? The cop? Maybe then you can share your heroin with him? I'm gonna keep your toy champ because if this night pans out the way I think it will, I'm gonna need this more than you," Peter said. Josh turned and looked at Stephen who still said nothing and was still standing inside the door of the washroom.

Peter flashed his best business-man like smile and pointed at Stephen. "This guy! This guy I like. He's quiet, he's staying out of everyone's business, and you don't give a hot damn if I'm packing some heat do you, doc?" Stephen looked at both men and shrugged. Then he walked to one of the stalls, closing and locking the door behind him. Peter winked at Josh again and strolled out of the washroom.

"Stupid prick," Josh mumbled. His head was swimming and the interaction with Peter completely killed his buzz and now he lost his gun which could only end badly. Josh turned on the faucet and splashed some water on his face again. Stephen came out of the stall and shuffled over to the sink beside Josh. Josh glanced at him and turned off the faucet. “You don’t say much do you?” Josh asked.

“Not much to say,” Stephen said, washing his hands.

“Where were you heading, before this storm?”

Stephen looked at Josh. “Nowhere, this is where I was supposed to be. This is where we are all supposed to be.”

Josh laughed despite himself. His positive buzz was coming back. “Alright dude, whatever.”

15

Ethan had no idea how Mike knew where he was. Mike insisted twice that they were going west on the highway and he was fine so Ethan let him do what he was doing. It felt like a half an hour before Ethan spotted something on the shoulder of the road facing away from them. In fact it had only been fifteen minutes that they had been out there.

"Mike, there is something there, on the right." Mike tried to peer through the window but he saw nothing. His old eyes weren't quite as good as the young truck driver with him.

"Vehicle?" Mike asked.

"Could be."

Mike shifted down and began to slow the cat and move it away from the shoulder to avoid hitting anything, car or otherwise. It was a few more minutes before Mike noticed the buried object on the roadside. It was buried in what was already several feet but the dark colored Mustang was where Josh had left it when he abandoned the car to hijack the Green's van, or catch a ride depending on how you looked at it. The cat slowed and Mike pulled over as close as possible without being dangerously close.

"I'll go," Ethan said. "Keep the engine running," he joked.

Mike nodded but did not smile. His mind was occupied with his hallucinations and the raging storm. Ethan opened the door and jumped out of the cat. There was two feet of snow on the highway and the wind felt like ice pellets against Ethan's face. He got his bearings and then pushed his way through the snow to the Mustang. He peered into the dark windows. It was chillingly black. Any outsider might assume this car had been there, abandoned, for months. Ethan tried the driver's side door and it popped open, but not without icy protest. He had to haul on the door to drag it through the snow that had built up under it. He stuck his head inside and looked into the back seat and then the front. The interior was a mess, a pig sty, with old fast food wrappers and drink containers everywhere. Despite the cold, there was the unmistakable smell of booze and pot. He had been in enough truck stops to recognize the smell.

He leaned further in the car and saw a woman's purse on the passenger side floor, on top of more trash. He grabbed the purse and pulled it onto the driver's side seat. Under the circumstances he felt like he needed to go through the purse...the lack of actual logic was not lost on him but he ignored it and rifled through the bag. His hand shot back when he noticed an uncovered syringe near the bottom. He shook his head and tossed the purse back into the passenger side. Ethan looked around the car one last time before standing up and feeling the wind push him violently. He looked over the car, into the wasteland on the far side of the road. He could just barely hear the snow-cat rumbling behind him and could see nothing in the field. "Hello!" he screamed as loud as he could, into the storm. "Anyone...?" he called again. As he expected there was nothing. Ice was forming on his face and there was literally nothing else he could do where he was. He turned and pushed his way back to the snow-cat.

He jumped inside and slammed the door closed. Mike had undone his jacket and the heat inside the cab felt incredible, now that the machine was warmed up. It almost made the snow outside seem less brutal than it was. "Well?" Mike asked. Ethan shook his head rubbing his gloved hands together.

"There was nothing. There was a purse in the passenger side...and... nothing else," Ethan stumbled. Mike looked at him curiously. Ethan noticed his gaze. "The purse had a syringe in it."

"Diabetic?" Mike asked.

"No...I think this was a...recreational needle. I mean, I don't know, but I think it was."

Mike seemed to think about this for several moments but said nothing else. He shoved the cat into gear and they rolled forward. Neither man said anything to each other although Ethan wondered how far Big Mike planned to go into this monstrosity before turning back to shelter. Finally Mike cleared his throat and spoke.

"Another mile and we'll turn around and go back. I just want to make sure we cover as much ground as possible."

"Alright, fair enough," Ethan replied.

"I'm not feeling very positive about this search and rescue."

"Too much search, not enough rescue." It was only moments after Ethan uttered these words that they spotted another car on the deserted highway. This one was sitting across the road, the passenger side directly in front of them. The car had spun out and there was significant damage to the front end fender where it had bounced carelessly off the median. "Car!" Ethan said, and although Mike didn't verbally respond he nodded. Ethan was impressed with Big Mike's concentration on safely maneuvering the cat. Although, truth-be-told, Mike's mind was still on his potential delusions. The snow-cat slowed and Mike shifted the beast into park. "I think its Peter Oswald's car," Ethan said. Big Mike only nodded. It seemed to fit the description that Peter had given them of his accident. He had insisted they not look for his car, and they hadn't, they had just stumbled on it.

"I'll go this time," Mike said, pulling his coat around him.

"I don't mind going again," Ethan replied.

"No I'll go," Mike said firmly, and Ethan nodded. Ethan didn't know the man from Adam but he felt like something was bothering him. Once Mike had his coat and hat pulled comfortably around him, he threw open the door. The wind shoved its way into the cab and howled. Ethan thought it seemed even worse here than at the last car, how could this storm keep getting progressively worse? Shouldn't there be a turning point, a break in this mess? Mike jumped down, closed the door and hiked his way towards the abandoned vehicle. Ethan watched the burly man move towards the dark car.

Mike had pulled the cat closer to this car than the last one so it took even less time for him to get to the vehicle. It was almost completely buried, there was at least four feet of snow piling up against it. As he approached the vehicle, he tried to peer into the icy windows. No matter how bad the weather, or how icy the car was, Big Mike Otterman's eyes could plainly see someone...someone? They were sitting in the passenger side and it looked as if their head was against the window. Mike picked up speed and leaped the last few feet to the door. He pulled on the door handle but it didn't move. The snow was at his knees and made it hard to position himself so he could pull on the door. Perhaps it was frozen shut like everything else.

Ethan could see Mike's urgency in getting to the car. Had he seen someone? Surely there couldn't be anyone in the car...not in this cold. Ethan opened his side door of the cat and leaned out. "Mike!" he screamed. "Mike, do you need help?" Mike couldn't hear him. He couldn't even hear his own voice over the howl of the wind. He leaned out further trying to see what Mike was doing.

Mike had given up on the passenger side and started to trudge his way through the snowdrift to the other side of the car. Much to his relief the driver's side door was already open just a crack. Enough that the snow had started to invade the inside of the car. If there was someone in there, they'd be in bad shape and suffering from awful hypothermia or not suffering at all anymore. He yanked the driver's door and still had to pull on it to make it move through the snow, but he was strong and got the door wide open. Big Mike dove inside the car. Inside the car was a young woman. She was completely still and Mike knew right away she was utterly dead. Her long dark hair seemed brittle and frozen. He reached over to her. He felt the fear in him rise and a knot in his stomach develop. He didn't think he had ever touched a dead person before, especially not one frozen to death, but he needed to know if there was a pulse, some color, anything. His hand was inches from her face and he swallowed hard. He stopped and tried to look at her face. Her eyes were closed, but not clenched, almost like she was just sleeping. He shifted his body weight and the car groaned from the movement and from the brutality of the storm. He took a deep breath and prepared to feel her neck for a pulse.

Suddenly there was a face at the window in front of him at her side of the car. Mike hollered out loud despite himself and his hand shot back before he could touch her face. Ethan peered through the passenger window. His voice was muffled and barely audible. "Mike…." he said something else but Mike heard nothing over the intense noise of his heart pounding and his heavy breathing and of course…the storm… always the storm. Mike collected himself and waved Ethan over to his side. It was only a few moments before the young man bounded over to him. "Are you alright?" Ethan called.

"Scared the crap outta me boy," Mike replied.

"Sorry." Ethan leaned down and peered over Mike into the car. He looked at the woman and frowned. "Is she…?"

"I don't know, I'm afraid to…ya know…touch her."

"Want me to check?" Ethan said.

"Oh damn it boy, I'll do it." Big Mike moved back into position and decided this would be better to perform like a band-aid removal, quickly and without thought. He reached forward and touched her neck. He may have never touched a dead body before but he had prepped and dressed plenty of turkeys, and the feeling of that woman's neck was the exact texture of touching a defrosting turkey only he figured she was going in the opposite direction of defrost. He pushed around on her skin but felt nothing. Gently he touched her chin and turned her to face both of them. Ethan was still huddled over the driver's side door. The inside of the car was dark, the windshield completely blocked by the thick snow. It was clear to anyone that the woman was dead. Mike stopped and took another breath, exhaling a cloud in front of him. "She's dead," Mike confirmed and Ethan said nothing. Mike prepared to back out of the car but paused. He looked closer at her face and once again reached out to her chin to move her head slightly.

"Mike?" Ethan said questioningly.

"Gimme a minute," he responded. He moved further into the car towards her. He reached up and pulled the corners of her jacket down. The jacket was more of a spring coat that shouldn't have been worn in this mess. Ethan leaned down further into the car to see what was taking so long.

"Come on Mike, we gotta go. We gotta tell Officer Harrison about this."

"You think this is that Oswald guy's car?" Mike replied, yelling over his shoulder.

"I dunno. I imagine given where it is and how it's placed, but he said he was alone. Maybe she jumped in here for shelter after he abandoned the car," Ethan said.

"Maybe," Mike replied too quietly for Ethan to hear him. Mike reached into her coat pocket and pulled out a small red wallet. He pocketed the wallet into his own coat and then just looked at the woman's quiet, frozen face. His own face felt like ice and he was beginning to lose feeling in his toes even though he was wearing thick boots. This weather was even getting through their protective clothing.

"What's wrong?" Ethan asked, getting impatient. Hanging out with a clearly dead person wasn't going to help any of them.

"Ya ever seen anything like this?" Mike asked. He leaned his body as far towards the dashboard as he could. Her coat was open slightly and her head was still turned towards them exposing more of her neck. Even in the dark car, with the only light around them being the distant glow of the snow-cat, Ethan could see a distinct, red, clotted line across the woman's throat. She was dead. But her throat was also slit, unmistakably.

"Her throat is cut," Ethan said.

"I think she's been stabbed too. I think there is a stab wound just below her collar." Ethan looked at Mike, not knowing what to do or say. Mike pushed Ethan out of the way and lumbered out of the car. "Let's go," Mike said and turned to walk back around the car and towards the cat. They could just barely make out the lights on the snow machine.

Both men knew they had to get back to that stop and talk to Mark Harrison. Something wasn't right but things were about to get far worse for the two men. Ethan walked only a few feet behind Mike. He was basically only following Mike's footprints and the outline of him in front because anything else was unseeable. It almost felt like a shiver to Ethan when he heard the whisper for the first time. It wasn't anything intelligible; he wouldn't have sworn that he heard actual words. However, Ethan was becoming accustomed to the noise of the storm, the howling, the whipping, maybe even the clink of the chain on the flag pole outside the rest stop. The noise he heard this time made him pause. He held his breath for a moment and he was certain of distinctive whispering. He heard it again and actually stopped walking. The crunching of the snow drifts beneath his work boots stopped although Mike continued walking. It was a moment still before Mike stopped and turned, realizing that Ethan was no longer right behind him.

They were both passed the crashed car and almost in front of the snow-cat. The bright white lights of the machine drenched them in a glowing spot light making the snow look even heavier around them. "Are you coming?" Mike yelled, but Ethan was listening intently. He looked at Big Mike and then over Mike's shoulder. He would have thought he was seeing things but Ethan knew his own senses and he knew what he was seeing.

There was a woman, or what he was certain was a woman. Even in the wall of white snow he could see her pale skin. She had long dark hair and seemed to be standing several feet behind Mike. She had a long flowing dress on and her deep red lips stood out against the snow. "What in the hell?" Ethan muttered, his eyes widening.

The whisper was louder now in Ethan's ears. "*Fukushu shite yaru*," the hissing noise seemed to cut through the ice and snow. Mike cocked his head and looked at Ethan curiously. It was too damn cold to be standing out here and right now he just wanted to get back to talk to Officer Harrison about his findings. All he knew was that woman in that car didn't freeze to death and he had a bad feeling about it. But right now all he could do was look at Ethan who was staring blankly over his shoulder. Mike turned around and looked in the direction that Ethan was staring and he felt his stomach drop. She was there again, the woman, and it seemed as though she was moving, almost gracefully, towards him and the feeling of dread and fear filled his lungs. He whirled around and looked at Ethan, immediately bounding back through the snow to his side. Ethan didn't move but continued to stare. "Ethan!" Mike called out. He said nothing and did not move. Mike grabbed Ethan's arm and shook it firmly. "Ethan! Do you see her?" Ethan finally turned to him and the look in his eyes made Big Mike's stomach sink further. "You do."

"Who is it?" Ethan stuttered.

"What is it?" Mike replied. The two of them turned and looked at the woman. It seemed as though she was now floating several feet off the ground and moving inch by inch closer to them. "We need to go," Mike exclaimed, and tried to step forward but Ethan didn't move.

"She's beautiful isn't she?" Ethan said mindlessly.

"Snap out of it boy, let's go!" Mike called, pulling his arm.

Mike looked at his reappearing female guest and she was still rising and moving forward but now something was changing. Her blood red lips seemed to be parting and her face elongating as she moved forward. Her face looked horse-like and her mouth was getting wider. "Shit, Ethan let's go," Mike called out again and pulled on his arm, hard. It seemed to have worked because Ethan nearly toppled over but finally snapped out of it and looked at Big Mike.

"What in the hell?" he hollered over the storm which was encircling them. The snow swirled and it was as though Ethan, Mike and their strange visitor were in the center of a snow tornado.

"I've seen her before, this isn't right...she is not right," Mike hollered back.

She was nine, maybe ten feet away now, and several feet off the ground. Her white dress was entwined with the snow so you couldn't see where one ended and the other began. Her dark hair whipped behind her and her skin almost shone against the snow. "*Fukushu shitai*," she hissed again, her face stretching out towards them. Almost on cue the snow-cat lights died and the engine sputtered and shut down. The two men stood side by side in the snow, ice caked on their face, darkness completely surrounding them, watching this thing moving towards them. Mike finally got his bearings but kept his eyes firmly on her.

"On three, we run for the snow cat," Mike hollered. Ethan said nothing. "Ethan! On three," he repeated louder.

"Yah okay," Ethan said just loud enough for Mike to hear.

"One...two..."

"*Fukushu shite yaru!...*" she screamed suddenly at such a frequency that both men's gloved hands covered their ears. The woman raised her hands above her head and with that motion the snow around her rose in perfect cylinders beneath each of her hands. They looked solid, but the swirling cylinders were snow and ice tightly wound. She controlled them effortlessly.

"Run!" Mike hollered and bounded to his left, leaping over the snow drifts as best as he could. He was overweight and getting old but he could still move when he had to. He wasn't even sure if Ethan followed him but he couldn't wait any longer. There was a screeching, it was the sound of tires on pavement, obviously impossible in this storm, but that was the only noise it compared to. It was immediately followed by the sound of angry crying but it was deep and guttural. You know what they say about a woman's scorn, well it was very clear...she was pissed. Mike glanced over his shoulder but didn't stop moving towards the snow-cat. Ethan was only a few feet behind him, pressing through the snow, and beyond Ethan was the psycho snow woman with her face completely elongated looking like an angry dead horse coming at them. The pillars of snow that she had created with her bare hands were still floating beside her in perfect form.

Big Mike spent too much time looking over his shoulder and an especially large drift of snow caught his feet. He stumbled a few steps before falling on his side and coming to a stop. Ethan was on him in seconds sliding to his knees beside him. Mike knew immediately, that, with Ethan stopping, she would be on them in seconds. "Keep going, just go!" Mike yelled. Ethan looked up at the horse faced woman and back at Mike. It was clear Big Mike was serious so Ethan stumbled to his feet and bolted towards the snow-cat. Mike rolled onto his elbows to watch this thing coming. Would she hurt him? Possess him? He had no idea. Big Mike Otterman wasn't a religious man, or even a superstitious man. Up until fifteen minutes ago he thought seeing this woman was some sort of mental breakdown or a physical issue of some kind. But unless both he and Ethan were suffering from the same ailment, this thing was something of a different nature.

There was another screech and Mike watched the woman roar again opening her ghastly mouth to reveal razor sharp, disgusting, brown teeth with spittle drooling from her mouth. She roared and Mike swore he could feel the warmth of her breath and the stench of, what smelled to him, like rotting tomatoes and eggs, a lovely combination. She was hovering only two feet away from Mike now and he realized that she wasn't looking at him, or maybe wasn't seeing him, but had her attention completely on Ethan who had just reached the snow-cat. She stopped directly above Mike. His heart was pounding, his chest heaving, and he couldn't even feel the snow around his body as he propped himself up on his elbows. She raised her pale, white, left hand and the snow cylinder moved into the air and changed direction. The cylinder formed itself from her hand out into a cone shape with the fine point aimed towards the snow cat. Mike's face fell and his heart sank. She was attacking.

He rolled over onto his stomach and looked into the dark shadow of the dead quiet snow-cat. He couldn't see Ethan but he thought he might be inside already. The machine was ready to be started up again so they could get out of there. Maybe being bathed in light would change this situation. "Ethan!" he screamed as loud as he could but began to cough and choke. "Ethan!" he called again.

Ethan stood at the door of the snow-cat. The snow was flying into his face and he was peering back into the dark looking for Mike and looking for that freakish monster. At the moment he saw neither. Through the sound of the driving snow he was sure he could hear his name being called. It was Big Mike, he was certain, but he couldn't actually make out any distinguishable voice. The monstrosity was still hovering in the air over Mike as the cone of snow built up in her hand. "*Fukushu shite yaru..!*" she hissed again and she looked down straight into the eyes of Big Mike Otterman. Her eyes were completely red now, as red as her lips, without any sign of humanity in them at all. Mike's mouth gaped open.

"Stop," he whispered hoarsely. The image of the woman in that crashed car flashed through his mind. Her throat had been slit. Straight across, slicing through her artery. It was deliberate and Mike was no expert, but the wound had killed her. Someone had sliced that woman's neck. Was it this snow beast that had done this? He couldn't understand how that could be. This wasn't exactly your average serial killer floating above him. Big Mike was distracted from his thoughts when she roared, and there was a cloud of condensation pouring from her mouth. She looked away from Mike and her hand shot out in front of her. The enormous icy cone shot from her hand and into the darkness towards the snow-cat...and towards Ethan.

"No!" Mike screamed and reached for her dress. His hand touched the hem of where her dress would be, but disappeared into her snowy apparition. He pulled his hand back and his black glove was covered in ice and frost. Inside the glove his hand throbbed and he pulled the glove off desperately. His hand looked nearly blue as though it had been buried in frigid water for hours. It was time to move.

Mike turned over and pulled himself up and moved away from the woman.

Ethan heard Mike distinctly this time, but it sounded as though he was screaming...in terror perhaps? It was time for Ethan to move. He threw open the snow-cat door and, no sooner had he done this, than there was a sound of metal tearing open inches away from him. Ethan felt the pressure of the door pushing against him and it made him stumble back only seconds before an enormous sharp chunk of ice tore through the metal door and stopped with the tip inches from Ethan's stomach. He was completely shocked by the piece of ice, as solid as steel, protruding from the door. Mike barreled around the corner and stopped by Ethan's side. He looked at the gaping hole in the side of the machine with the enormous ice shard piercing it. "We need to go now!" Mike said. Ethan nodded and both men scrambled into the passenger side door. There was no way the door was going to close but it didn't matter.

Mike turned the ignition but there was no response. "For the love of... " Mike muttered. He turned the key again, only this time the old snow-cat sputtered and the lights on the front dimly came to life blinking with the engine trying to turn over. Mike stopped and the cat shut down again. The two men looked at each other and they couldn't help but look down at the enormous ice piece. It encouraged Mike to focus his attention back to getting the cat to start. He turned the ignition again and the cat sputtered, louder this time, and as if feeding off Mike and Ethan's insistence, it turned over. The lights splashed out into the blizzard and right into the face of the monster woman who was levitating towards the front windshield. Both men screamed.

16

"...finally, God told Noah it was safe to leave the ark. Noah opened the door to the ark and all those animals rushed out," Father Patrick said smiling at Hannah Green and running his fingers down his own arm to Hannah's and tickling her playfully. Hannah smiled and Andrea Green smiled too. She was beginning to think Hannah would never calm down enough to get any sleep.

"Time to lay down baby and try to get some sleep," Andrea said to Hannah. Hannah frowned and stuck her thumb firmly in her mouth, something she hadn't done now for several years. Tears welled in Andrea's eyes. She was so tired and scared and just burnt out. Father Patrick smiled compassionately at her and reassured her with his arm on her shoulder.

"Hannah, why don't you lay down and I'll sing to you, would you like that?" Patrick asked. Hannah seemed to brighten at this idea and nodded excitedly. She used her own coat for a pillow and curled up in the booth. Patrick knelt beside her as she closed her eyes almost instantly. "What a friend we have in Jesus...," Patrick began to sing quietly. "...all our sins and griefs to bear..."

Mark was pacing the floor nearby taking stock of the situation and stopped momentarily to listen to Father Patrick singing. Peter Oswald cautiously moved up beside Mark and stood there unassumingly. Mark glanced at him. "My mother used to sing this to my brother and I,"

Mark said, mostly to himself.

"Yah? Mine too. What's your brother's name?" Oswald asked.

"Kevin...," Mark said, absent-mindedly.

"You and I are like two peas in a pod Officer Harrison," Peter said, smiling. Why did it always seem like this guy had a perpetual smirk?

Josh Barton glared across the room at Peter Oswald. He had not stopped thinking about his gun being in the waist band of the skinny insurance salesman's pants and it was making his blood boil. Of course it didn't help that the small shot of heroin was not giving him the high he hoped. Apparently he would be forced to deal with these people, and this shitty weather. He didn't even care if Big Mike and Ethan came back with Sheila, or news of any others out there. He just wanted to leave.

Peter Oswald was feeling pretty good about this situation. He could tell that the cop and the priest thought it had been far too long since Otterman and Ethan had left. Both of them had been pacing the rest stop, taking turns consoling Andrea and the little girl, and peering out the front windows which was pointless as there was absolutely no vision outside anymore. The skylight overhead was completely blanketed in snow, and worst of all the lights in the rest stop had angrily flickered, threatening to give up completely.

Stephen Camp was sitting by himself at a table away from everyone else. He was writing feverishly in his notebook and had his computer open at the same time. Despite everything else going on he seemed to be completely content working with whatever it was he was doing. Paul and Heather were sitting together at a table against the wall. Heather had brought out sandwiches, everything she could put together, and spread them on another table like a low-budget buffet but she doubted that anyone had eaten more than a few bites.

The little girl had eaten half a chocolate chip cookie, Paul had eaten nothing, and only Josh Barton had eaten two sandwiches hungrily.

Other than that it was just going bad. Heather sighed and stretched. Paul glanced out of the corner of his eye at her firm taut body and small breasts poking through her uniform. She caught him looking and smiled. "I suppose I should clean up the sandwiches. It doesn't seem like anyone wants to eat and it's all going to go bad. Big Mike will have my head when he sees the food we wasted." She stood up and turned back to face the table. "Wanna help," she asked.

Paul shook his head and looked away from her. "Nah," was his only response.

What a moron, Heather thought. She thought she'd give him the opportunity to spend some time with her, especially in the back of the eatery where they would be alone. If anything fueled a little make out session it was boring isolation. She was even bored and antsy enough that if he was a good kisser she might have let him grab her breasts...on top of the clothes...she wasn't a slut. Heather tried to look at Paul with an 'are you serious' kind of look but Paul did not even notice. She frowned and headed towards the table of sandwiches.

Peter Oswald left Mark's side and watched Heather from where he stood by himself. He licked his lips playfully and suddenly the urge began to rise. He never had urges so close together. He always tried to leave a week between his 'dates' and had no problem doing so, but here he was sitting in a rest stop, bored out of his mind, and standing only a few feet from him, bending ever so provocatively over the table, was Peter Oswald's next potential date. He leaned back and just stared at her tight little ass. He wondered if maybe the young convenience store clerk was hitting that but he hadn't seen anything that would imply such, not that it would matter. She wasn't exactly Peter's type, but she would do under the circumstances.

Heather had gathered an armload of dishes and food and was expertly carrying them towards the eatery on a large circular tray. Peter glanced around the area and then walked towards the spot where Heath had.

Mark and Father Patrick were now talking by the vending machines and they were the only ones Peter felt he needed to keep an eye on. No one else cared what he did or said and paid little to attention to anyone else other than the priest and the cop. Peter sauntered over to the eatery counter and peered into the back where Heather had vanished. It was only a few moments before she returned and was startled only slightly by Oswald standing there. She smiled, very friendly, very warm...very sexy...Peter thought.

"Hey. Mr...Oswald right?"

Peter waved his hand at her dismissively. "Peter, Pete, Petey...call me anything but late for dinner, sweetie," Peter said charmingly. Heather smiled politely at his lame joke. She knew his type, fast talker, sexist, thought they were God's gift to...well...everyone. She didn't understand how men like him actually sold insurance or cars or whatever questionable type of service they provided. She thought his style came across as slimy. However, Mr. Oswald...Peter, Pete, Petey, seemed nice enough, Heather thought.

"Do you have a telephone?" Oswald asked Heather, smiling.

"They're dead Mr. Oswald, we tried earlier remember?" Heather replied.

"Oh yes, that's right," Oswald said and Heather thought he seemed disappointed. "I'm going to go back to the table and enjoy one of those delicious sandwiches you made honey." Peter turned away from the counter knowing full well that Heather had cleaned up those sandwiches. He was throwing a curve ball and he hoped to catch her with a low strike.

"Oh...Mr Oswald," Heather said. Oswald stopped and smiled without turning around, a swing and a miss for her, strike one.

"Yes?" Peter said turning slowly.

"I cleaned up the sandwiches. They were going bad and I didn't think anyone was eating them. I'm really sorry," Heather explained.

She had pulled out a white terry cloth and was wiping down the counter.

Peter frowned, a dramatic and over-played reaction. "Well shit...," he looked disappointed. "Do you have any of them left?"

Heather leaned over the counter and he noticed how her uniformed blouse fell open just a little, enough to see the swell of her breast and he felt himself going hard for her. "I put a few in the fridge for Mr. Datsun and Big Mike when they got back. I'd be happy to go get you one," she whispered, and smiled. Her dimples were adorable. Oh man, he wanted to cut her in all the best ways.

He realized he was staring and nodded at her innocently. She didn't seem to notice his awkward behavior and disappeared back into the kitchen again. He looked around back at the other travelers. It was the best situation he could possibly imagine because no one was paying any attention whatsoever to him, or Heather. He double checked, triple checked and then effortlessly and quietly jumped the counter by placing two hands firmly on the wood and pushing himself over it. He hit nothing, and made no noise doing so. Peter Oswald slipped behind the appliances and rows of pots and pans hanging from steel racks.

He spotted Heather. She was standing at a back counter next to one of three enormous stainless steel refrigerators. She had a knife in her hand and appeared to be adding some fresh mayo to one of the sandwiches for Peter. Peter felt his mouth moisten, he was actually drooling. Oh, he wanted to cut her so bad. He wanted to cut her and throw her body out in the snow and then feign ignorance when everyone started to look for her. It was risky, it was insane, it would be amazing fun. As he crept across the back area towards her, towards that tight ass, that pretty little ponytail, he spotted another of his favorite things in the whole world, a knife. It was unused, glistening in the dull fluorescent lights of the kitchen and it called to him. "Hey Peter, I slice real good," he imagined it saying. Gingerly, with every effort to be deadly silent, he slid the decent sized kitchen knife into his hand. It was a bread knife with a serrated edge and a nice feel to it. It had a sturdy plastic handle. It was about to become a perfect weapon for him.

Peter was only a few feet behind Heather and she hadn't stirred. She was placing the sandwich and a fresh pickle on a new plate for Peter. Geezus, she was a hard worker. What a stupid bitch, Peter thought. He raised the knife preparing to wrap his hand simultaneously around her mouth. This was like a natural talent for Peter, hand over mouth, pull back slightly on the neck, knife in the other hand down over the shoulder and into the chest puncturing the vital areas in the front that usually prevented pesky alarms like screaming, crying or breathing. Then they would turn and look at him in horror and one look at those eyes, those terrified eyes, with blood running down their chest, would get Peter off for a week. Then stab again from the front, and again, and again...usually four or five stabs was enough to truly satisfy him. Heather Morton would be the first white girl he had killed. He had a thing for minorities. They had lovely skin, dark eyes, he especially liked Asians. But he was primed and ready for Heather.

He moved in for his kill. The lights flickered and buzzed and Peter froze, as did Heather. She didn't turn, thank goodness for Peter, but she looked up at the lights. The whole rest stop buzzed and flickered and then their worst fears were realized, the power went dead. "Damn it," Heather whispered and turned away from the counter. Peter had frozen in his place and her eyes caught his and she screamed. Then she screamed again. Peter slid the knife into his back pocket somewhere on the other side of where Josh Barton's gun was and reached out his hands for her to see.

"Shhh Shhh Shhh," he insisted trying to console her. "It's Peter... Heather its Peter..."

Finally she calmed down clutching her chest, the chest he wanted to stab her in, that lovely heaving chest. "Jesus!" she exclaimed.

Her calm and happy demeanor was all but gone for the moment. She cursed again breathing heavily. "You...you scared the shit out of me," she said.

Peter chuckled. "I guess everyone is entitled to one good scare," he said. Then added, "you just disappeared back here and I was worried about you. I came to make sure everything was okay and then the lights went out."

If the whole evening wasn't already stressful enough and she wasn't so tired she could have easily spotted the hole in Peter Oswald's story. Why had he sneaked up on her so quietly? Why didn't he call out for her? Why did he have a bulging gun in his waist band and a sharp bread knife in his pocket...or was he just happy to see her?

Someone called Heather's name from the counter in the other room. It sounded like Mark. Heather reached knowingly underneath a counter and pulled out a big industrial flash light. She clicked it on and shined it into Peter's face, who flinched from the light. She smiled. "I'm sorry," she whispered. Peter nodded and the two of them walked to the front of the eatery where Mark, Father Patrick and Paul were trying to peer into the pitch dark kitchen. Presumably Stephan Camp cared very little about the lights being out. He stayed alone at his booth and his laptop was running on battery power now and was the only distant glow in the entire eatery.

If the rest stop was eerie up until now, darkness ramped that up to new levels. Shadows were cast everywhere and the place seemed even quieter with only the wind outside more pronounced. Heather appeared followed by Peter and the men were relieved after hearing her scream. "Sorry, Peter scared me...completely by accident," she explained. Peter shrugged apologetically.

"Ya got any more flash lights?" Mark asked.

"Supply closet, by the washrooms," Heather replied. She grabbed her key ring and walked around to the other side of the eatery. Paul glared at Peter. Why had they been back there together? Peter was like forty, why would Heather be with him? Stupid ass he was, he should have been back there with Heather. The four men and Heather made their way through the darkness of the rest stop. They could both hear little Hannah Green stirring and her mother tending to her but thankfully she did not wake up.

"Are you alright Andrea?" Father Patrick asked.

"Yes Father, we're fine," Andrea replied.

"Where's the physicist?" Mark asked.

"Stephen?" Father Patrick called out. They looked in his general direction where they could just barely see his face in the glow of his own laptop. He glanced over at them but said nothing.

"Does this place have a generator?" Mark asked Heather. He was first behind her and walking close.

Heather nodded and then realized that under the circumstances no one could see her nodding. "Yes, out back, near the motel but Big Mike has the only key. We've only needed it a handful of times but it's a good gennie!" Heather said. They were turning the corner to go down the hallway towards the washrooms when there was a distinct rumbling sound. All of them stopped and listened carefully. "You guys hear that?" Heather asked. No one responded.

"That's the cat," Paul said, speaking up finally. They listened for a few more moments but he was right. The distinct sound that they could hear getting louder by the moment was definitely the sound of the snow-cat. They abandoned the quest for the supply closet and all followed the beam of Heather's fat orange flash light. They all stumbled to the front door and peered out. They could see nothing. The five of them huddled around the big glass front doors for what seemed like an eternity. There was a roar and a sudden bright light as Big Mike Otterman's snow-cat pulled up directly in front of the rest stop. It was so close that they were staring into it. It was still hard to see out the windows and into the snow-cat but they had no reason to doubt that it was Big Mike and Ethan inside. They were right. It was a few minutes later when it powered down and they came through the front doors. Paul pushed on the door and Ethan pulled in order to get inside. The door was blocked now by almost three solid feet of snow. Ethan stomped and shook and pulled off the winter clothing that was obstructing his face. Heather shined the light at him and he winced and shielded his eyes. She apologized.

Big Mike was right behind him and performed the same ritual of shaking himself out. Heather shined the light on him and she immediately noticed he looked very disturbed. She had worked with Big Mike Otterman long enough to know when something was bothering the big man, and he looked awful.

"Lights are out, boss," Paul blurted. No one commented on his stupid observation. Mike stepped forward and reached into his coat producing a key ring. It had easily a dozen keys on it.

"Can you start the generator?" he asked Paul. Paul nodded. He had done so for Big Mike a few times before. It was usually in the summer when the rain, lightning, or the tail end of a tropical storm knocked out their power and Big Mike was too busy. Heather handed Paul the flashlight and Paul headed over to the convenience store counter to grab his coat and hat. The generator building was probably only a hundred feet behind the rest stop on the south side of the old motel.

Ethan and Big Mike seemed to have caught their breath and they were warming up now. Everyone's eyes were adjusting to the dark so it didn't really feel like they were in complete darkness. The snow outside was so bright that it almost seemed to give off some light. At least there was one good thing coming out of this damned snow. They all made their way back to the tables where Andrea Green was sitting with the sleeping Hannah. She spotted Ethan and Mike in the darkness and immediately stood. She hadn't even opened her mouth before Mark stepped between her and the men. He wanted details before she got to them and lost control yet again. He needed to keep this situation under control.

"Any luck?" Mark asked quietly.

Ethan looked over his shoulder at Mike. Both men looked shaken up. It must have been really rough out there. In the dark room, Peter Oswald and Big Mike Otterman locked eyes. When their eyes locked...Peter knew...that Mike knew...Big Mike Otterman had found Peter's car, and his date.

"Can we talk...over there," Ethan said to Mark. Unfortunately Andrea overheard Ethan.

"You found my family!" she said, pushing past Mark and in front of Ethan. "Where are they, what happened?" she demanded to know.

Ethan held out his hands in front of him.

"We did not find your family, Mrs. Green, I'm sorry. We did however... ," Ethan cleared his throat. "We did find Barton's car." Ethan motioned towards Josh Barton, who was sitting in a booth with his head against the wall paying no attention to any of them. If he closed his eyes tight enough he was seeing a terrific light show squeezing his heroin induced high out.

"My husband was with Barton's girlfriend," Andrea insisted. For the first time in the entire evening, Andrea Green seemed calmer. She was insistent and worried but far more in control of her emotions. Although no one would say, everyone was relieved they would not have to console her anymore. Ethan leaned in so everyone wouldn't hear his horror story and get upset.

"There was no one at his car. There were no people, not your husband and not Barton's girlfriend but I promise you that kid over there," Ethan motioned towards Josh, "is higher than a kite and probably coming down from something and could be dangerous, so please let me talk to Officer Harrison."

"Mark," Mark said. Ethan nodded. Andrea backed off and went back to Hannah's side where she was snoring softly. There was a thump outside of falling snow from the roof and they all looked up. Mark and Ethan stepped aside to the outside of the convenience store. Big

Mike and Peter were still having a stand-off with their eyes and neither was willing to look away. Big Mike broke the glare first. He wasn't about to let this smarmy schmuck intimidate him. He turned away from the group and walked towards the back hallway where the washroom was.

Mike carefully felt his way up the hallway but he knew his way even in the dark. He found the supply closet and opened it. Inside, hanging on a series of hooks, were several flashlights of varying sizes. Mike grabbed one and checked its status. It turned on immediately, sending a column of light into the dark closet. Mike put the flashlight into his coat pocket and tried the next one. They all seemed to work fine. He grabbed two, stuck them in his pocket and turned to head back to the rest of the travelers. As soon as Paul got that generator running they wouldn't need these, he hoped.

Big Mike Otterman took a deep breath. He just wanted to talk to Mark and tell him what he had seen. Whatever had happened to that woman in that car, he would feel a lot better once it was in the hands of a New Jersey state trooper. He turned away from the closet and likely didn't even feel the cold hard metal of a chair against his face. Most of the chairs in the stop were bolted to the ground but there were a few that Mike had always left free so that families could move them around if they needed more seats. Ultimately, that tiny decision, which had always made people happy, would be his demise.

The chair was made of solid heavy metal, with a plastic seat and backing which only helped to smother the noise of the chair catching Mike across the head. With the wind and snow pounding against the building, no one could hear much of anything from the hallway. It was a good swing too, and it clanged dully and sent Mike sprawling against the wall. It did not, however, knock him out. Big Mike was stronger than that and had a thick head, he would joke often. Peter Oswald, standing over him, his eyes wide and his nostrils flaring, was holding the chair, gripped tightly above his head. Mike could feel a stream of blood coming down his forehead. He reached up and touched the blood and looked at his hand. The blood, even in the dark, looked red and thick. One of the flashlights had fallen out of his pocket and spun on the ground in the hallway sending shadows dancing. It made Peter Oswald look like an insane monster...or was it the light doing that. Big Mike looked up at Peter Oswald and opened his mouth to speak but the chair came down again with a sharp crack and Big Mike Otterman's world went black.

17

"A syringe?" Mark said. Ethan nodded. "And in the other car there was a woman's body? Frozen?"

"Talk to Mike about that. Although I'll warn you, he's clearly upset about it. There's something else about the body…." Ethan began.

He was interrupted because, just as quickly as they had gone out, the rest stop lights and electricity kicked back in. Everyone winced at the sudden burst of light but there was a definitive sigh of relief. Paul had got the generator on. Mark spotted Stephen Camp. He hadn't seen him for some time; he wasn't much for joining them in groups, even when the lights went out. He had left his booth and was standing away from everyone else pacing the floor and looking around. He would glance outside, although there was nothing that could be seen except the snow building on the panes, and then back to the floor. He had a pen sticking out from his ear.

"What do you think his story is?" Ethan asked, noticing Mark watching him. Mark shook his head contemplatively.

"I don't know but I think it's time I spoke with him." Mark walked across the room examining everything in the newly generated light. The generator's power wasn't as strong as the actual electricity so everything seemed to have a slightly dim quality to it. He popped out his cell phone just in case service had returned but, where the bars should be, it still said "No Service." The digital time on the front also read: 9:43. That wasn't right. He knew it wasn't right. This storm was messing with everything. It had to be well after midnight. They had all been there several hours now. "Anyone have the time?" Mark called out. His voice echoed across the rest stop.

Those who had cell phones looked at them. Josh Barton did nothing, still propping his head against the wall with his eyes closed. "Mines busted," Ethan said. "It says 9:43, but its way later than that."

"Mine says the same?" Heather replied looking concerned.

Father Patrick pulled up his sleeve and looked at his watch. He crinkled his brow and shook his head. He looked at Mark and his face was worried. Mark decided not to press the matter at the moment. He turned back to where Dr. Camp was pacing. "Do you have the time doctor?" Mark asked. There was no response and he did not look at Mark. "Doctor?" Mark said, louder this time. Stephen Camp looked at him as though he had heard him all along but chose not to respond.

"Are you familiar with John William Dunne, Detective?" Camp asked. He pushed his glasses up his nose. Mark looked at him straight faced.

"I'm not a detective, you can call me Mark, and I asked if you had the time."

"And I asked if you knew John William Dunne," Camp replied, emphasizing each word in an almost condescending tone. Mark took a few steps towards him but Camp did not back down.

"No," Mark responded. Camp seemed pleased with that answer and sat down in a chair nearby. He assumed that Camp would not say anything else but after several moments he spoke again.

"Dunne was an author who believed, among other things, that he had precognitive dreams. He would say that he would readily dream about a time on his watch and wake up to see that time. He began to write, almost exclusively, that dreams were all precognitive and time was relative to the person who was dreaming."

"Meaning," Mark said, losing his patience. He wasn't sure why he was entertaining this man. It was, however, the most Camp had spoken since any of them had arrived. Camp turned to face him again and smiled, perhaps for the first time.

"Meaning, that we all can see things in multiple dimensions of time. What one person's conception of time is, might not be another's. Someone out there," Camp motioned to the windows, where the wind and snow were still beating against them, "might not be experiencing the same things in the same time that we are." Mark said nothing. He was evaluating the man in his own mind and hardly listening to his blather. Camp seemed to notice that Mark was sizing him up. He smiled again. "Multiple time dimensions, its physics."

"And it so happens you are a physicist?" Mark said, immediately. Camp smiled again and nodded. Mark leaned in close to him, hovering over the chair where he sat. "Do you have the goddamn time...right now...in this dimension."

Camp did not falter, despite seeming so sensitive and quiet earlier, he continued to smile. "The time YOU are looking for is probably around thirty past midnight." Camp emphasized "YOU." He produced his notebook from inside the jacket he was wearing. Mark looked at the chair beside Camp and slipped into it watching the doctor scribble in his notepad.

"Why do I feel like you know why our clocks aren't working on our phones?"

"The clocks are fine, so are the watches, and the digital read outs...the time is correct for where we are."

Mark banged his fist firmly down on the table and forcefully got Camp's attention. He jumped and had to push his glasses back on his face again. He was looking at Mark now. Sweat was beading on his forehead. His cheeks were a bright red and fear was in his eyes. It was Mark's turn to smile at him eerily. "Do you have any theories as to what is going on here, doctor," Mark said, his emphasis on 'doctor' sounding almost sarcastic.

"Not yet, but I will keep you up to date as I figure this out," he replied, and cleared his throat. Then he turned back to his notebook again. Mark was too tired and far too annoyed to deal with this little shit.

Father Patrick walked over to where Heather was sitting alone. She was playing nervously with her hair. She seemed to be distracted. "Are you alright, Heather?" he asked.

"I was just wondering where Paul is. He should have been back already, the generator isn't that far."

"Where is it?" Patrick asked. Heather seemed to think about this for a moment.

"Out the back doors of the stop, where Mike and Ethan left from earlier. Back to the left of the rest stop is an old motel. Big Mike never ran the motel; it hasn't been used since the seventies. It's only about six rooms but it's been boarded up for a long time." Heather realized she was rambling. "The generator shed is just on the south side of the motel. It's only a hundred feet maybe. Even in this mess, he should be back."

"I'm sure he is fine," Father Patrick said smiling. "But maybe Mike will pop out there and bring him back in?" Heather nodded and Father Patrick walked over to where Mark had finished speaking with Dr. Camp. "Do you know where Mike went?" Mark shook his head, and the two men walked together towards the hallway where the washrooms were to look for him.

***

Paul, who was likely one of the laziest people you'd ever know, only wanted to turn on the generator for Big Mike because he hated the dark. He would never ever tell anyone that, but Paul Janson was afraid of the dark. He would rather brave the crappy winter storm than stay in the dark. He actually thought that everyone was making a big deal out of this shitty weather anyways.

He pulled on his jacket and threw on a scarf and headed for the back door. No one bothered to join him and the hallway in the back was very dark. He swallowed hard and felt his way up the cement walls to the door and wasted no time pushing it open. It took two solid shoves before the door flew open. Fortunately, it wasn't completely blocked by snow because Ethan and Big Mike had gone out that way earlier. The snow flew into his face like he had dived into a pool of ice. He was still trying to convince himself that everyone else was over-reacting. He pulled the scarf tighter around his face and headed in the direction of the shed that housed the generator.

By the time Paul got to the shed, he was second guessing his own opinion about the weather. It was more than bad. He was what would normally be two minutes away from the rest stop and he felt like he'd been out there for an hour rather than five minutes. A shiver ran through his entire body but he tried to ignore it. He pulled out Big Mike's key ring and fumbled with it. His hands were turning red already and he wished he had brought gloves. He pulled the key he needed, marked GS (generator shed), and moved his hands towards the lock but his hands were frigid and barely functioning. His eyes were full of snow and he couldn't see the lock properly. Murphy's Law took effect and the metal key ring slipped from his hands and into the snow. "Dammit!" Paul yelled, as the keys vanished into the snow drift that was building at his feet. "Shit!" he yelled into the storm. He punched the shed, open handed, and the loud bang was barely audible over the howling wind.

Paul took a deep breath through his scarf. The cold wind still burned his throat even with the scarf over his face. He leaned down and stuck his bare hand into the snow where the keys had vanished. Fortunately, they were easy to find and he pulled them out and stood up.

"*Fukushuu...*" hissed something behind him. Paul stood up straight, still facing the shed and tilted his head.

"...the hell?" he whispered, turning the keys in his hand.

"*Fukushuu...*" the voice said again. Paul turned, not quickly, but he still turned to see where this noise was coming from and she was there. She was beautiful, stunning, pure white skin, blood red eyes and lips and she was less than a foot from Paul's face when he turned. He could lean in and kiss her if he wanted to, which he did not. He froze, not literally; in fact he couldn't even feel the icy cold weather for a moment. This beautiful Asian woman in a flowing dress was hovering in front of him, her face only inches from his. Paul looked at her and his eyes widened. He said nothing. Her head tilted to the side and she looked at him through her blank bloody eyes. The next thing uttered was hardly a whisper and yet seemed to ring in Paul's ears. It was the same thing he had heard before.

"*Fukushuu.*"

Paul was about to respond, whether vocally or just to turn and run like hell, but she wasn't going to allow either. Her hand shot forward towards him too fast for him to realize that it was not her hand at all. What should have been her hand was a long, thin, razor sharp piece of solid ice. It glistened and entered Paul before he even knew what was happening, or could process the situation. The long slender piece of ice sliced through Paul's abdomen with a thin '*schick*' sound causing Paul to jump. His scarf fell off his face and blood spurted from his mouth. He dropped the keys back into the snow and stood with his hands outstretched. She was still in his face and he could see her breath in the air. Their eyes locked, only her blood red eyes were normal now, but still as empty as any he had ever seen. Paul felt so warm which was ludicrous in this weather but he felt nothing else. He did not even feel the three feet of razor sharp ice that had sliced through his abs that he worked so hard on. He looked down for the first time but registered nothing.

In his mind the only thing to cross it was..."I'll be damned," and he looked up at her. The woman, the ghostly figure that had stabbed him, pulled her hand back and the icy weapon pulled out of Paul like a sharp knife from boneless meat. It made the same "schick" sound coming out as it did going in. More blood spurted from his mouth as he tried to breath. The wound bled excessively onto the ground and was making a Picasso type display on the snow canvas around him. But Paul did not fall. He stood in shock thinking about what was happening. He looked down again and saw his coat was drenched with his blood and Paul laughed. It wasn't out loud and it wasn't a giggle, just more of a shock induced chuckle. Blood bubbled from his lungs and out his nose and mouth.

"Bitch," he whispered, saying something for the first time.

She leaned in even closer to him. She looked as normal as anyone, although she was slightly more transparent. Her transparency was not representative of her reality, Paul's gaping stomach wound could attest to that.

Her hands shot forward again and both of them landed squarely on Paul's chest just above his wound and launched him backwards into the generator shed. The small tin door of the shed crumpled behind him and he was tossed through it like paper into a wastebasket. Paul's body tumbled against the inside of the shed and he found himself propped between the wall and the generator. The shed was no bigger than an out-house, its sole purpose was to hold the generator.

He tried to get his bearings. He still felt nothing, not the wind and the cold, or the snow, or the fatal wound to his gut. He was bleeding out quickly and yet he still had no thought that his life was over. His mind was spinning and he looked out through the torn tin door into the snow. The snowstorm was bad, he decided. He was wrong, everyone was not over-reacting. He would never be able to drive home in this, he thought. Damn he wanted chips...*Ruffles*, with dip. His mouth was watering. Paul spit inadvertently and more blood splattered out onto his coat. The woman was leaning into the shed now and he could see she was floating in the air. There was at least four feet from the ground to the beginning of her dress. What a pretty dress, he thought. She was moving towards him again, coming into the shed and her eyes had turned back to the blood red color. She was coming to finish him off, Paul finally realized. She didn't need to, Paul Janson was already dying. He looked around him, it was dark and the snow was the only light thing anywhere around him.

He finally realized his life was over and yet he had no idea how or why, nor would he ever. There was only one thing left for Paul to do, maybe one thing that would be like retribution for all the laziness, the poor work ethic, the scamming on girls...there was only one thing he could do. Paul leaned over, reached up with everything he had left and flipped the tiny red switch on the giant generator. Lights blinked on. He felt around the top of the generator and found the soft yellow button and pushed it. It was the last ounce of strength he would ever have. The generator kicked in immediately. Big Mike was right, this was worth the money, Paul thought. He could just barely see a glow behind his ghostly friend and he knew the lights were back on. He looked up at her again and Paul Janson smiled, his best, most charming smile. "Bitch," he said again.

The woman, the spirit, this evil bitch that was haunting them, said nothing else. She took her hand back and brought it down across Paul's head and cut his face from his neck to his left ear exposing his throat, his jaw and much of the inside of his nose. Paul slumped back.

18

Ethan Datsun was pacing back and forth when the lights came back up. He was relieved, because right now the dark was really getting under his skin. Big Mike had gone to get flashlights, he figured, but flashlights only made things look creepier. Father Patrick passed by Ethan and nodded. He looked like he was heading to the washroom or maybe the convenience store for something.

"Father," Ethan said, hoarsely.

Father Patrick stopped and looked at him. "Yah Ethan?" Patrick suddenly noticed that Ethan looked downright pale, he looked awful. He quickly went to his side. "Are you alright, Ethan?" Ethan lowered his head and shook it. When he looked up again at Patrick he had unmistakable tears in his eyes. Patrick put his arm around the young man and led him away from everyone else. "What's going on?" he asked.

It took Ethan a moment; he swallowed hard and looked at the priest. "I need this to stay between us...for now...is this confidential?"

Ethan asked. Father Patrick smiled warmly.

"Everything you say to a priest is confidential, it's in our handbook."

"Mr. Otterman...uh...Mike and I, we went out to look for those people," Ethan began. Father Patrick nodded encouragingly as he had so many times before during counseling sessions. He had a charisma about him that made him easy to talk to. It was one of his greatest God given talents that helped him in his work. "We found the first car, it was that kid's car," Ethan said nodding to where Josh Barton was still propped comfortably in the booth. It looked like he was sound asleep now but sitting straight up.

"Josh," Patrick said and nodded again.

Ethan nodded back. "Yes, Josh's car was empty and then we found another car and there was a woman in it."

Patrick was taken aback by this news. "A woman? Where is...," he started to ask where she was but he suddenly knew by Ethan's face that this woman did not return with them to the stop. "She was dead."

Ethan nodded. "Mike's real upset about it I think, but then there was something else," Ethan said nervously, swallowing the lump in his throat. Patrick was very concerned now. Ethan was obviously distraught. "Another woman...something...out there... came after us." Patrick peered at him curiously. Ethan took a deep breath and began to tell Father Patrick John everything.

***

That ice felt sharp on his face. Mike Otterman was coming around and he could feel icy pellets biting his cheeks. He opened his eyes and realized his head was throbbing. He also knew very quickly that he was outside. The snow was driving around him everywhere, begging to know why he was out there. Mike gradually began to come around but only his head was hurting him. He couldn't feel anything else. It was probably another two or three minutes before he really began to see and understand his surroundings. Mike was bathed in the slightest, dull yellow light. When he looked straight up in the air he could see there was a parking lot light above him. He also noticed when he looked up there was a repeating '*clink, clink, clink*' sound that he knew right away was the chain from the flag pole hitting the mast outside the rest stop.

He knew that sound as well as his own voice. Summer, spring, winter, fall...any hint of wind or weather the flag pole would sound the relentless '*clink, clink, clink.*' Some would find it annoying, but somehow Big Mike always found it rather soothing and relaxing. Some people liked ocean sounds, he liked the sound of that flagpole. Mike's head was finally clearing. He was sitting on the ground with his back against what he suspected was the flag pole. His hands were not bound. He couldn't even feel his hands, they were so frigidly cold without gloves, but he was not tied up in any way. He did vaguely remember what had happened. He had been hit at least twice with a metal chair by...he paused. It was Peter Oswald. He had seen his face. Now he was outside against the flag pole, like he was part of some sort of fraternity prank. It was then that something else came to Big Mike's realization. He was against the flag pole, he was sitting in the snow, and he was also completely and utterly head to toe naked.

"What in the hell," he whispered, his teeth chattering. His large belly jutted out in front of him and he didn't even know where his balls were because he couldn't feel anything below his chest. "You gotta be shittin me," he said, the situation hitting him all at once. Now he was pissed. If this was a joke, it was cruel and stupid and he was literally going to kill that little glasses wearing salesman bastard. It was time to get out of this situation. Mike slowly tried to sit forward. He could not. He moved his back slightly but something was pulling on him. He lifted his hands and waved them in front of his face to confirm that he was not tied up.

Mike shook his head and leaned forward but again without success. Big Mike's stomach turned. He felt nauseous and terrified as he realized that his naked back was solidly attached to the icy cold flag pole. He did not know how long he had been sitting here but it would only take seconds for skin to freeze firmly to steel, and he was frozen solid. He began to panic, his eyes darting around. He was scared and his heart was pounding. He looked down and saw that even his feet were bare. His shoes and socks were gone and his feet were blue. He moved them around and they moved, but he could not feel them at all. He was sure he had hypothermia and he began to think this wasn't a joke at all, and that Peter Oswald was really screwed up.

The woman...in the car...with her throat cut, he had done that. They had locked eyes in the rest stop and Big Mike knew he had killed that woman and worst of all Peter Oswald knew that Big Mike knew. Mike moved slightly, trying to sit up, his skin was being pulled by the metal. It wasn't painful because the skin was frozen solid. He couldn't even feel the metal pole attached to his back. Mike's eyes filled with tears as everything became clear. "HELP!" he tried to scream for the first time. His voice was hoarse. He was barely audible even if the storm wasn't howling around him and blocking all noise, let alone his pitiful plea.

He would die here. He had no idea how long he had been here but his feet were blue, he couldn't feel anything below his chest and he knew he was dying. He would not die, he thought to himself. This could not happen, not like this, not in his beloved rest stop. He had all those other people to think about in the stop. Peter Oswald could prey on them and Mark Harrison needed to know what was going on. Also there was that apparition, the woman who had tried to kill Ethan and him was some sort of demon. What in the hell was going on? It was time for his survival instincts to kick in. He had to get off this damn flag pole. Mike looked around at the snow. He spotted something he hadn't seen before. It was laying half buried but something was there. It was a blanket, an emergency blanket. It was gray and made from rough material that could be used to put out fires if need be, or keep someone warm...or drag an oversized 250 pound man down a hallway and into the snow. That's why it was there. Peter Oswald had moved Mike on it. It still must have taken him a lot of time and a lot of risk that no one would come down the hall to the washroom. Then again, it was pitch-dark in the rest stop; people weren't going to move until Paul got that generator on.

Mike moved his foot as best as he could to the right, towards where the blanket was. He tried to stretch out his frozen blue foot. He could just barely touch the blanket with his big toe but he didn't even know he was doing that because he could feel nothing. He strained his entire body and felt his skin pulling away from the pole, stretching inhumanely. In some ways it was actually a Godsend that Big Mike Otterman was so overweight. He had plenty of skin on him to stretch. It wasn't, however, helping him in this case. He could not get close enough to the blanket and even if he had been able to get his foot on it he didn't think he'd be able to get his frozen appendage to do what he wanted and bring the blanket to him. He would have to crawl to the blanket once he got off this pole.

Could he actually build himself up to ripping his back off this? Mike took a deep breath and reached behind him to try and feel how much of his skin was attached. His hands were numb and turning color now too. What would it be like to pull his skin from this pole? Would he bleed? He suspected he would. It would have to be done like a band-aid, just as a parent would tell their silly youngster who puts their tongue on a flag pole out of a dare. That was in a movie wasn't it? Big Mike couldn't remember. He put his hands into the snow, on each side of himself, and pushed down into it until he could feel the ground, or at least where the snow was packed enough to be sturdy.

He felt almost relieved that he could actually feel the icy cold snow on his hands ever so slightly. Any feeling was a relief to him at this point. He took as deep a breath as he could, but his breathing was shallow and his lungs felt icy. He positioned himself closer to the pole, and then used his hands to get some leverage, and began to push off the ground and away from it.

His skin pulled, it stretched away from his back keeping solidly hold of the flag pole. Mike grunted as he pushed. He wasn't giving it his full strength that much was obvious. He should but, without a doubt, he was scared. He had no idea what it was going to be like to rip his naked body off frozen metal. The storm seemed to suddenly escalate and it whipped around Mike's head. He spat the snow away from his mouth and shivered. He stopped pushing and took a moment to reassess his surroundings. And then, she was there again. His heart sank, and he wanted to cry out in pain and anger and agony. It was the Asian woman, the spirit. She wasn't floating this time; she was standing twenty feet in front of Mike, in the snow looking into the sky. It was as though she didn't even see him and he hoped that was the case.

This woman, that he and Ethan knew for certain was the furthest thing from human, would not leave him alone and now she was back and he was in an incredibly vulnerable position. He wasn't even thinking about the fact that he was sitting here, balls out, facing her but rather that she would destroy him like she had tried to do on the highway. He still didn't know what had stopped her when they sat in the cat side by side desperately trying to start the machine. When it had finally turned over and she was moving towards them like the driving storm, just like that...she vanished. No reason, no explanation and no excuses. The cat had turned on and both men were fine, despite her attempt at impaling Ethan on a cone of razor sharp ice. It took them no time at all, to turn the cat around and get back to the rest stop. Neither man said a word to the other for the entire ride back.

Mike had tears welling in the corners of his eyes. "Please," he whispered, clearing his throat and trying to yell, "please, leave me alone!" he hollered at the ghost. She stopped looking into the sky and looked right at him. She could hear him obviously which was interesting information. He wasn't sure why or how it was usable but it was interesting nonetheless. Interesting, like being frozen to damn metal by the skin of his back. Mike hollered into the snow angrily, raising his head up to the sky. He screamed, until he couldn't scream anymore, and then pushed on his hands, sitting forward as hard as he could.

It was only by God's grace that the skin on his back was frozen solid and had no feeling in it at all, so the only thing Mike felt when his skin began to rip and shred off the pole was a released feeling. The skin tore from his back. Mike continued to scream as he pulled harder. The thought of what was happening was making him nauseous and woozy and he was worried he would pass out. The skin ripped grotesquely, tearing thin strips from the big man's back. The hanging skin stuck to the pole like strips of tape. Mike pushed harder on his hands and the he shot forward face first into the snow. Blood began to pool out of his back from the ripped skin. Mike crawled with all his strength through the snow, naked and bleeding. He didn't know how bad his back was, he only knew that blood was running down his sides and into the snow. His arms and hands were blue and the snow was threatening to bury him.

As he crawled through the snow, he looked to where the woman was. She was closer now, not a lot, but several feet. She was still walking rather than floating which Mike knew she could do. The cold didn't seem to effect her at all. In fact, she seemed to be controlling the weather around her. The snow parted when she moved and her feet stayed effortlessly on top of it. There was a distinctive pattern around her where the snow simply refused to fall.

The woman walked towards him as he crawled across the ground. She was looking at him curiously. Mike looked up and he reached for her. He didn't know why, the shock was taking over now and she seemed like the only person or thing that could help him at this point. "Please," he whispered. Big Mike's naked body crawled closer to the woman and he could see the corner of the emergency blanket which was almost completely buried. Mike reached out with his frozen hand and tried to grab the corner of the blanket. He had to force himself to close his fingers around it but even then he couldn't get a good grip. He began to cry out again. The woman was suddenly standing over him. When he looked in front of him, her pale, white feet were at his head.

He tried to look up at her, tried to see her face clearly, but he could not. His eyes were dimming. "Please, help me," he whispered, and reached up as far as he could towards her, begging for her help. "Please," he cried again. Her left hand came down like an ax. As it fell, it began to morph from flesh to ice and then to flesh again, changing forms as it came down towards him. By the time her hand crossed Big Mike Otterman's outstretched arm it was like a sheer, icy blade and it lopped off his hand like a razor through wax. Mike did not scream as his freshly amputated hand spun into the snow somewhere he could not see. This was like a horrible horror film, he thought, and this is where the camera would zoom in on his decapitated hand, only he didn't know where it was. The woman stood over him, her razor sharp weapon no longer visible and instead she had two hands again. Where his other hand had been, the hand he had worn his wedding ring on, held hands with, shook hands with, eaten with, jerked off with, was now a bloody stump. The icy wind and snow was actually cauterizing his wound but not quickly enough. Blood was spurting from his stump and his ripped back now.

Mike lowered his arm to the snow and lay there naked, practically frozen, looking at the place where his hand had met his wrist so perfectly for sixty years. Physical shock and complete utter disbelief had taken over Mike's world now and he didn't even know where he was or what was going on. The woman was still looking down at him, the blood pooling in the snow like a bright red cherry snow cone. Unable to do anything else, his strength draining from him, Mike lowered his head to the snow putting his cheek against the crunchy white powder. He took a deep breath and when he exhaled blood spurted violently from his mouth and he choked. His vision was cloudy and he was dying. He did not know where the ghost went or whether she still stood over him watching, it did not matter to Big Mike. He had suffered long enough and it was over. The last thought he had was of his wife and then Big Mike Otterman died.

19

"Say something," Ethan insisted. He had finished his tale of the ghostly woman they had seen and been attacked by. Patrick had said nothing. He was beside Ethan staring into the corner nearest to where they were standing. He looked very serious which partially relieved Ethan who was thinking if anyone would think he was crazy it would be a priest.

"I honestly have no idea what to say."

"I swear it is all true."

Patrick looked at Ethan closely and nodded. "I know. I believe every word." Ethan's relief was obvious on his face. Patrick put his hand on Ethan's shoulder encouragingly. Mark approached the two men and they both looked at him.

"Paul didn't come back from the generator shed," Mark said.

"Where is Mr. Otterman?" Patrick asked.

"I think he went to get flashlights," said Ethan. "I'll go look for him." Ethan hurried away from the men towards the hallway where the washrooms were and the supply closet.

"Something is very wrong here," Mark said, looking into the eating area.

"I think we have no idea how wrong things are," Patrick said in agreement.

"Where's the insurance guy, Oswald?" Mark asked, making a mental note of who was currently sitting in the eating area. Andrea was sitting at a booth with Hannah's head on her lap. Hannah was sleeping soundly, covered by her pink fuzzy winter jacket like a blanket. Josh Barton had literally not moved from the booth all night where he was sitting, still seemingly fast asleep with an odd and eerie smile on his lips. He was dreaming about something. Heather was sitting near Andrea and Hannah playing with her hair, looking mostly bored and chewing something, presumably gum. Stephen Camp was sitting at a table with two chairs, his laptop and several notepads open in front of him and what looked like a textbook of some kind. Something about that guy really got under Mark's skin. His intuition told him something was off about him. Mike Otterman was missing from the room as was Paul Janson, Ethan was in the hallway and Peter Oswald was nowhere to be seen. Mark could not recall the last time he had seen him.

"I haven't seen Mr. Oswald since the lights went out, since Ethan and Mike got back from their excursion," Patrick replied, seemingly reading Mark's mind. Ethan walked the hallway and could see there was a door open half way between the men's and women's washroom. When he got to the open door he could see there were brooms and cleaning supplies all very neatly organized. This was the supply closet that Mike had gone to get the flashlights from but Mike was not there. Ethan looked down and spotted a flashlight on the ground several feet away from the door. It was still turned on but barely lighting up anything now that the regular lights were on. Ethan bent over and picked up the flash light. He clicked it off and on a few times and pondered why it was there. The men's washroom door swung open and Peter Oswald strolled out, smiling at Ethan.

"Greetings boy," Oswald said. His hands were damp and he was wiping them on his cream colored khaki's. Ethan nodded. "I don't think you need that, lights are back on." Ethan looked at the flashlight and nodded again.

"It was sitting on the floor in this hallway." Oswald smiled, shrugged and walked past Ethan towards the main eating area. "Hey Mr. Oswald?" Peter stopped and turned to face Ethan. "Have you seen Mr. Otterman?" Peter looked thoughtful for a moment and shook his head.

"Not since you guys got back from your little venture out there." Peter paused for a moment and then walked a few steps back towards Ethan. "Speaking of that...what'd you fellas find out there?" Ethan cleared his throat and noticed how close Oswald was to him.

"Well Mr. Oswald, we found your car, and we found Josh Barton's car. The thing is...well...there was someone in your car." Peter seemed to think about this for several moments.

"Hmm, you don't say? Where are they?"

"Well...the person, it was a woman," Ethan stuttered, "...she was dead."

Peter's face twisted in remorse. It was a good performance. "Oh god, that's awful! I don't know of any woman though. What happened?"

"We sorta figured that she got into your car to get out of the storm but we don't know where she came from. Your car, well, it's a write off, I'm sorry to tell you."

Peter looked thoughtful again. "I understand. Well that's just awful about that woman. Have you spoken to the cop...uh...Mr. Harrison about the woman?"

"Yes, we told him. He needs to be kept up to date on everything."

Peter chuckled defiantly. "I don't know about that. I never got a vote on him being mayor of our little isolation community." Peter realized that Ethan disagreed with this statement and he felt like this little shit was sizing him up. He could cut him; he could slit him from top to bottom or better yet pull this gun from his waist band and blow him away. Peter imagined the little shit's body being blown backwards by the force of the gun, his guts spreading all over the hallway. He composed himself and tried to smile again. "Then again, he is an officer.

I suppose it is best in this situation."

Ethan seemed satisfied with that answer. The men seemed to stare each other down for a few more seconds and then Oswald turned and walked away. Ethan looked around the hallway. The south wall had large plate glass windows along it several feet above him. He stared up at the windows and if only he could see through them and beyond, he would see the body of Big Mike Otterman, bleeding out on the snow right outside those windows. Even from where Ethan stood he could hear the same "clink, clink, clink" of the flag pole where Mike had died.

He was just about to walk back to the eating area when he noticed a spot just to the left of the supply room door and to the right of the women's washroom door. The floor in this area was wet, it looked almost like it had been mopped or wiped up but only in this small spot. The thing that caught Ethan's attention was the stain above the wet floor. It looked like something had splattered on the wall. It may have been some time ago, as it was barely existent now, but there was definitely a dark brown stain on the wall. Ethan leaned over and put his hand to it. The wall felt damp like it had been wiped down as well. This was really strange.

Ethan heard someone calling out. It was Mark Harrison. He was calling everyone together again. He stood and walked out to the main room. Mark, Patrick, Andrea, Peter, and Heather were sitting together, this time at a larger table. Hannah was sleeping soundly and Josh Barton was stumbling his way over to the table, having been roused from his drug induced sleep. Dr. Camp, probably very reluctantly, was also sitting at least near the table with everyone else. He had left his laptop and other pads at the other table but he still had one notebook with him and a pencil in his ear. Ethan joined everyone at the table. Mark stood when everyone else had found a seat. He stood at the head of the table leading them all as though it were a Wall Street business meeting.

"I need to make sure everyone stays calm. I know this is a bad situation we are in. The landline phones are still dead and the storm is still keeping us from using cell phones. The problem is...we have more missing people." This got Andrea Green's attention. "Mike Otterman seems to be missing and Paul did not come back from starting the generator although clearly he was successful at it. Now, who saw Mike last?"

Everyone looked at each other but no one spoke. "He was here when the lights went out, he sent Paul outside," Andrea spoke up. Mark nodded and no one else said anything. It appeared that was the last time anyone saw Mike.

"He isn't in the hallway," Ethan added.

Mark appeared thoughtful for a moment and paced a few times in front of everyone as they watched. He cleared his throat and turned to them. "Alright, well we need to go find Paul. We know he was going to the generator shed and we know that he made it there," Mark held up his hands motioning to the functioning lights.

"I'll go," Ethan said, standing up. Mark was very impressed with Ethan Datsun. This was the third time he volunteered to go out looking for people that he didn't even know. Mark nodded.

"Alright, Ethan can head out back. Heather can you give me an idea as to where the shed is?" Heather nodded. Oswald looked from Ethan to Mark. Big Mike was out of the way and he just wasn't sure what Ethan knew or thought. He didn't think Ethan had said anything to Mark about him being responsible for the dead woman but could he risk that? Oswald stood up and everyone looked at him.

"I should go too," Peter said.

"Go?"

"With Ethan. No one should be going anywhere alone out in this mess, so we should go together," Oswald explained. It seemed to make perfect sense and it would give Oswald the opportunity to find out more about Ethan or if necessary put a stop to him. Mark looked from Oswald to Ethan. Ethan shrugged and nodded. It did seem to make sense. Mark didn't care for Oswald much. It wasn't the same bad feeling he got when he thought about the physicist Dr. Camp, but there was still something off about him. Then again he was a salesman and they tended to give off that vibe.

"Alright, Ethan and Peter will go out the back and see if they can find Paul. Maybe he just wanted to make sure the generator stayed running," Mark said. He was trying to make everyone feel better but everyone, including him, had a feeling that Paul wasn't just sitting around out in the frigid winter storm.

"What about Mr. Otterman?" Heather asked.

"We find Paul first. While we are waiting everyone spread out here. We're going to check the washrooms, the hallways, the eatery,

Heather check inside all back areas of the stores...the eatery, the bakery, the coffee shop and the convenience store."

Ethan was pulling his coat around him again and zipping it up to be as protected as possible. Peter Oswald had grabbed his winter gear and was putting his on as well. Heather was heading towards the eatery. "I'll check the hallway again and the washrooms," Father

Patrick volunteered and Mark nodded.

"No one leaves this rest stop except Ethan and Peter. And on second thought Patrick, don't do the hallways alone. I'll come with you."

"I'll wait here...cuz...well I don't give a damn," Josh Barton said, lying down completely outstretched on another bench. Mark looked at the junkie and shook his head. He walked to Patrick's side and the two men turned away from the table.

"You really think we have to stay together, even in the rest stop?" Patrick asked.

"As far as anyone can tell Mike was in this rest stop the last time anyone saw him."

"Good point."

Ethan and Peter followed Heather to the eatery and down the hallway. Ethan knew the way, having left here with Big Mike earlier in the evening. Ethan thanked Heather, and Peter winked at her. Heather felt a chill go up her spine. There was something undeniably creepy about him especially after he had nearly scared her to death only a short while ago. "Ya ready pal?" Peter asked Ethan, smiling boldly. His constant smile was wearing thin on Ethan. It seemed inappropriate under the circumstances. Ethan pushed his feelings aside, this was about finding Paul and he pushed the doors open.

The snow was like a curtain, it was coming down so hard and so heavy it almost looked like one big sheet in the air. The wind was frigid, even worse than before, Ethan thought. He could feel the icy chill cutting right through his heavy coat. He pulled a pair of gloves from his pocket and put them on. He needed to be as protected as possible.

Heather looked out the open doorway and shivered. She wrapped her arms around herself and Peter gave her a once over again. "Just go straight out and to your left, you'll find it. It's a small shed that looks like an outhouse. If you find the motel you're too far left. It's just on the right of the motel," she said raising her voice. She had to yell above the incessant howling of the wind.

"Thank you!" Ethan hollered back. "Ready?" he confirmed with Peter, who nodded. His jacket was definitely not as heavy as Ethan's, in fact it looked absurdly spring-like, but he did have a scarf and honestly Ethan didn't care whether he was cold out there. Maybe it would chill that inappropriate smile off his face. Ethan led them outside, unlike before when Big Mike had taken them out to the much larger shed where the snow-cat had been. Peter reached behind him and made sure the gun was still tucked safely in his belt. He felt the bulge and knew it was still there. He hoped he would never have to use it because he preferred to be more creative. He certainly didn't have to use a gun on Big Mike and he smiled again but this time no one noticed. He envisioned the look on Mike Otterman's face when he had hit him with that metal chair. He had hit him so hard, he had swung that with all his might, he thought he might even break Big Mike's neck but it had only knocked him out and that was only after a second shot. He wondered if Mike had woken up out there and found himself positioned against that pole...oh that had been such a perfect idea. It made him happy thinking about him waking up against the pole and feeling his naked skin against that metal.

It hadn't been easy work that was for sure. That fat bastard had at least one hundred and fifty pounds on Peter and that was being generous. Peter was getting good at handling dead weight even though he had never dealt with that much weight. An emergency blanket had made for some easy dragging, that was really using his brain, and as cold as it was out it took no time to drag Big Mike across the snow. Then he stripped Mike's clothes off. The hardest part was hoisting him up against the pole. By the time Peter had come back inside from putting Mike in that position, he looked like a blueberry he was so cold. The hand heaters in the washroom had defrosted him quickly and he ditched Mike's clothes into a stall in the men's washroom. He wasn't worried about the emergency blanket because anything he left outside was buried and gone in seconds. He had propped Mike up against that pole, turned around and the emergency blanket was practically gone, so he left it there. By the time anyone found any of that crap, including Big Mike, Peter intended on being long gone from this place.

Ethan and Peter were already fifty feet from the rest stop doors. Ethan trudged ahead, pushing through the snow, his hand in front of his face trying to block the wicked wind from getting into his exposed eyes. Peter did the same several feet behind Ethan. Ethan peered through the snow and spotted a dull glowing object. It looked like a single light bulb. Perhaps the shed had a light on the front of it. It never occurred to Ethan that the shed might be open. The two men finally reached the shed and through the intense snow Ethan could see that, not only was the shed door open, but the shed was crushed in like a tin can. It looked as though the front of it had collapsed in some way.

"The shed's busted," Ethan hollered over his shoulder. Peter heard him yell something but couldn't clearly hear him and didn't care. Peter's mind was racing on to what his next step should be. He felt like he was still fully in control of the situation and had plenty of time to keep things going his way. Ethan placed his hand on the side of shed and looked in. Paul's bloody corpse was lying skewed on the floor of the shed in the corner. His arms were propped on either side of him where he had reached to turn on the generator. "Geezus," Ethan muttered and rushed into the dilapidated structure. Peter reached the door of the shed and stood in the doorway as Ethan attended to Paul.

Ethan looked at Paul's face which was ashen and frozen. His head, cheek to cheek, had been sliced wide open. It looked like he had been split in half. Parts of his skull hung horrifically from his face. "He's dead," Ethan said to Peter without looking over his shoulder.

Peter stood there looking down at Ethan's back practically ignoring Paul's dead body. He didn't even care how he had died or why he was there and it never crossed his mind to wonder who else was killing off the travelers. It was time for Peter to act. He reached behind him, lifted the back of his jacket and gripped the butt of the pistol. He slid it out and clicked off the safety.

Ethan turned to see why Peter was not responding. The gun came down fast towards Ethan's face but he was young and spry and had always had really good reflexes. He had played high school football and baseball and still worked out regularly, never knowing his response time would be put to the test defending his life. Peter brought the barrel of the gun directly towards Ethan's forehead with the intention of catching him squarely in the brow and incapacitating him. Ethan's left hand went up and instinctively blocked Paul's right hand holding the gun. With his other hand, Ethan pushed up towards Peter pushing him backwards. Unfortunately, he did not drop the weapon. Peter cursed, backing off slightly and pointed the gun at Ethan who dived out of the shed, cut to the right, and tumbled through the snow. Peter followed Ethan for several feet and then held out the gun and fired. The gun blasted, muffled only by the weather, and the flash exploded. The bullet vanished into a snow bank as Ethan put distance between them.

Unable to run back towards the rest stop, Ethan pushed right having to march his way through nearly four feet of snow in some places. Peter cursed again and began to plow after the kid. Ethan didn't dare look behind him but his instincts told him to just keep going. It was only a few feet before he could see a long, gray, stone building. There was an old rickety Adirondack chair buried in the snow outside of a red door with gold numbering that said, 16. He was at the motel. He pushed his way past 16, 15, 14...there was no 13...there rarely was. Ethan jumped and hollered as something above his head exploded. A bullet fired from Peter's gun had caught one of the burnt out lamps outside room number 14. Clearly Oswald wasn't far behind.

Ethan turned to the door marked 12 and turned the handle. Nothing, it was locked. He turned the handle again while putting his weight behind it. Ethan was not a big man by any means but the motel doors were worn and weakened. The door splintered and the lock burst open and Ethan fell, arms whirling, into room 12. The room stank of mildew and wet dog for some reason. The carpet was an ugly, torn up, puke green color. The walls were an off yellow but who knows what color they had been before. The lower halves of the walls were decorated in a faux wood that probably looked good in 1977. The bed was made with a dark red bed cover. There was an old television, which probably didn't even have the capability of having a remote, on a small TV stand at the foot of the bed. There was a desk, a very old brown chair and nothing else. Ethan wondered momentarily if there was still a Gideon's Bible in the desk drawer. There were two other doors in this room, one was open slightly and the other closed.

Ethan grabbed the knob of the closed door and to his surprise it opened. Inside, was the room next door. The two rooms were connected. The other room, which was room 11 he assumed, was much bigger and actually more tastefully decorated but did not smell any better. It was a light blue room with matching bed cover and a slightly better looking television that you would still have to turn channels by hand. Ethan spotted a door on the other side of the room and hoped that maybe all the rooms were connected and all the connecting doors would be open. He rushed to it and turned the knob and it did open! Unfortunately for Ethan it was a closet.

There was a crashing noise as Peter stomped into room 12 where Ethan had busted the door. Peter stopped. He had to re-group and think. Thinking was definitely Oswald's strong suit and he did not want to make a mistake at this point. He took deep breaths, gulping in the snow free air but also the stench of a closed up motel room. He had stayed in rooms like this; sometimes they hadn't smelled any better. He had killed in rooms like this. He had screwed hookers and smoked dope in rooms just like this. Not lately...he had given up dope a long time ago. He had to take care of himself after all. The room was dead quiet, the wind stayed outside despite the door being busted open. Still, he couldn't hear himself think, so he closed the big red door which was only slightly off its hinges and still clicked close despite being broken open.

Peter stood in the doorway, silently, taking everything in. He knew Ethan had to be in here. His eyes narrowed and he inspected the room. He saw the other open door and peered around into it. It led into another room. Everything was a go and he would blow a hole into Ethan Datsun's head. It would be the first time he had ever shot anyone.

He was looking forward to it. Peter slowly walked through the motel room, his head cocked, waiting for some sign of his prey. He began to whistle quietly, it helped him concentrate. Ethan had decided the closet was a bad idea but had ducked into the bathroom which was not a pretty sight. He had to plan carefully if he was going to not only escape Oswald but get the jump on him. Ethan had ducked into the disgustingly brown and rusted bathtub and laid flat into it. There was a curtain, which was partially open, and it would help conceal him enough that when Oswald came into the bathroom Ethan should be able to jump him, at least that's how he hoped it would play out.

He could hear Peter in the other room and then he heard him whistling. Peter was whistling an old hymn that Ethan recognized but couldn't remember from where. Peter looked into the bathroom of room 12, nothing, he looked under the bed and moved towards the other room. "*What a friend we have in Jesus,*" he began to sing. He paused in the new room and scanned it quickly. *"All my sins and griefs to bear..."* Peter fired the gun and it exploded twice ripping holes into what was the closet door where Ethan had considered hiding. Still nothing, silence. *"...what a privilege to carry..."* the gun exploded again this time into the bed. The stuffing from the mattress flew into the air, but no one or nothing moved. "*...everything to God in prayer.*"

Ethan could only guess where Peter was in the room. The shots were close but did nothing to help him know where he was exactly. He needed to know where Oswald was or this wouldn't work. He very cautiously lifted his head and peered over the cracked, dirty side of the bathtub. He could see Peter Oswald's back facing away from him. He was going to check under the bed first, Ethan thought. This was his chance to get him from behind. Ethan slipped from the tub and moved lightning fast towards Oswald's back. Oswald, shockingly, did not see it coming. He hollered and his song was cut short as Ethan wrapped his arms around the man's back and tried to lift him off the ground. Most importantly, the gun was at such an angle that he would not be able to fire it at Ethan from here.

"You bastard!" Oswald hollered. He was practically foaming at the mouth. The two men struggled and Oswald pushed back driving Ethan into the wall but he did not let go. He spun again and tried to roll Ethan off of him. Ethan desperately hung on to the psycho.

Peter would not go down easily. He ran backwards again and Ethan tripped on the carpet, losing his balance and his grip on Oswald. Oswald also lost his balance and the two men fell over each other. The gun slipped and skittered across the floor. Both men fell to the carpet and stopped. They were regaining their energy. They looked up and their eyes locked and then they both looked at the gun which had fallen only a few feet from them. There wasn't much of a stare down before Peter rolled his entire body towards the gun and at the same time Ethan jumped to his feet and bolted for the exit from room 11, praying the door would open easily. He opened the lock and threw open the door before another bullet exploded to the left of his head, into the door frame, which splintered and sent small shards everywhere.

Ethan was in the snow again and tried to pounce through it but it was far deeper here and he fell down into the snow. When he pulled himself back up he stumbled a few steps and then dropped to his knees. "Oh geezus," Ethan said. He was staring into the face and body of the mysterious Asian ghost woman. She was hovering again, several feet above him, but she was staring down at him, her dead eyes completely red yet again. "Oh no," Ethan whispered. He felt frozen metaphorically and literally as the icy wind slapped his body. He was sweating profusely from his struggle in the motel room. Peter appeared at the door of the motel room and held up his hand in a salute, trying to block the snow from his face.

He could see from where he was that Ethan was on his knees in front of a beautiful, young, Asian woman, in what looked like a long evening gown. She had long dark hair that stood out against all the white. "What in the hell?" he said out loud, peering through the snow. He hadn't said it loudly, no one could have heard him anyway, and yet she suddenly turned her attention away from Ethan, on his knees, and was staring straight at Oswald. She moved just like a plastic bag blowing in the wind but more graceful. She passed by Ethan without even giving him a second glance. Ethan swallowed hard and looked over his shoulder where the woman was moving towards Oswald. He could see Oswald standing in the doorway of room 11 looking perplexed but not terrified... yet.

As the woman got closer Peter Oswald felt a knot building in his stomach. She was floating...there was at least three feet between her and the ground, her eyes were a solid bright red, like demon's eyes, and her face seemed to pulsate and change shape as he stared.

Finally he leveled the gun at her when she was fifteen or twenty feet away. "Stop!" he yelled, like a TV Cop. "Don't come closer."

Obviously, the woman didn't care. "Shit...stop...you bitch," he blurted. She wasn't stopping. Ethan stood facing the two of them.

"Shoot her!" he yelled at Oswald, although he felt like it would do nothing. Something told him she was hunting Oswald and would not stop, much like she did on the road with him and Mike. She was only ten feet away now and moving towards him quickly. It was then her face truly began to change, elongating and opening her mouth to show the razor teeth. Oswald's eyes widened and he began to scream at the top of his longs, one long terrified scream. He squeezed the trigger and the gun fired several times into the woman. The bullets passed through her and vanished. They didn't come out the other side, they simply vanished inside her. Oswald continued to scream and continued to fire, until the woman was standing directly in front of him. She reached out and Oswald felt an icy grip on the wrist holding the gun. It felt like putting his arm into a frozen river. He stopped firing and looked up into the red eyes of this beast woman just in time for her to yank his arm up so fast and so hard the arm snapped in two like a pencil being broke. Oswald's blood curdling scream cut through every noise of the winter storm. His arm was snapped in two with the bone protruding through the skin and her icy hands still holding his wrist which was now twisted and misshapen.

The gun dropped into the snow and Oswald dropped to his knees staring up at the ghost and screaming, one long horrifying screech. Ethan had seen enough. He turned and began to hurdle his way across the snow, back towards the rest stop. He thought he could just barely see the rest stop lights, maybe even the parking lot lights. Was he far enough over that the front of the rest stop was closer than the back? He did not know. He didn't care either, his potential killer had just had his arm snapped in two like a twig and he didn't want to stick around to see the encore performance. Oswald deserved what he got but Ethan didn't want to watch. Oswald was still screaming and he looked up into his attacker's monstrous face. She was looking down at him and staring into his eyes. She leaned closer, still gripping his arm. "*Yatto mituketa yo*," she whispered into his face.

20

Patrick and Mark walked off the hallway for a third time. They had checked both the women's and men's washroom twice and found absolutely nothing. The supply closet was just your average supply closet and the only thing Mark noticed was a dark brown stain on the wall but it didn't concern him quite yet. It was a rest-stop with thousands, even millions of travelers every year, things would get dirty and there would be some strange spots. The two men met half way in the hall for the third time. "Anything?"

"Nothing," Mark replied.

"Maybe he went back out to the snow-cat?" Patrick suggested. It seemed as likely an idea as any. Mike and Ethan had parked the cat right outside the front door when they had returned. It was more important to get inside then to worry about pulling the snow-cat around back and into the garage.

"I'll go look," Mark said. Patrick moved to protest and Mark held up his hand cutting him off. "You're too worried about keeping me in here; the cat is just outside the front door. Let me look and you can watch from the doors." Patrick was defeated in trying to argue. The two men made their way to the front door and tried peering through the glass now almost entirely frosted over. The wind was beating relentlessly against the glass panes, and snow was piling up in a hill formation against the door. They couldn't even see the snow-cat from where they were but they knew it was there, just a few feet outside.

Mark looked at Patrick but neither man said anything. He pushed through the double doors into the frosty foyer. Then he pushed again, harder this time, to get the ice and snow away from the front of the doors, and the cold air blasted in. Patrick shielded his face propping the door open for Mark to slide out. Mark ran out into the snow, not wearing his winter gear as it was only a few feet but that was a mistake. His heavy jean shirt was soaked in an instant and provided no protection against the horrific elements.

Within seconds Mark was at the dark, looming snow-cat. He noticed the massive hole in the door where something had pierced the side. He really needed to talk to Ethan and Mike about what happened out there. He made his way to the driver's side and hoisted himself up on the treads and pulled the door open. The heavy metal door groaned as he pulled on it and he looked into the vacant interior. It looked as dark and cold as it was outside. Mark swept the interior with his eyes twice but saw nothing. He jumped down and headed back towards the doors where Patrick was waiting. It was then that Mark's eyes caught something at the corner of the building. The parking lot lights were just strong enough to enhance the snow but also form shadows over anything nearby. Someone was coming towards Mark. Mark stopped and wrapped his arms around himself. "Hello?" he shouted. He was certain now that someone was coming and they were coming quickly, running in fact.

Mark stepped forward and brought his hands to his forehead trying to see what was going on. As the person got closer Mark felt sick to his stomach. Something wasn't right here and was about to get worse. Ethan had basically made a near circle around the building and was coming up on the north side to the front. He was sprinting and bounding through the snow, hindering him at every step. He stumbled, nearly falling face first into the drifts, but caught his balance at the last moment and continued pushing on. He looked up, his face was caked with ice, and he could see a shadow standing near the entrance of the stop. "Hey!" Ethan shouted. It was pointless, his voice wasn't carrying and even if it was they would never hear him. He wondered only briefly if that psycho Oswald was still following him or even still alive. The way that his arm had been snapped like a piece of plastic, he was certain Oswald was stopped in his tracks. But that meant that other thing, that woman, could be following him and he could be next. This was his second run in with that thing and he didn't think he'd survive another round.

It felt like he wasn't making any progress but his thoughts about Oswald were abruptly answered when he heard screaming from behind him. Ethan stopped and turned. Less than a hundred feet behind him, Oswald was bounding through the tracks Ethan had left. He was screaming...Ethan wasn't sure what and didn't care...but Oswald was screaming. His arm was pulled up to his chest and looked excruciatingly painful. In his good arm Oswald had the gun again. Oswald and Ethan's eyes locked once again and Oswald screamed at him incoherently. The gun flared again but the sound of the shot was lost in the storm. Ethan had no idea where the bullet went and had no intention of waiting to find out. He turned and continued his trek towards the front of the stop and the shadowy figure watching them.

Mark did not hear the shot either but he saw the flash in the snowstorm and his sickening feeling got worse. He had seen enough muzzle flashes to know that it was a gun. He looked over at the frosty double doors where Patrick was waiting for him. Patrick looked at him curiously, encouraging him to come back by waving his hand. Mark held his palm up and took a few steps towards Ethan. "Hello!" he called again. "Mike?"

Ethan was finally making some progress and he could finally make out the man standing in the snow in front of him. He was almost certain it was Mark Harrison. "Mark!" he called out, "Oswald has a...." he tried to yell. His throat and lungs were filling with ice but he had to get Mark inside. Ethan would never be able to understand how Oswald gained distance on him but next thing he knew he felt Oswald's skinny frame ramming into him and knocking them both into the snow.

"You dick," Oswald was spewing. Ethan wondered where the gun was right at that moment as Oswald tried to roll over onto him. Ethan had several pounds on Oswald and was in better shape, so it didn't take a lot to shove him backwards into the snow and get up again. When Oswald tried to regain his balance Ethan reached out and grabbed his snapped arm and squeezed it. Oswald hollered in pain and dropped to his knees. As Ethan turned to run again, Oswald's right hand came out from behind him, still holding the pistol. He shot blindly in Ethan's direction and clambered to his feet. Ethan was finally in the light of the parking lot and could see Mark walking towards him.

"Gun..." he sputtered. "Gun!" he yelled.

Ethan collided into Mark grabbing his denim shirt. Mark looked into his eyes, which were wide with terror and his face was nearly blue in some places. "Ethan? What's going on?" Ethan could not respond. He couldn't get his breath or his words together. Finally, he looked up at Mark and took as deep of a breath as he could and the exhale was a cloud of mist.

"Gun...Oswald has a gun..." Ethan stumbled and began to fall into Mark. Mark looked down and saw a pool of dark blood on Ethan's beige jacket. The wound was below his right shoulder, and he didn't even seem to notice it but he was falling. Mark propped him up and grabbed him.

"Shit, Ethan."

"He...shot me," Ethan said, finally realizing what had happened. Mark turned to Patrick and tried calling out to him. Ethan was losing consciousness and becoming dead weight against Mark. He had to get some pressure on the wound if Ethan was to have any chance at all. Patrick could see Ethan collapse into Mark and rushed outside to help. Mark looked up to see another snowy figure pushing his way towards them. It was Oswald. He could just barely see the outline of the gun in his hand. Patrick slid into place beside them and Mark moved Ethan onto Patrick's shoulder.

"Take him inside, pressure on this wound until I can get in there. He's been shot, Oswald has a gun." As if to prove this point, a bullet whizzed past them in the snow. They didn't hear the shot again, it was lost in the storm, but the bullet was close enough that both Patrick and Mark knew it had passed them. Patrick did not hesitate. He hoisted Ethan up and began to pull them both towards the rest stop. Mark turned and bolted out to the middle of the parking lot. He was heading to his SUV. He didn't know exactly where Oswald was but at the moment there was only one goal in his mind, get to his car, and get his gun which was tucked into a leather holster in the side of his driver's seat.

He slid twice and almost went down but got to his car. He suddenly thought maybe his keys were inside his winter jacket but a quick pat to his pants pocket revealed his keys on the car starter key chain. He fumbled in the cold but quickly got the door open and lunged inside. It only took a moment before his hand closed around the handle of his state issued glock. He pulled it out, slammed the SUV door and moved to the front of the vehicle just in time to see Oswald standing where they had been only moments before. Mark pointed the gun in front of him, as years of training had shown him to do, and began to walk towards Oswald in measured, slow paces. It wasn't easy in the drifting snow. When he was close enough that he thought his voice would carry, he stopped and aimed the gun. A driving burst of wind stung his bare face.

"Oswald!" he cried. "Drop the weapon."

Oswald was standing in place, panting, there was some blood on the snow which was being covered as though it had never been there. He was holding his gun at his side and his other arm was still bent across his chest. He turned slowly towards Mark and raised his weapon. "Oswald, don't! Put it down and tell me what's going on!" There was only ten feet between the men now.

"What's going on? What's going on!!" Oswald repeated. "That damn kid attacked me! I barely got this gun away from him! He broke my arm!" he screamed.

"Let's go inside and talk about it. Put down the gun." Mark took a few more steps towards him, not lowering his gun at all. His hand was freezing to the metal grip of the glock. "Who are you, Oswald?" Mark asked.

The screech was deafening. As much as Mark didn't want to lower his weapon, he almost lowered it completely and crumpled to the ground from the extreme noise. It was deafening, it was like having your ear against a blue whale when they bellowed. It sounded like the roar of thunder right next to them in the storm. The screech was everywhere around them like amplified nails on a chalkboard. Oswald screamed and turned in the direction that he had been running from. The beautiful, monstrous woman was moving towards them, riding on the snow around her. Her face was grotesquely disfigured and the screech coming from her was like metal against metal. Mark looked to where Oswald was looking and saw the beast for the first time. "What in the..."

"You bitch...you bitch! I know you!" Oswald screamed at her. He raised the pistol towards her.

"Oswald don't!" Mark hollered, not knowing what this woman was. He was in sensory overload and had no idea what was happening. Oswald ignored his cries.

"Bitch!" he screamed again, firing blindly at her. The shots were nothing against the screeching noise and did nothing to stop her from moving towards him. Finally, the gun clicked and then clicked again as

Oswald tried to continue to fire. He screamed in frustration and, with nothing left to do, tossed the gun through the storm at her. The gun seemed to simply disappear into the white blizzard. The screeching stopped but she did not. She was only feet away from where Mark and Oswald stood.

Mark knew, all at once, that this thing, this woman was going to hurt them. He lowered his weapon and moved towards Oswald grabbing his shoulder. Oswald whirled around and looked at Mark. His eyes were wide and looked nearly black in the darkness. "We need to move now!"

The beast was hovering in the snow, her white dress flowing around her. Her eyes glowed red and her face was still twisted in an unhuman form. "*Fukushuu*," she hissed. Her hand raised and her finger pointed. She began to wave her finger seemingly drawing something in the snow. Mark had enough and he wasn't going to stick around to see anymore.

"Move now!" he hollered at Oswald and shoved him harshly. Both men clambered through the snow towards the door. Mark looked over his shoulder to see the woman or monster, whatever she was, was close behind and the screeching was beginning again. Mark only hoped to get inside before she reached them. They hit the glass doors and bumped into each other like a comical three stooges' skit before finally getting the double doors open and flying inside. The sound behind them as the doors closed was like a huge snowball hitting the window violently. Mark expected the doors to shatter but they didn't. Both men were able to get through the second set of doors and collapse into a heap onto the wet floor mats meant for people to stomp out their boots. Their chests were heaving and both men were certain, in their own minds that the cold and ice in their chests was going to stop their hearts. Finally beginning to recover,

Mark noticed Heather Morton standing over them.

"What in the hell is going..." Heather began but she could not finish. On the north side of the dining area were several large windows for patrons to look out of while they enjoyed their lunches. The windows rattled suddenly and then two of those enormous glass windows shattered into the rest stop. There was screaming...Heather was screaming and little Hannah Green was startled awake and screaming too. There was a lot of commotion. Snow was driving into the rest stop and glass spread out over the floor. Mark stumbled to his feet and hurried to the gaping holes.

Before he could even fathom what was happening, the monster woman burst through the broken windows. Her upper body and twisted face hung through the window and she screamed and roared like a beast caught in a trap. Mark stumbled back and his feet caught the corner of a table sending him down hard on his back, his head clipping the side of a bench. His head was swimming now but he knew he had to stay focused although on what he had no idea. His glock was tucked into his denim coat pocket and he scrambled to take it out. But even in his own mind he knew that it would do no good. He had watched Oswald unload that gun in this thing's direction with absolutely no effect.

He aimed the glock at the looming figure. She turned and looked down on Mark, the barrel of his gun pointing up at her. Mark had no other option. He fired twice in succession. The shots echoed through the inside of the rest stop. Several people screamed in shock. The monster hung over Mark and it seemed as though everything went silent. The storm raged on, the wind and the snow angrily licking its way into the broken windows, but it seemed as though everything had gone mute. As quickly as it had all happened, it ended. The monstrosity slipped out the broken windows the same as she had come in. There was a quiet sucking vacuum noise as she disappeared, leaving Mark on the floor with his gun pointed in front of him and snow covering the linoleum around him. He took deep breaths and lowered his weapon to the cold tile floor.

It was several moments before he got up and turned to face the dining area. Patrick had Ethan laid across two tables pushed together. He was standing over him with a large white towel pressed onto his gaping bullet wound. The blood was already starting to turn the towel crimson colored. The priest was looking at Mark and the broken windows and where the beast had been. His face was ashen and scared. They had gathered what blankets they could and any coats not being used to try and make Ethan as comfortable as possible.

Heather Morton and Josh Barton were standing several feet to Patrick's left staring with their mouths open. Heather was crying silently. Josh made no attempt to console her. He looked as though he was witnessing his own drug induced nightmares come to life and Mark wasn't entirely sure that that wasn't what was happening.

Peter Oswald was slumped against a Pepsi machine near the front doors where they had stumbled in. His arm was still crooked against his chest and his face was red and swollen from the cold but he was clearly starting to thaw out. Andrea Green was the only one smart enough to take cover when the windows had broken and the bizarre visitor had barged her way into their desolate hiding spot. She was cowered behind a booth away from everyone and her daughter, Hannah was clutched close to her chest. Hannah was also crying but mostly silently, though Mark assumed she was probably the one doing most of the screaming since he and Oswald had came back inside. And finally...the doctor...the physicist...Dr. Camp, was standing closest to Mark but on the other side of a planter with a large indoor tree growing from it. For the first time Mark noticed he was showing some real emotion, his mouth gaped open and his glasses were fogging over from the abrupt weather change inside the stop.

Mark took another deep breath and turned his attention to Oswald. He didn't seem to even care that he had shot Ethan and had acted like a maniac in that parking lot. Mark moved quickly and vigorously across the expanse of the room and was on Oswald faster than any of them could even fathom. Mark's fist came out and caught Oswald clear on the right side of his face. Oswald groaned and crumpled against the pop machine, still coddling his busted arm. Before Peter could slide to the floor, Mark pocketed his weapon again and grabbed him violently by the collar. There were some gasps from the onlookers but no one said anything or moved to stop him.

"You son of a bitch...you crazy son of a bitch...you shot him." Mark brought his arm back and sent another dizzying punch into Oswald's face. It was probably still frozen enough that he barely felt it. His face just seemed to bounce off Mark's fist and his head thumped against the plastic on the front of the Pepsi machine. He seemed to slip a little more out of Mark's grasp. Mark winded up again but this time a voice stopped him. "Officer Harrison...don't." It was the least likely person he had expected to speak up, it was Josh Barton. He didn't even think that kid would care what any of them did as long as it didn't affect his next fix of whatever he was hooked on. Then again, Mark didn't think he was picky when it came to getting his fix. Oswald looked at Mark and the son of a bitch smiled. There was blood in his teeth and his nose looked broken. Mark dropped him and Oswald slid to the floor again using the soda machine as a brace.

"Fascinating!" Dr. Camp whispered. Camp was staring at the broken windows, the snow pouring in and the wind groaning. Mark ignored him, or didn't hear him, either way no one paid any attention.

Mark quickly went to Ethan's side where Patrick was trying to make him comfortable. Ethan was whiter than a sheet. Mark hadn't seen anyone that pale in a very long time. He was conscious but barely and his breathing was raspy. Mark put his hands over Patrick's to make sure he was putting on enough pressure, which he was. The blood did seem to be slowing.

"Anyone have medical training?" Mark asked.

"Big Mike does..." Heather began, and then realized Big Mike was still missing.

Mark looked over at where Dr. Camp was still gaping at the broken windows. "You have any medical experience doctor?"

Camp looked over at them and seemed to almost sneer. He didn't give a damn that someone was dying right there in front of them. "I am a physicist Detective, not an MD."

Mark walked over to him and stood only inches away. He towered over him by at least two feet and meant to intimidate him. "A doctor is a doctor and I'm not a detective, can you help or not?" Stephen cleared his throat and pushed his glasses up his nose like a cartoon character's trademark move.

"I'll see what I can do." He walked quickly, head down, to where Ethan lay on the tables. Mark suddenly felt dizzy and had to steady himself against a support beam. It was frigid in here now and they were going to have to block off those broken windows...especially before she came back, if she came back. If they could keep her out it would be a miracle because that thing was the furthest thing from human that Mark had ever seen or heard of. Heather and Josh had made their way over to Mark and were standing there, gaping, looking at him, probably for direction or leadership but his patience was wearing thin and he didn't want to give direction. He wanted to be

home.

"Sir...what do we do?" Josh asked.

Mark's head was spinning. "Well, Josh, first you should stop dropping whatever dope or drug it is that you have been on since you got here. Once you've assured me that you have no other issues with that then maybe you can help me get some things accomplished."

Josh seemed taken aback but he said nothing, he only nodded. "Heather, any chance you have some large pieces of plywood or something to block those windows?"

Heather thought about this for a few moments. "There are rolls of plastic covering in the back of the diner. We had some renovations a few months ago and the rolls are still there."

Mark nodded. "Perfect, it'll get that gap covered. Can you and Josh bring them out here and any tools that Mike has to put them up." Both of them nodded. Before they went to get the supplies, Josh turned back to Mark and cleared his throat as if he was afraid to speak.

He had certainly humbled himself since the strange attack on the rest stop.

"Sir...Mark...what about that thing, whatever it was, what if she comes."

"Let's worry about getting that window covered," Mark replied. Mark walked over to where Stephen Camp was looking at Ethan's wound. Hannah and Andrea were sitting at a booth now and Mark smiled at Hannah trying to relieve some of the tension. She still looked terrified. Patrick was standing close to Dr. Camp looking over his shoulder. Camp had removed the blood soaked towel and was looking closely at the wound. Ethan's shirt was ripped wide open and his face was sweating profusely. He was still unconscious but his head was jerking involuntarily.

"How's it look?" Mark asked Camp.

Camp looked at him, his glasses pushed down to the end of his nose. "I told you, I am not an MD. However, it would appear that the bullet perforated the lung. Outside of that, it seems to have missed any major arteries."

"Is the bullet still in there?" Father Patrick asked.

Dr. Camp glanced over his shoulder where Patrick was hovering. "Yes Father, there is no exit wound."

"So what can we do?" Mark questioned.

Camp shrugged. "If I had some tongs, some rubbing alcohol...maybe I could take it out. And if there is a first aid kit, maybe we can sew him up. He'll likely live, for whatever its worth."

Mark looked at him curiously. He seemed to have this habit of making rather odd statements like that. Heather and Josh were carrying out a very large role of plastic sheeting and a stereotypical red toolbox. "Can you handle that Josh?" Mark asked. Josh nodded and waved his hand. He immediately began to unroll the plastic and appeared to be ready to work. It crossed Mark's mind that Josh was in serious danger hanging out that window with that thing out there but the window needed covering and he had other things to worry about. With that thought, he looked down at Ethan who was looking very pasty with each passing moment.

Patrick was returning to their makeshift gurney with a large red and white bag with "FIRST AID" emboldened on the front. In his other hand he had steel salad tongs and a large bowl. It looked funny seeing him carry those completely unrelated items but under the circumstances it made sense. He set the stuff down beside Stephen Camp. Camp looked at it all and nodded approvingly. "You can help him with this?" Mark asked Patrick and he nodded.

Mark returned to where Andrea Green and her little girl were hunched down at a booth. Andrea was holding Hannah tightly and the little girl seemed to be finally calming down. Mark knelt down beside them and took a deep breath. "How are you holding up?" Andrea asked.

Mark looked at her. She was weary and tired. Her face was streaked with tears and her eyes were bloodshot. He smiled faintly.

"We're all hanging in there."

"Ethan?" she asked with genuine concern in her voice. Mark looked over to where Patrick and Dr. Camp were putting the salad tongs into the bowl and pouring a bottle of rubbing alcohol over the top of it.

"He's hanging in there too."

"Ya doing okay kiddo?" Mark asked Hannah. She had stopped crying but her body convulsed with a leftover sob every once in awhile. She shook her head and buried it into her Mom's side. "Maybe you and your Mom can sing that song that you and Father Patrick were singing earlier?" Andrea nodded and not really knowing the words simply hummed the tune.

Hannah finally seemed like she was drifting off to sleep from pure exhaustion. Mark envied the sleep of a child, who could quickly overcome any intense situation and drift off. He was past that point now. He couldn't sleep even if he tried, not that he could try anytime soon. "What the hell is going on?" Andrea asked, whispering. Mark looked into her eyes again and sighed. He ran his hands over his face and through his hair.

"May I be blunt?" he asked her. She nodded. "I haven't got a clue."

"I can hardly believe that...that thing...that woman...it doesn't even feel like that was real," she said and tears began to well in her eyes again as she looked over at the broken window. Josh was standing on the top of a booth using a staple gun to attach the top corner of the plastic. Heather was helping by holding the rest of the plastic and handing him whatever tools he needed.

"I like to think my investigative skills are pretty good but I'm at a complete loss," Mark replied.

"Mark!" Patrick called. He looked up and Patrick was feverishly waving him over. Camp was standing over Ethan with the tongs hanging just over his wound. Ethan's body was rocking back and forth now. Perhaps he had come around which would make removing the bullet near impossible. Mark jumped up and hurried over to them. Ethan was definitely awake or more awake than he had been. "He's asking for you," Patrick said. Then he stepped aside for Mark to move in closer to him.

"I need to get into that wound," Camp insisted. He might not be an MD but was suddenly very determined to do his make-shift operation. Mark waved at him to step aside and knelt beside Ethan, who turned his head and looked right at him. His lips were moving and it sounded like breathy whispers but Mark could not hear him. He leaned in closer.

"What is it Ethan? We're going to patch you up, good as new, just hang in there."

"Ossswald...," Ethan whispered, barely audible.

"I know Ethan, he had a gun. It's okay, everyone is okay."

"Oswald killed a girl."

The words were still breathy but they were also unmistakable to Mark's ears.

"...Ethan...what do you mean?"

"Officer, please, we need to do this now," Dr. Camp insisted.

"Hold on!" Mark snapped back, and leaned in closer to Ethan.

"...his car, there was a girl in it...stabbed. Been dead awhile. Mike has her wallet."

Mark's mind raced, dead girl, stab wounds... "What did she look like Ethan? What ethnicity was she?" Ethan sputtered and tried to speak. A line of blood came from his mouth threateningly. Mark tried a different approach to the questioning. "Mid-twenties, dark hair, light complexion, an ethnic minority?" Ethan looked at him and their eyes locked. He heard the next word loud and clear because it wasn't even whispered.

"Yes."

"Ethan, listen to me...stay with me Ethan..." Mark leaned in, and whispered back at him, "was her throat cut?" "Yes," he said again and then his head went limp and he passed out.

"Did he just...," Patrick asked.

Camp reached down and put his fingers on his pulse. "No. He's still alive, God knows how, but he's passed out now so let's do this." Mark stepped back and let the two men back in and they began to work feverishly on preparing everything.

Mark walked backwards away from them until his back hit a large foundation pillar in the middle of the dining area. His face was flushed, his head was spinning, and his mind was pumping. Coincidence...it had to be...this was insane...but then everything was insane right now. Mark had to compose himself. He looked over to the soda machine where he had left Peter Oswald slumped against the machine after hitting him, a momentary relapse in anger control. Oswald was not there. He was gone.

21

Peter Oswald was in the men's room with his arm carefully balanced against him. The pain was subsiding now but it still felt numb and swollen. So did his face from where that dick cop had punched him. He didn't care that he had shot that little prick Ethan. He felt like the world around him was just losing its balance. Oswald walked to the stall at the furthest spot in the washroom. He pushed open the swinging dark blue door and grabbed a pile of clothing on the ground. It was a large, warm, plaid winter jacket, the sort of thing a hunter might wear. It was Big Mike Otterman's jacket, and under that was the rest of his clothing.

Oswald carried the coat over to the sink and threw it down. It made a clunking noise and Oswald dug through the pockets. Inside one of the inner pockets was a long slender wallet. It was red in color and was emblazoned with a trendy designer's emblem on it. It was a woman's wallet. He struggled to pull the wallet's clasp open with one arm and eventually he got it open. There was a clear window in the wallet with the woman's Pennsylvania Driver's License in it. Moira Lopez declared the license. She was 24. She was lovely.

"Moira...that's your name!" Peter said, smiling to himself.The doors to the washroom banged open violently, the back of the door hitting the wall. Mark Harrison stood in the doorway. Oswald looked over at him and smirked. "Come back for more officer?" Mark stepped inside the washroom letting the door swing closed.

"How's your arm?"

Oswald looked down at it and shrugged. "It hurts."

"What happened out there?"

"That thing...that woman...snapped my arm, just broke it right in half after that little shit attacked me in the old motel."

"Oh Mr. Oswald, Ethan Datsun did not attack you."

"Excuse me?"

"You heard me. He did not attack you. That thing that was out there, our uninvited guest, she may have broken your arm but whatever happened in that motel...Ethan wasn't the instigator."

Oswald looked at Mark, searching him up and down without fear. "He told you."

Mark looked at him innocently. "Who told me what?"

Oswald reached behind him and tossed the wallet with his good arm and sent it skittering across the floor. The wallet landed in front of Mark, Moira's face staring up at him from the driver's license. "Don't play games with me officer." Mark surprised Oswald by laughing out loud. He nudged the wallet with his foot and looked down at her picture. She was the exact type for the King City Killer, long dark hair, pale creamy skin, mid-twenties and Latino.

"That is the exact definition of irony Mr. Oswald, you saying that. You love playing games, that's what your entire killing career has been all about. What are the sheer odds that I would end up here...with you...in a men's room, stuck at an Interstate rest stop with this storm and that thing out there, all of us here."

"You gonna read my rights Officer or are we gonna banter back and forth like a Shakespearean tragedy?"

Mark reached into his jacket pocket and slowly removed his weapon. He did not aim it at Oswald but held it to his side making sure Oswald could see it. "I should kill you like you killed those women, you sick bastard," Mark said, his voice lowered. Oswald scowled and then smiled.

He was enjoying this.

"Don't forget Big Mike. He was the first man I ever killed." Mark flinched at this information which made Oswald smile even more. "Oh yes Officer Harrison, Mike Otterman is dead. His body is probably only a few feet from where you were standing out there." This time Oswald took two steps towards Mark. Mark did not move. "I stripped him, dragged him outside and I imagine he froze to death in a matter of...twenty minutes. I knew he was on to me."

"Same with Ethan, which is why you tried to kill him?"

Oswald nodded sheepishly. "So what happens now?"

"I find a place to keep you locked up until we can get out of here."

Oswald was now standing only two feet away from Mark. "Oh no sir, I don't think I want to do that with you." Mark now raised his weapon and had gotten it at the height of their chests when the lights flickered ominously. There was a zapping noise as the fluorescent bulbs fought against a power outage. Mark's stomach began to sink. The generator was done. It was about to die he suspected and there would be no more lights anywhere in the stop. As if agreeing with him, the lights buzzed again, there was a popping noise from outside the washroom and the electricity died. The washroom was completely swallowed in darkness.

Peter Oswald was not stupid. He had made some minor mistakes in his career as a killer but he was not stupid. He couldn't take on Harrison even if he had both arms which he didn't. His arm was a weak point, an Achilles tendon, and this sick bastard cop would use it against him. He needed to get out of here, even out in the winter storm and against that crazy floating bitch would be better than here. Oswald made his move the moment the lights went out. It was a sign from the gods that they wanted Peter Oswald to succeed in life. He grabbed Big Mike's enormous plaid coat and ducked to his right. Oswald was small, wiry and fast. Even Mark's quick reflexes couldn't stop him from getting out the washroom door.

Mark turned and followed him quickly. Oswald thought fast and decided to go to the left in the long hallway, away from the main dining area. There was a secondary exit at the very end of the hallway usually used by truckers, who pulled their rigs around to the side of the building to park and sometimes sleep. The hallway was completely dark but it was long and straight and there weren't any issues for Oswald running for his life. His arm was beginning to ache but he could not stop. He would worry about getting Big Mike's coat on when he was outside. Would Harrison follow him outside? He didn't know but he suspected not. He heard the washroom door bang again as Mark followed him out.

"Oswald, I'll shoot!" he yelled. Oswald smirked. He wouldn't shoot blindly into the hallway. He was not stupid. Suddenly he was at the exit door and pushing hard on it. The door groaned but swung open reluctantly, dragging ice and snow with it. Within seconds Oswald was outside, feeling the blast of icy air on his skin...again. He turned right and ran towards the parking lot. This time he was on the opposite side of the building where he and Ethan had been only a short while ago. He ran through the snow flailing. Desperately, he pulled the coat around his good arm and then his shoulders. There was no way he was going to put his broken arm into the coat. Now wasn't the time to bring back all that pain.

Mark flew out the door only moments later. Already it looked as though Oswald had disappeared. The parking lot lights were out too and the snow and the darkness ate up everything within a foot of the rest stop. Mark stopped and was trying to look out into it. He wanted him bad and he had no intention of letting him get away but going out unprepared into this storm was suicide and stupid. He cursed and put his gun back into his coat pocket and went back inside.

"Clank!" " Tink!" The noise of the deformed bullet hitting the metal bowl beside them as Dr. Stephen Camp, who was not an MD, removed the bullet fragment with a pair of plain old stainless steel salad tongs. Patrick was amazed. Camp had worked diligently and silently and found that bullet. Patrick was holding Ethan down in case he woke up but he was passed out cold and had lost a lot of blood.

Several times, Camp would ask Patrick to check his already thready pulse. It was there but barely. Camp reached into the first aid bag and removed a small curved needle and thread. This was not even remotely meant to be used inside the body but they had no choice. It was literally this or nothing and Ethan Datsun would die.

Camp leaned over Ethan, took a breath and moved towards him with the needle, right before the entire power grid died yet again in the rest stop. "Shit!" Patrick said. He immediately felt bad and filed it in his mind to do his confession and prayers later on.

"Quite." That was all Dr. Camp said.

"Can you do it by flash light?" Patrick asked.

"Do I have a choice?"

"We need flash lights! Right now, quickly," Patrick called out. He heard Heather and Josh making their way across the room from their window project. As far as he knew they had at least gotten one solid covering across the broken window. Now they were all standing over Ethan. Heather had kept the flashlights handy and was shining one down on Ethan. His wound looked awful, maybe even worse having had Dr. Camp digging around inside of him.

"I need you both to hold a flash light," Camp instructed Josh and Heather. "I need you to hold them at 30 degree angles from his body, one to the left and one to the right." They both tried to stand somewhere but it wasn't where Camp needed them to be. "I said 30 degrees!" he responded angrily. It was the first time Patrick had heard him show any emotion whatsoever.

"Hey doc, that means nothing to us," Josh replied.

Annoyed, Camp stood up and grabbed their arms with the flashlights and aimed them approximately where he needed them. Without another word, he went to work stitching meticulously, quietly and determinedly. There were several banging noises from the washroom hallway but none of them noticed or turned to look. Ethan was the only thing on any of their minds. "Should that generator be out already?" Patrick asked, directing his question at Heather but without saying so.

"No definitely not," Heather replied.

"Hold the lights still," Camp snapped.

Mark walked into the large eating area and looked around. He could just make out their faces in the glow of the flashlights. Did Ethan have a chance in hell? Mark didn't think so. Not under these conditions. He could also just faintly see the outline of Andrea and Hannah Green resting in the same spot he had left them. At least they were safe and quiet for now. He walked over to the group and Patrick looked up at him as he approached.

"Everything alright?" the priest asked.

"Sure. Yah everything is fine," Mark lied. "Except for the lights being out again. Is the broken window covered?" he asked.

"We got one covering on completely but if we really want to be sure we should put another one or maybe two on it," Josh replied. Camp glared at him for moving slightly with his flashlight but Josh didn't even notice.

No one else spoke for some time. Mark found a place nearby to sit down so he could gather his thoughts. The rest stop seemed deadly quiet. There was hardly a noise other than that awful howling wind outside which had literally not let up once even for a moment. Mark didn't know exactly but it seemed like another fifteen or twenty minutes before Dr. Camp sat up and took a huge deep breath. "Done.

Live or die, he's sewed up and the bullet is out of him."

"Hell of a job Doc." Father Patrick said with genuine respect in his voice. Camp blushed, though no one could see. He released Ethan's shoulders and checked his pulse. It was still thready but somehow seemed slightly stronger and he was breathing normally.

"Anyone got any antibiotics?" Camp asked.

For whatever reason, Andrea, Dr. Camp and Patrick all looked at Josh. "What the hell?" he said, annoyed. "Believe me, what I take has nothing to do with antibiotics. Amoxicillin isn't exactly a street drug."

"What he needs is cephalosporin but we don't have that so anything would do," Camp explained. In the dark shadows, he was cleaning his glasses with tissue.

"Excuse me," said a woman's voice. None of them heard her at first so she spoke again louder. Heather shined the flashlight in the direction where Andrea and Hannah were resting. Hannah was still lying in her mother's arms. Her arms were probably asleep but

Andrea never complained. "Inside my purse, my daughter has been on erythromycin for strep throat."

They all looked back at Camp and he shrugged. "I told you I'm not a medical doctor." They didn't stop looking at him. He was clearly the best they had in the situation. He sighed. "Fine. It'll do. It's better than nothing." Josh turned to go get the medicine. "Maybe we don't send the crack addict," Dr. Camp said, smirking. Josh stopped and faced the man.

"Hey, screw you, dude. I'm clean at the moment and I'm not going to take some kiddie medicine to get my high."

Heather ignored the cock fight and made her way over to get the medicine.

"Calm down son," Father Patrick said to Josh.

"No. Screw you all. You don't know me and I don't know any of you. I don't wanna be here with you people either and you're giving me a hard time about my recreational drugs. I'm sure you all have some messed up issues too."

"Not like you," Camp said. It was strange. Dr. Stephen Camp had spent most of the evening ignoring everyone with his head buried in his notes and now he seemed to be provoking Josh on purpose.

Josh took several steps towards him and Patrick cut him off as best as he could. The flashlights were the only thing lighting anything around them but it was enough for now. "Like you'd know," Josh sneered.

"I know that bullet on the table didn't come from Mr. Oswald's own personal weapon. I think he took it from you didn't he?" Dr. Camp said suddenly. Josh's eyes widened. Camp had been in the washroom when Oswald took his gun. He had seen the whole thing.

"You son of a bitch."

"Whoa, hold on now. Is that true?" Mark had stood up and joined the conversation. Josh looked at Mark's shadowed appearance and then back at the tiny little hunched over scientist. "Did Oswald get that gun from you? Did you bring a gun in here?"

Josh backed down and away from them. "Fine. Alright, I did. It was my gun and that crazy little shit...he took my gun in the bathroom. I didn't give it to him and I sure as hell didn't tell him to shoot Jethro over there." Josh continued backing away from the group towards the convenience store. They were all staring at him and he was sweating profusely, his body aching for some sort of high. This was not a high. This was as low as he could get. This was like sitting with his sanctimonious family while they judged him. He was almost at the front doors now and he had to speak very loudly for them to hear him. "I don't need this shit. I'll go sit in the damn van and wait for some real help."

It was Mark who stepped forward. "Josh, don't do that. Just sit down. No one should be out there." He was thinking of Oswald being out there somewhere but also that other thing that was out there too. The kid didn't have much of a chance.

"I'll go where I want to go alright. This isn't a military state. It's a freakin' rest stop and you are not a cop here, you're just a guy with a gun who keeps bossing us around."

"At least take my keys...turn the heater on," Andrea said, standing up and gently placing Hannah down on a bed of coats she had made for her on a booth. She tossed the keys high and wide and it was a perfect shot as Josh caught them effortlessly with his left hand. With that he saluted sarcastically and turned, pushing his way through the front doors. There was a 'woosh' as he pushed open both sets of doors. Then, as they say, all hell broke loose.

22

Hollywood uses a harness when an actor needs to be thrown from an exploding car or blown backwards by a breached door. Josh Barton needed one of those harnesses. Only it wasn't an exploding car and he wasn't blown backwards as much as he was tossed like a Raggedy Andy doll with his limbs flailing. Someone, or something, seemingly had scooped him up as soon as he exited the second set of double doors and tossed him violently and easily back through the doors. Both sets of double doors broke and shattered like thin ice as his body flew through them. The sheer power it would have taken to throw that body through those doors was unimaginable. Josh Barton's body didn't stop there. While everyone else shielded their eyes and ears from the sound of breaking glass and shuddering metal, Barton's body continued through the air thirty feet into the rest stop, then hit the ground with a sickening thump and continued sliding and rolling until he came to rest against one of the many tables. His arms were broken, his legs were practically dismantled and his neck was bent at such an angle that it was clear it was snapped, possibly and mercifully before he was even thrown.

The wind and snow pushed its way through the double doors. It was Heather who screamed first when Josh Barton's body came to rest finally. The pressure from the broken doors seemed to steal Heather's scream from her and pull it outside as violently as Barton's body had come back in. It was pitch dark but their eyes were adjusting to that now and they could see as much as was necessary. The snow also seemed to glow in some places giving them some very soft makeshift light to train their eyes on. Mark stood up and ducked as low to the floor as possible, making his way to Josh. It was pointless because he was dead and anyone could see that but Mark's training said he had to check. He reached over and touched Josh's neck and could feel bones protruding under the skin. No surprise, he was truly dead. Mark pulled Josh's fingers apart in his left hand and pulled Andrea's keys from him. His hand, remarkably, was still clamped around the car keys. He had tightened his fist only moments before being flung to his death. When Mark looked up again, Dr. Stephen Camp was walking slowly towards the broken doors. The snow was swirling around his feet as he got closer.

"Camp, stop!" Mark screamed but he did not. He kept walking. Beyond the doors, a figure began to form. It seemed like she was being put together by pieces of the snow and ice until she was fully formed... the beautiful woman. Her face was human now with her deep red lips and her dark eyes, all shadowed by her long flowing hair. Her Asian features were stunningly beautiful and in any other circumstances she should have been a model from a magazine. "Stephen, get back here," Mark called again. Stephen stopped but he did not back off. He was watching the woman in the white dress seemingly made from snow. She was walking now, very slowly, gliding closer. She was coming into the rest stop. Her form flowed through the first doors which were no longer doors but a gaping hole with broken pieces everywhere. She was barefoot which comically made Mark worry for her safety on all that broken glass. That was foolish because she wasn't human and her feet weren't even touching the glass or broken door parts. She was floating a foot above the tile floor, although she still took small steps mid-air.

As if the situation could not get any stranger, Stephen Camp stopped, reached into his jacket pocket and removed a very small digital camera.

Without another thought, he began to snap pictures of the ghostly woman. There was a small flash each time he clicked the camera. Mark cursed under his breath and moved towards where Camp was standing. Remarkably, and surprisingly, the woman didn't seem to care or notice Camp taking the pictures. After taking a dozen or more, he glanced at the screen on the digital camera and then slipped it back into his pocket. He did not back away from the woman.

She was through both sets of doors now and was moving into the main area. Everyone else stood around where Ethan was laid across the tables, watching. The woman seemed to pause and the air in the rest stop was distinctly chilled. The wind and ice was pouring through the missing front doors. She looked around the room, her head moving slowly, looking at everyone and everything around her. Mark wondered how much she could see in the room or whom she could see in the room. Everyone was huddled around Ethan to her right except for him and Camp. She was beautiful and the most disturbing thing any of them had ever seen. She was standing only a few feet from Dr. Camp now, still floating off the ground. Finally, her attention turned back to him but he didn't seem to be concerned at all despite the fact she had clearly been responsible for Josh's body being shot-gunned through the doors and into the room amongst them.

Mark moved very slowly behind Dr. Camp. The last thing he wanted to do was draw this thing down on all of them. "Doctor...," he whispered. Camp did not seem to hear him or acknowledge him. "Stephen," Mark tried but still nothing. The awkward scientist and the spirit seemed to be staring at each other and Mark was beginning to feel like it was a silent battle for territory. Camp reached into his pocket again and Mark's stomach fell. Was he actually going to take more pictures? This time Camp removed a small bundle out of his pocket. It was the size of a light bulb, maybe smaller, and looked as though it were cloth that was folded up and tied off with string of some kind. Camp took it out and looked at it, turning it over in his hands. Then without another thought, he held it out in front of him.

The woman seemed to look at it curiously, her head cocking ever so slightly. Camp cleared his throat and began to speak in a surprisingly firm and loud tone for him. He sounded almost confident and strong willed. "I call upon the blessing of Kotomatsukami, blessed spirits, bind this woman in the name of the night and darkness. So they may not harm me or send ill will." Mark looked at the apparition. Her face was changing distinctly. It wasn't the monstrous face she had shown before, it was still her human face but she looked like she was in pain. His words were clearly affecting her and she began to slowly back away. Camp took a defiant step towards her and held out the small bundle in front of him and above his head. "Make it so!" he yelled. Her face changed again, instantly twisting and contorting. She roared at him, which sounded like an angry cat only much larger and much angrier. But without incident she vanished, sucked back out into the storm, leaving them all in the darkness. The lights flickered yet again but they did not stay on. There was dead silence in the rest stop from the people. The wind howled and the single layer of plastic sheet that Josh and Heather had put over the broken windows made a snapping sound but held fast.

It didn't seem to matter now that the entire front door of the stop had been obliterated. It was freezing cold inside now and that wasn't going to change. There was a soft moaning noise from behind them all. Patrick looked down and saw that Ethan was quietly making a

comeback into their party. His eyes were opening only slightly and he was moaning softly under his breath.

"Ethan, can you hear me son?" Patrick asked. He knelt in close and listened to him. His breathing was shallow but it was there.

Mark finally gained his composure and grabbed Camp's shoulder. He had not turned away from where the ghost had vanished. He had lowered the small bulb though and held it in his hand tightly. "What in the hell was that?" Mark demanded.

Camp turned to him and much to Mark's shock and annoyance seemed to be no different than if they had ran into each other at the grocery store in the produce department. He pushed his glasses up his nose and shrugged. He then stepped around Mark and began to walk back to where his things were on a table, untouched. His laptop was still on battery power as the screen glowed in the corner. Mark headed him off and stopped him. "Did you just shrug at me? What in the hell did you just do to that thing?"

"I was asking her to leave," Camp replied, as though answering what movie he wanted to see at the multiplex.

"And you knew how to do that? How?"

Camp smiled and for the first time Mark felt like Peter Oswald wasn't the only seriously disturbed individual amongst them. This whole time while worrying about little Hannah Green and Andrea Green's hysterics over her missing husband and son, Big Mike's disappearance, Ethan getting shot, Oswald being a serial killer, the storm, the ghost...he had hardly stopped to even glance at physicist Dr. Stephen Camp. He was quiet and odd but the absolute least of Mark Harrison's problems tonight or that's what he thought until now.

"What in the hell is that?" Mark motioned at Camp's hand which was still clasping the mysterious package shaped like a small onion.

"Not important," he replied unconcernedly. He tried to step around Mark but Mark was tired, angry, pissed off and he had enough of all of this. His hand fired out quickly and grabbed Dr. Camp's hand turning it towards him. Camp shouted in surprise and the others looked over at them curiously. "You cannot touch me," Camp insisted, trying to pull his hand away. Mark used his training to squeeze Camp's hand just the right way to force it open, dropping the bulb into his own hand. Mark released Camp and looked at the parcel he had taken from him.

"What in the hell do you think you're doing?" Camp demanded. He was showing some flare now. Mark turned the package in his hands looking at it. It was just a small piece of cloth with something relatively firm inside of it, tied off with string. It was clearly homemade. He smelled it, thinking it looked an awful lot like a wacky homemade drug of some kind. He shuddered at the smell and pulled it away from his face.

"What is this?" he demanded. Camp said nothing. Mark moved forward and grabbed Camp by the collar on his shirt and pulled him up into Mark's face so that they were quite literally nose-to-nose. "You little pissant, I've got at least two people dead, two more missing, someone shot, and my 'are ghosts real' inner dialog is suddenly leaning towards hell yes, so you tell me what this is and what you know or I'll beat you with an inch of your life. Understand!?"

Camp's breath smelled like mint and perhaps cheddar chips of some kind. He smiled again, that crooked annoying smile and Mark relieved some of the tension in his grip. "Officer, I will tell you precisely what is in that bag but you cannot open it or she will come back sooner than she should."

"Or she'll not come back at all."

"Oh she'll be back regardless. It's only a question of when she'll be back. She won't stop until you are all dead." "And what about you?"

"Acacia leaf, althaea root and aspand seed," Camp replied.

"Enough of this bullshit," Mark said into his face and released him. He walked over to where everyone else was and Ethan was stirring.

The lights flickered again casting shadows over the whole place. "We're leaving," he said firmly.

Everyone gasped and talked at him at once. He held up his hand. "You want to stay here, fine. I'm not the leader here. But I am leaving and Mrs. Green," Mark turned to face the woman who was still rocking her little girl, "I suggest you and Hannah come with me." "Mark, where are you going to go in this?" Patrick asked.

He thought about it for a moment but only a brief moment. "I'll take my chances in this storm, in my own truck, then staying in here and getting picked off by whatever is out there. Oswald is dangerous and he's out there now too. That...thing...whatever it is...may come back and I don't even know what's going on with Camp." "What about Ethan?" Heather asked.

Once again Mark appeared pensive for a moment. "Mrs. Green has a van, I have the keys," he explained, thinking about prying them from Josh Barton's dead hands. "We can make a convoy with whatever cars we have. We bring the van and my SUV up to the door...,"

Mark motioned to where the ripped apart door frame was. "We put Ethan in the back of the van lying down. Andrea, Hannah, and Father Patrick will go in the van so someone can watch over Ethan and help Andrea if need be. Heather, you and I will go in my SUV and lead the way. I have four wheel drive and a GPS although it wasn't co-operating earlier this evening."

"Where are we going to go? How far are we from a town, a city, a gas station, anything?" Andrea asked.

"There's a gas station on the property right Heather?" Mark replied.

Heather nodded. "The pumps are likely still on. I don't think either Paul or I turned them off tonight. There are two islands, six pumps, and a huge propane tankard out there," she explained.

"So we fight the weather, fill both cars and any gas canisters we can. There was a man out on the road when I was driving. He had me turn around and come back here but maybe he can help us."

A chuckle echoed through the dark stop. It was Camp again. Mark looked over in his direction. He was back sitting with his laptop open making notes again. "You are more than welcome to sit here and cast spells you ass," Mark said sharply.

"That man on the road is why you're here," he responded. "He is why we are all here actually." Mark looked at Patrick who frowned and looked concerned. Mark rubbed his eyes. He was so tired and the temperature was dropping far too fast inside this place. The darkness was making his temper rise.

"Everyone, please collect everything you can. We need blankets, emergency items, first aid kits, food, and drink, whatever we can reasonably carry and get your jackets on. Heather, see if you can find something that will help us move Ethan...maybe a strong blanket or crutches or something." Heather nodded and headed towards the back room of the diner with a flashlight. "Andrea, get Hannah ready, we'll pull the van up out front for everyone alright?"

Mark leaned over Ethan and then looked at Father Patrick again. "You ever seen anything like that thing out there Father?" "Not ever in my life."

"Wanna do an exorcism?" Mark asked jokingly, but also not.

He shook his head. "That wasn't a demon. That was a woman... a ghost maybe? Sounds to me like Dr. Camp had his own exorcism happening." Mark nodded. He tossed the bulb package on the table beside Ethan where Patrick could see it. He looked at it curiously and picked it up, smelling it as well, and then turning it in his hands. "What is it?" he asked.

"He won't say what it's for, only what's in there and I don't recognize any of it." "It looks like a black magic bag of some kind." "Meaning?" Mark asked.

Patrick looked closely at it again. "Well I've seen cultists or dabblers in the black arts, witchcraft, New Age-ism, things like that use these for spells or incantations."

"Can you tell what it's for?"

Patrick shook his head. "Unfortunately, these items can literally be anything. It all depends on the person who makes it, packs it, what's in it and what they say when they use it. I'm not an expert in black magic,

Mark." Mark looked over at Camp who was typing feverishly.

"Do you feel like he's writing some sort of journal or report when he gets going like that?"

Mark was silent for what seemed like a long time though it was probably only moments. "Father, can I just say that I feel like he has something we need to know and we might not have a lot of time to get it out of him...what if I needed to...put on some pressure?

Some...intense pressure?"

Father Patrick looked at Camp and then at Mark. He lowered his head and for a moment Mark thought he was praying, not that they couldn't use a healthy dose of that. "The Lord is a forgiving spirit Mr. Harrison. Just make sure you confess your sins if you know what I mean." Mark nodded and moved to stride towards Camp. Patrick stopped him and lowered his voice. "Don't kill him."

"He's no good to any of us dead. He's the only one with the nursery rhyme that makes our guest go away," Mark replied and then smiled reassuringly. In just seconds, Mark was sitting across from Camp but he did not look up from his computer.

"Want your bag back?" Mark asked, showing him the magic bag. He glanced at it and shook his head.

"Just don't open it...ever," he replied.

"Any chance you're going to answer my questions honestly, as I ask them?" Mark asked, legitimately hopeful. Camp grinned yet again and peered at him over the top of his laptop.

"No. Although that was honest so I suppose you've created a paradox of sorts."

The next movement happened so quickly that no one could have sensed or seen it coming, least of all Stephen Camp. Mark pushed back his chair, swept aside the laptop and moved into a solid offensive hold on Camp's right arm, left arm and neck. Camp grunted in surprise and then began to yell out in pain as he moved him from the table to the far corner where the pay phones were and not far from the window Josh and Andrea had attempted to repair. He held the man solidly, though he suspected Camp could not have gotten out of much of anything, let alone this hold which had kept three hundred pound plus men at bay. He pressed Camp against the far wall and shoved him violently against it. He suspected everyone was watching, except Ethan, but he didn't care. He hoped the darkness would be enough to keep them from seeing exactly what was going on.

"I will literally choke the shit out of you. I will leave you dead on this floor and every single person in here will back me up that you attacked me and no one will give a shit about you. Or better yet maybe I can feed you to that thing out there since you don't actually have your voodoo bag on you," Mark whispered into his ear.

Camp looked terrified and that was good, thought Mark. Not because he took joy in this but because the doctor was withholding something and this might loosen his lips. He tightened the grip so that Camp's breathing was reduced significantly. He began to sputter. "What's the bag for?" Mark demanded. Camp actually managed a weak shrug through the hold so Mark pressed harder. The inner workings of this hold were that the wrong move...or the right one...could snap his arm and it was already bending in ways that weren't necessarily considered natural. "The bag!" Mark insisted.

"I told you what was in it," he cried through clenched teeth and developing tears.

"I want to know what it is, now!" Mark exclaimed. "Give me something!"

"You can't know...it ruins the experiment."

Mark released the grip and Camp collapsed to the floor sucking in mouthfuls of air. Mark looked across the dark room. He could see the shadows of his fellow travelers and he thought they were looking at him. Camp stumbled to his feet again and Mark sucker punched him solidly in the stomach. He doubled over immediately, crying out in pain, but Mark wouldn't let him fall to the floor. "We aren't your damn experiment," he whispered in Camp's ear.

23

"That is enough!" boomed a voice from behind Mark. Everyone in the stop looked towards the front door where that thing had busted through earlier. Snow was swirling inside and the lights flickered ominously. Standing inside the rest stop was the yellow coat man Mark had met so many hours ago out on the highway. Mark did not let go of Camp. He looked at the shadow of the newcomer. "Mr.

Harrison," the man droned, just as he had out on the highway. "Let Dr. Camp go." Mark shoved Camp against the wall and he slumped to the ground still trying to catch his breath. Mark walked towards yellow coat man and he could see that Patrick was also walking towards him. The three men met in the middle of the room.

"Who are you?" Mark demanded.

"You've done very well here, Mr. Harrison."

He hated the way this guy droned his name. He reached into his pocket and produced his weapon. He pointed it out towards the man. He had never pointed his weapon at a person who was not a threat. He was past his threshold of normal routine and training. "Who the hell are you?!" Heather and Andrea both gasped when they saw Mark's gun. Andrea was holding Hannah's head against her chest to block her vision of what was happening.

Patrick held up his hand towards Mark and his other towards yellow coat man who had not moved and was in fact smiling at Mark and down the shaft of his gun. "Let's just talk about this, gentlemen," he said calmly. "Sir, I'm Father Patrick John from Atlantic City, New Jersey. This is..."

"He knows who I am," Mark replied glaring at him.

The man chuckled.

"And you know him, I'm guessing?" Mark said, lowering his weapon and motioning towards Dr. Camp. Camp was still slumped against the bank of phones. The man nodded. Mark lowered his gun completely. "Why won't you just tell me who you are and what is going on,"

Mark said nearly begging. The man finally stopped smiling and seemed to look more serious.

"Mr. Harrison, you have done so much for me, I think I can give you some of what you seek. My name is Dr. Thomas Raines. I am a physicist."

"Oh excellent, another one," Mark groaned.

"Dr. Camp, works for me. He is observing."

"He's observing the phone booths from the floor," Mark spat back.

Patrick sighed. "Do you intend on giving us any real answers or do you even have any?" The man smiled yet again and the intense desire to plow a fist into this man's face came over Father Patrick this time. "This guy doesn't know anything," Patrick replied to Mark.

"Is that an attempt at reverse psychology, trying to make me tell you more?" the man asked.

"What is a physicist exactly?" Mark asked.

"Physical phenomenon. Light, dark, particles, protons, building blocks of life and all that jazz. See Mr. Harrison, it was several years ago when I realized that what I have studied since I was just a young man was all about the phenomenon of life. But what about beyond that? What about the phenomenon of everything in the universe." Heather had left Andrea, Hannah and Ethan and walked closer to the three men. Dr. Camp had actually managed to pull himself up and make his way back to the table where his books and computer were. "I began to collect observances from all over the world of customs and strange rituals that gave people a completely different physical being. There are ancient cultures and teaching of reincarnation where they believed the soul, an eternal being, could be reborn into another being whether it is human, animal or even spiritual. You understand this concept, though you reject it." Raines was speaking to

Father Patrick.

"I don't reject the eternal soul. But reincarnation in this world...I do reject that."

"Can we all sit?" Heather said suddenly. The three men looked at her and then Mark and Patrick looked at Raines. The ice and snow

was still building rapidly at the broken front doors. Raines nodded. As they walked towards a table away from where Andrea and Hannah were watching over Ethan, Raines called out to Dr. Camp.

"Stephen, will you join us please." Dr. Camp scowled and closed his laptop. He did not want to be anywhere near Mark Harrison. But he did as he was told and the five of them took a long table. "Where were we?" Raines asked rhetorically.

"Reincarnation," Heather replied. She actually seemed interested. Mark glowered at her.

Raines smiled. "You are awfully pretty," he said. Heather stared at the man and wrapped her arms around herself. She was cold but the guy also gave her chills. "Reincarnation implies that the soul must exist on another plain of existence before it is reborn into another being. I sought to find that plain. Multiple plains of physics." "You're talking alternate dimensions," Patrick said.

"Exactly!" Dr. Camp said, showing very sudden excitement. Raines looked calmly at Camp who very quickly calmed himself.

"You can't find alternate levels of reality. Not without being a spirit," Patrick said. Mark noticed Camp and Raines both smiled at that.

"You found one," Mark said. He felt sick to his stomach. Things were coming together in his mind and yet not coming together at all.

"You found some sort of science fiction rip in reality."

"No," Raines said firmly. "Absolutely not. There is no rip and this is no science fiction. There are alternate planes of reality."

Mark scoffed. "Reality? There is only one reality. This is reality," Mark said, standing up from the table and spreading his hands. Dr.

Camp laughed out loud and this time Raines didn't stop him.

"You are in our newfound reality, Mr. Harrison. We brought you here. This is a completely different physical plain of existence than where you were earlier this evening, prior to say...9:43," Camp replied. "Dr. Raines found this place; he found this and created a way to get here." Mark stared down at Camp. Camp avoided eye contact with Mark. His arms, neck and stomach still hurt.

"What does he mean?" Heather asked, directing her question at Raines.

"Darling, I think we've talked enough. Dr. Camp and I are going to leave here now. Unfortunately, you all must stay here."

Dr. Raines felt a cold prodding length of steel on the back of his neck and it caused him to stop moving. Mark had produced his weapon again and was holding the muzzle flush against Raine's bare neck. "Patrick, take Heather and go back to Ethan and Andrea," Mark instructed.

"Mark..." Patrick began but Mark looked at him and he stopped speaking. He saw determination, anger, exhaustion and the look of a man at the end of his rope. "Heather, come with me," Patrick instructed. Heather looked at the men around the table but allowed Patrick to usher her away.

"How's this for reality Dr. Raines. I am very willing to pull this trigger unless you tell me where all the missing people are."

"I believe I said Dr. Camp and I were done here," Raines replied. Mark did not hesitate or make any further comments. He took the gun from

Raines' neck and shot a single bullet into Raines' left thigh. Raines screamed and Dr. Camp toppled from his chair and skittered away from the table. Patrick hollered Mark's name and Heather and Andrea screamed. Hannah began to cry. Mark heard nothing. He placed the gun barrel into the bullet hole and pressed. Raines hollered again.

"You stupid son of a bitch, you shot me," he blubbered. Mark pressed harder.

"No one leaves here anymore. Now answer me right now...where are the missing people...all of them."

"If they aren't in this stop, she's probably killed them and hunted them. She wanted Oswald, we gave her Oswald." Mark pressed into the wound harder. Blood poured from his leg, saturating his heavy pants. "The others are fine," he screamed. Mark released the pressure on the wound and Raines sighed heavily.

"What others?"

"The woman's husband and son, the other priest, the trucker... anyone who didn't come through with us."

"Come through?"

"Camp told you. This is the alternate reality. I discovered this place. I could open a doorway to an area separate from what you would call the real world. It's not a whole new earth or anything stupid like that...it's an area...isolated from the rest of the world where there is nothing, only we can bring things here."

"How big an area?"

"Sixty two square miles."

"It encompasses this rest stop and the surrounding area?"

Raines nodded feverishly.

"What happens outside this area?"

"I'm still toying with that. Most things...most people...can't go outside of the area. It holds them in. It would be like an invisible wall.

Others...can pass through it and return to the regular world."

Something fell into place for Mark. "Hours ago, on the highway, a light passed over me and it felt like a migraine. Did you cause that?"

Raines was silent. Mark pressed the gun against Raines' temple. "Did you cause that?"

"It's the doorway. It's an electromagnetic pulse in layman's terms. Some can come through it. Others can't."

"How did you know it would bring us...all of us...here?"

Raines actually smiled. It made Mark sick. "You don't remember me do you, Mr. Harrison? I didn't know who it would bring here when I set off the pulse, I only hoped for a handful of test people. You were a bonus. We met at your conference. I was working with the FBI forensics team and we spoke briefly. This is how I recognized you when you pulled your car up to me at that barrier. You want to believe you are special and here for a reason...well you're not. You're a random choice by the universe, and a coincidence for me."

"A coincidence? A coincidence that I ended up here with the killer that I have been looking for?" Raines looked up at Mark and his mouth opened slightly. He winced from the pain of his gunshot wound.

"The King City Killer, Peter Oswald was the only person we tracked and made sure was here. He needed to be here to draw her in." Dr.

Camp appeared yet again creeping out of the shadows. He was holding that damned notebook he had been scribbling in for hours.

"Dr. Raines, I have all my notes here for you. You'll find them quite complete."

Mark turned to face Camp who cowered back a step from him. Mark reached out and ripped the notebook from Camp's hands. "I'm bleeding out for God's sake," Raines said, mostly angrily.

Mark scoffed.

"The bullet went clean through your thigh. Use your belt above the wound, pull it tight." With that he leafed through the notepad. Camp wasn't kidding about it being complete. It appeared as though he had started the journal even before Mark had arrived. The book was scribbled in legible short hand. It detailed all of them, names were added as Camp learned them. Prior to that, it was descriptions, opinions, where each of them went in the rest stop. The book was chronological up until 9:43 PM when Camp had written "*ENTRY POINT.*"

It was clear from his descriptions of Peter Oswald that Camp knew exactly who and what he was before any of them did. The notebook detailed the run in between Oswald and Barton in the washroom which Camp had walked in on. The notebook also detailed each time the ghost woman had attacked them inside the rest stop. Mark clenched his teeth and threw the book on the floor in front of Raines. "This doesn't make sense. Why is he chronicling us? Even if what you say is true and you've brought us through to this alternate bubble of reality, what is the point? What do you want from us?"

Raines was pulling his belt around his thigh above the wound as Mark had instructed. He pulled it tight, though not as tight as he could have, and looked over his shoulder at Mark. "You? I don't want a damn thing from any of you. I assume even you have heard of the rat in a maze experiment?" Raines asked. Mark nodded affirmatively. "Well, you, all of you...are the cheese."

"What in the hell does that...," Mark began. Patrick had escorted Heather back to where Ethan laid and then returned to where Mark was questioning Raines.

"It's that thing, that spirit. She's what you're studying," Patrick said. Raines shifted his gaze from Mark to Patrick and smiled, only this time the smile was strained. He had never been shot but it would all make for interesting observances in the stranded travelers behavior.

"All of this is for her," Raines replied nodding. Patrick looked at Mark. Mark leaned forward and took one end of the belt that was wrapped around the doctor's thigh. He pulled it hard and Raines screamed in pain as the belt pulled his leg violently. Mark continued to pull the leather harder. "What do you want?" Raines cried. "I've answered your damn questions!"

"Why are we here?" Mark demanded.

"I needed fodder. I needed prey to see how she hunts. I needed to know how she eliminates and kills. I needed to know if she would kill you all even if she found Oswald. This bubble is to trap her here to observe her." Mark loosened the pressure on his leg and he breathed a sigh of relief. "She is stunning, Mr. Harrison. She is unbelievable and built on pure vengeance."

"Meaning?"

"Dr. Camp, would you care to explain?" Raines said. He needed time to catch his bearings from all the intense questioning.

"Are you familiar with Onryo?" Camp asked. Mark's brow lowered and he shook his head. Camp actually snickered. He was clearly being condescending to Mark but Mark didn't care anymore. "Onryo is Japanese folklore. It is an enraged spirit who unleashes themselves on the living, driven by pure and unbridled vengeance. Ancient stories on Onryo have them controlling natural disasters and wiping out entire villages just out of pure hatred for what has happened to them."

Mark rolled his eyes. "Ghost stories. Enough of this. What is that thing out there, that woman?" Mark asked.

"She has a name," Camp muttered.

"Fine. What is her name?"

Raines looked up at Mark. "Her name is Riko Nanami."

24

Riko Nanami was 21 years old. Born in New York City in 1991, she was a first generation American. In fact, it was only two years before she was born that her mother and father immigrated from a small fishing village on the eastern coast of Japan. Her father and mother had operated a laundry service in Japan and, with meager savings, they were able to open another laundry service in New York City in the late eighties. Her mother Miko was soft spoken, elegant and well versed in the old ways of Japan. While helping her husband diligently with their laundry service, she also continued her own family's tradition as generational spiritual healer.

Spiritual healing had been a part of her family's history for centuries. The women in her family believed they had gifts passed on from the gods that enabled them to channel the spirits to help with fortune, health and warding off evil. Throughout the generations, they had been branded 'fox-witches' and often chastised for their practices. In Japan a fox-witch was someone who used a fox as a familiar to bestow certain abilities and powers to manipulate and trick others. Riko tried to distance herself from her mother's spiritual side at first. Clients would often come by the laundry and disappear through a suede green curtain where her mother would speak with them for anywhere from a few moments to an hour or more. There were no crystal balls or tarot cards or anything like that. Instead it was prayer, incantations, and special herbs considered "mystical" by Japanese culture.

It wasn't until Riko was in her late teens when she began to take an interest in their family culture and history. Her mother was more than willing and eager for her young daughter to learn about everything spiritual. At 18, Riko spent two years at a college for journalism, something else she had found a passion for. She wanted to write for magazines and newspapers and maybe work on the great Japanese-American novel. It was the summer following her graduation that she decided to get away with her thoughts and her writing and take some time for herself. With only a few clicks online she found what she thought would be the perfect quiet getaway.

Wolf's Head, New Jersey was a small town of less than 500 people. It was over 60 miles from the nearest big city and it was 20 miles from the main highway. It was located on the corner of a large bay and was generally a busy location for tourists looking to camp, spend time on the small family beach, rent cabins from the nearby campground or just generally get away from the hustle and bustle. Aptly named, Wolf's Head was surrounded by several rock formations and if you were to stand on the waterfront, closest to the beach, and look across the bay, you can see a jutting rock formation that looked distinctly like a wolf. The permanent residents of Wolf's Head tried to live their lives around the few months of tourists that trickled through. They had one small motel that would fill up frequently in the midsummer. Even with all the tourists visiting in the summer, the beautiful young Japanese student was the talk of the small town when she arrived and checked into the motel.

The first evening she spent some time in the local diner and felt a little bit uncomfortable that many of the regulars and even the staff looked at her like she was a shiny new toy. The next morning she got up with the sunrise, put on some running shorts and her old college

T-shirt and went jogging. She started along the beach, through the park and down towards the marina where many boats were docked. It was still only mid-may so many of the yachts and small boats hadn't even been opened for the season. She hadn't seen a single person during her run and that was just fine. It was beautiful here, the sun coming up over the water, the cool morning air and being all alone with her thoughts.

She jogged down into the marina and to the very end of the docks. It wasn't until she was right on the dock when she saw the three men tying a small boat to the side. One young man with dark hair was standing on the dock tying off the line. Two other men, similar age, probably only a few years older than Riko, were on the boat collecting their fishing lines, pails, and a substantial line of fish. While some people would barely be half way through their sleep, fishermen were already full swing into their day. It startled her a little when she spotted them and they all looked over at her. She simply smiled and nodded and turned quickly and continued to jog back up the dock.

The men looked at each other and began to talk. She wasn't sure but she suspected they were likely talking about her but it seemed harmless enough and they said nothing to her so it slipped from her mind. After showering, she had a small breakfast in the motel diner where only two other people were eating. Then she went to the local market to buy some fresh fruit and water to have on hand while she wrote throughout the afternoon. Immediately, she recognized the same young dark haired man that had been tying off the boat earlier that morning. He had sharp green eyes and smiled at her when she walked past with her basket of apples and oranges.

"'Mornin," he said, showing nicely shaped teeth. He was handsome but scruffy and unkempt. He was loading fish and meat into a cooler near the back of the market. She wondered if it was the same fish he and his friends had caught that morning. She nodded politely but continued past him. "You not speak English?" he mumbled.

She stopped and turned back to him. “Excuse me?”

“I just wondered if you had a problem with English, bein’ Asian and all, and not speaking when you’re spoken to.” “I speak English just fine being I am American,” Riko replied firmly.

“Yep,” dark hair replied and then put his fingers up in the air in the familiar ‘rabbit ear quote motion’, “American.” “Racism is alive and well in Wolf’s Head I see,” she replied. “Do you work here?”

“Yes ma’am,” he replied, smiling again or still.

“Where’s your manager?” she demanded.

Dark hair laughed. Then he stepped towards her but she didn’t back away. He leaned in close to her and she could smell cigarettes and fish on him. His head was next to hers now when he whispered, “I don’t care who you are but don’t screw around me with sweetheart. This is my town.” Then he leaned back, smiled, winked at her and went back to his work. Riko turned and walked away from him fuming.

As she checked out at the register the older woman at the cash desk kept looking at her and smiling. Had this clearly dominantly white town never had an American of any color other than white here, Riko wondered to herself. “May I ask you something?” Riko said to the woman. The woman was clearly surprised at Riko speaking to her. She probably was surprised she spoke English Riko thought to herself and rolled her eyes. “The young man with the dark hair working on the fish and meat...who is he?” Riko asked.

“That’s Charlie West,” she replied, weighing Riko’s apples.

Riko looked at the paper bags stacked beside the cashier. “As in... West’s Convenience?”

“Oh he’s not the owner, he’s Mr. West’s son. He only works here and brings in the fresh fish every morning.”

Her items were bagged and she had handed the woman a bill, got some change, and was ready to go. “Well he’s a racist pig,” Riko said, matter of factly.

The woman laughed out loud. "Charlie West? He's not smart enough to be much of anything sweetie. We don't take him too seriously." Riko looked at her goofy smile and shook her head. Ignorance truly was bliss.

"Perhaps he just doesn't know how to speak to a beautiful woman," said a man behind her in line. Riko turned and looked at the complimentary gentlemen. He looked like he too would stand out in Wolf's Head. He was wearing a two piece suit, a white dress shirt and a tie which was loosened at the knot. He smiled and nodded politely. He was good looking, very well styled, the polar opposite of Charlie West. Riko returned the smile politely. He juggled the few items he had into his other hand and then offered his right one for shaking. Riko hesitated but then shook his hand. "I'm just passing through. Are you finding the folks here a little less than desirable?" the man asked, placing his things on the counter for the woman to check him through. Riko shrugged.

"I'm only visiting so it's no bother really. I just didn't enjoy Mr. West back there." The man nodded understandingly.

"I saw the two of you talking. You held yourself well."

"I like to think I'm a strong woman," she replied and laughed lightly. Now this man seemed polite, well spoken and friendly. He put her at ease...he was probably a lawyer...or a salesman, she thought. "Well, I must be going Mr..."

The man looked ashamed that he hadn't introduced himself. "So sorry. Oswald. Peter Oswald," he said, offering his hand a second time. She took his hand more firmly this time.

"Riko Nanami. It was a pleasure speaking with you, Mr. Oswald."
"You as well, Miss," he called after her, but Riko was gone.

An hour later and Riko was sitting at the cheap wooden desk in the decently decorated but inexpensive motel room. She had taken out her laptop and was ready to start writing. She tapped a pencil on the desk while she thought out the start of her project.

"The Racist in Wolf's Head," she said aloud, and then laughed despite herself. The small, not so funny joke, broke the ice and she began to write about something completely different and didn't stop for the better part of five hours.

The diner where Riko had had breakfast got much busier in the evenings. By six at night it was usually packed with locals and visitors to the area. Charlie West and his fishing pals all sat at the counter on swiveling stools nursing beers and cheeseburgers. West was regaling his friends with his run in with the Japanese woman. They laughed at West's cheap jokes about what he wanted to do with her. Their laughs only urged him on as he jumped from the stool and danced provocatively, pretending she was in his arms. "I'd screw the feminism out of her," Charlie West hollered, and his friends howled. Other patrons in the diner looked at him with disgust.

"I'd be surprised if you could get a woman, much less screw one." The comment came from a booth along the far wall. West stopped and looked at his friends who immediately averted their eyes.

"'Scuse me?" West said, approaching the booth.

Peter Oswald set his spoon down into his soup bowl. He smiled up at West. "You talk a big game son, but when it comes down to it, I suspect you'd be lost like a little boy in a corn field." "Who the hell are you?" West demanded.

Oswald wiped his mouth. "Where are my manners?" He stood up and put his hand out. "John, John Smith. I was just passing through your little town and was looking for a good time."

"John Smith eh? Well John, if by good time you mean me beating the living shit out of you, then you're about to have the time of your life," West threatened.

Oswald actually laughed out loud, throwing his head back. Then he lowered his voice and leaned in close to Charlie West. "I was thinking actually that we go visit that young lady that you met today. I understand she's staying right next door in the motel." Charlie West contemplated this and then looked at Oswald.

"You're a right twisted dude, ain't you?" Charlie West said.

Oswald, once again, laughed his infectious, exaggerated laugh. "I think you and I are cut from the same cloth," he observed.

By the time Riko stopped writing and looked at the time on her laptop, it was half past eight. She leaned back, stretched and yawned. Perhaps, she would stop for the night. The sun was set now and it was dark out. It was too late to go for an evening jog and she was sort of exhausted anyways from writing most of the day. She closed her laptop and went to the large double bed. She lay down on the floral patterned comforter and clicked on the TV. It wasn't a great TV, the furthest thing from a flat screen, but it did the trick. She tuned into a game show and zoned out for at least an hour.

It sounded like some May showers were starting outside. Nothing heavy, but she could hear the sound of the rain on the pavement. It was a little after nine when there was a thump outside. It sounded like a car door closing but closer to the room window. Riko listened for a moment, muting the television, but heard nothing else so she put back on a show and continued watching. A few moments later, another thump, this one sounded like it was at the door but not knocking, just thumping. Riko muted the television again, but this time got up and glanced out the window. The pavement was wet, the street lights shined off the watery road, but there was no one. The only car in the lot was hers and the only other light she could see was in the front office. She glanced to the right and saw something lying in front of her front door. It looked like a parcel or a large envelope. That was strange. She wasn't expecting anything and why wouldn't they just knock if she had something delivered. It wasn't that late.

She closed the curtain, walked to the door and unlocked the sliding chain. She opened the door just a crack to look outside. Small town or not, she was raised in New York City where you didn't just throw your door open. That was ultimately the last thing Riko remembered doing. She opened the door and someone stepped from behind it and drove their fist into her face. Her nose exploded and blood splattered on the door frame. She stumbled back until she hit a wall and three men filed into the room. It was Charlie West, and his two friends he had been with that very morning on the dock. Charlie was first through the door and had been the source of the devastating blow to Riko's face. The smallest of the three men closed the door behind them but did not lock it. Riko could see none of this as her eyes were blurred with tears and blood. Her teeth and nose ached and were bleeding profusely. One of them, probably Charlie, grabbed

Riko by the shoulder and tossed her towards the bed. She was stumbling and then fell onto the mattress on her side.

"Hi there girlie-san, 'member me?" Charlie hissed at her, standing over the bed.

"Leeb me alun," Riko begged through her wounds, her lip starting to swell.

"What's that? I can't understand a word you're saying ya foreign bitch," he said. The men all laughed loudly. It didn't matter how loud they were, Riko knew she was the only guest and it wasn't like anyone in the office would hear them.

Riko rolled over so she was on her elbows looking up at Charlie and his two friends, or whatever they were. Charlie moved over her and was suddenly on top of her. She struggled, tried to roll him off, the guys were hooting behind him, egging him on. "Settle down china doll, we just wanna welcome you to Wolf's Head," Charlie said. He was freakishly strong for a wiry guy. Finally, she felt like she got some leverage and twisted just right to throw him off. He lost his balance and fell to the floor beside the bed. The audience of his friends laughed even harder and Riko heard them both ribbing him for being tossed by a "chink chick."

This was her only chance. She rolled away from where he had fallen and off the bed and ran for the front door. Charlie's friends had moved into the room towards the end of the bed so the doorway was free. She threw open the front door and was startled backwards by the thin man standing in the doorway. He was still wearing his perfectly pressed suit that he had worn earlier that day. His tie was even looser at the knot than it had been in the market. It was Peter Oswald. His friendly smile appeared again, only this time it made her sick. She knew right away that he was there with them. "It's rude to leave the party that you're hosting," he said matter-of-factly. She turned away from him and jumped over the bed and towards the bathroom. Even if she could lock herself in there it would give her some time to think about strategy. She reached for the bathroom door but Charlie was on her again. His thin greasy hands grabbed the back of her neck and instead of reaching the bathroom door on her own volition. He pushed her face violently into the door frame. More pain, more blood, and a distinct welt on her forehead. He yanked her back violently and held her by her hair. His grip was like a vice and he stared into her eyes. His eyes were not the same clear green they had been in the store, they looked cloudy and dark and Riko knew she wasn't going to get out of this easily if at all.

"Lay down bitch, and let us welcome you to Wolf's Head," he spat. She could still smell the fish and tobacco on him. This time he didn't let her go and threw her to the bed. Peter Oswald had entered the room, closed the door, and was just sitting in a plush green chair to the side of the room watching. Charlie was fumbling with his pants. She could hear his belt clanging as he pulled it off.

She screamed and kicked but he wasn't going to let go this time. He put her down on the bed and used his hands and knees to hold her down. She began to cry, she begged him to stop, his friends stood to the side, cowards in their own right but not afraid to cheer him on. They sounded a thousand miles away to Riko. When Charlie's hands were on the waist of her own pants she shuddered and screamed and kicked at him. He was cursing at her and telling her to knock it off. She was not going to stop. His hand shot out and found the telephone just to the left of where they were. Before she could object any more he was beating her repeatedly in the head and face with the phone. The plastic on the receiver was cracking more each time he drove it against her skull. She fell still and could feel blackness setting in. She was going to pass out. She could not pass out. Peter Oswald was...he was laughing, as Charlie West stripped her pants off. Even Charlie West's friends had stopped hooting. Riko fought to keep consciousness. She was still awake but felt completely powerless as good ol' "we don't take him too seriously" Charlie West raped Riko Nanami. His friends did nothing. They did not rape her or touch her at all, they only stood there encouraging their buddy's every move. Peter Oswald laughed.

Riko would never know how long it lasted. It could have been a week or it may have been five minutes, in actuality it was probably somewhere in the realm of an hour. When Charlie West stepped away from her beaten, bloody and half naked body he actually looked down at her and smiled that creepy everyday smile. "Welcome to Wolf's Head," he said and then spat on her, his spittle landing on her exposed stomach. She looked at the wall, a painting of a forest with rabbits and a deer on it. Tears streamed down her bruised and beaten face. He seemed to pause, waiting for Riko to say or do something but she did not. He chuckled again and motioned to his friends. "Let's get outta here," he said. The three men walked to the door, only this time Charlie brought up the rear. Peter Oswald had not moved from the plush chair. He sat there looking from Charlie and his buddies and then back to Riko. Charlie stopped and looked at Oswald. "Thanks for the good time, pal," West said. Oswald nodded. "Wanna come back to my place and grab a beer?"

West asked.

Oswald seemed to consider this.

"You boys go on. I'm gonna stick around."

West shrugged and left the room leaving the door open slightly. Peter Oswald stood up and closed the front door of the room. His back was still turned when Riko mumbled something. Oswald turned around, "Excuse me?" he said.

Blood was in her mouth and on her face, everywhere. "Peter Oswald," she spat. She knew his name and she could describe him down to the last detail. "Peter Oswald and Charlie West," she said.

"You little whore," Oswald said turning towards her. He didn't say it angrily; in fact, it was a calm, meandering tone.

He went back to where she lay and stood over her, her naked body exposed to him. "Is that a threat, sweetheart? As in, you know who I am?" He chuckled and Riko realized he didn't care. Oswald reached into the front of his blazer and took out a long slightly curved blade. It was the sort of blade that one might use to debone fish or chicken. Riko looked up at him for the first time since the attack. He seemed to hesitate but Riko had no doubt he meant to use it. Peter Oswald had no desire to rape this girl. That wasn't what got him off.

After all, it had been fun to watch but his excitement came from thinking about slitting this girl's throat and having her bleed everywhere. And to top all of this off...he wouldn't even be considered a suspect. Charlie West and his buddies' had just left their DNA all over this room. It would be an open and shut case. When they explained that some drifter/businessman had been there, they'd be laughed out of the courtroom. He hadn't even given them his real name.

Suddenly he was on her, leaning over her, his hot, rank breath on her face. Before he could say anything, she leaned into his ear. "I will never leave this alone, I will kill you and every person who ever crosses me or tries to cross me....Onryō...," she whispered. He leaned away from her and looked into her eyes. They were black and the beating to her face made her almost unrecognizable.

"Shuddup," he hissed, and without another thought he drove the blade into her stomach three times, twisting each time. She shuddered and groaned as he stabbed her again and again. He got up and looked down at her. Blood was pouring from the wounds and yet she still moved but she was done. He would let her suffer. A smile crossed his lips. It felt so good. He decided at that moment not even to slit her throat. The fewer connections he left to his previous M.O., the better. The stabbing was satisfying. Peter Oswald turned and left the room closing the motel room door behind him. She was dying; she could feel her life draining from her. She thought about her parents, how they would suffer over this and she felt sad for them. But sadness was not the emotion that drove her at this very moment. Fukushuu...vengeance... pounded through her every pore. Against all odds, she pulled herself off the bed and fell to the carpet with a sickening heavy thud. Her bag was pushed nearly all the way under the bed. She had unpacked almost everything, but there was one thing she always kept close but in her bag.

With the last of her life draining from her, her hands wrapped around something. It was a small cloth ball, tied off with string. Inside was a very specific mixture of spiritual herbs her mother had painstakingly created for her. It was the essential ingredient for an ancient binding ritual. Acacia leaf, an herb symbolizing the afterlife and the power that can be harnessed, althaea root, to attract benevolent spirits from the afterlife to gain their abilities and help, and finally but most importantly, aspand seed, used in very old and ancient rituals to protect one from evil on every plain of existence. Riko's hand wrapped around it and held it tightly. She had no idea how she was still alive, she knew she had lost so much blood that she was rolling in it, sticky and hot.

She rolled onto her back and stared at the ceiling of the little room in Wolf's Head, New Jersey. Her breathing was labored; her blood was oozing out of her. She clutched the bag to her chest. "Sacred mother," she whispered, "...bind my spirit to this plain, for harming me and my loved ones, bestow unto me unlimited powers of the...," she coughed and blood spat from her mouth, "...unlimited powers of the Onryō. Bind my feet, bind my hands, bind my mouth, bind my mind and may my spirit never leave this realm...," Riko coughed violently and the bag slipped from her hands to the floor in the blood.

Riko died at 9:43 PM.

25

The chief of police in Wolf's Head had to be appointed by the local State Trooper's office because, frankly, no one wanted the job. Derek Smalls was in his late forties, a former Gulf War Vet, and was happy to do the job considering it paid alright and Wolf's Head was the furthest thing from a crime cesspool. There was the occasional drunk, whether driving or stumbling or starting a fight, and the occasional domestic dispute, mostly silly little things that never amounted to anything. This is why Chief Smalls had to fight to keep down his lunch when he was called to the Wolf's Head Inn, room 113. The bed was soaked with blood right through to the bottom of the mattress. There was blood on the walls, the carpet, and the telephone which was tossed to the floor. It looked as though someone had exploded in the room.

The motel owner stood just outside the door. "Do you see? What the hell is this?" he demanded. "What in the hell happened?"

"I have no idea," said Derek, scratching his head. He looked on either side of the bed and under it as well, but there was no sign of anyone or anything, just blood. "Could be animal blood?"

"Animal blood? She seemed like such a nice girl! What in the blue hell?" he screamed. He was freaking out. This would kill his business for the entire season if this got out. Derek Smalls stepped outside and took a deep breath of the fresh air.

"We can handle this two ways Jerry. We can call the State Troopers, have them come out here and test this blood. They'll try and track this...Jap woman. Or you can cut your losses and clean or burn that room cuz I can't see you ever rentin' it again. No one needs to hear about this except us." He paused and let the owner think about this. "State Troopers 'prolly have you shut down for a few weeks." Smalls pushed his hat back on his head and scratched his eyebrow thoughtfully.

After that moment, no one in Wolf's Head ever heard about room 113 at the Inn. Derek Smalls never found a body and they assumed that the nice "Jap" girl had spread her animal blood and then cut town. No one thought about Riko Nanami after her time in Wolf's Head. She was just another pretty face that came and went. Even Charlie West was surprised that there was nothing anywhere about it. He never saw "John Smith" again either and often wondered if they left town together. He never suspected that she was dead. The whole experience had been even easier than that little farm girl had been two summers ago. Granted he didn't beat her, just held her down and raped her in the field. She had blabbed, but there was little evidence and eventually the case had gone away just like Riko Nanami did. Summer came and went in Wolf's Head and the town prepared for winter as they always did. Winters on the bay were heavy at times

th but nothing they couldn't handle. This is why that following winter crippled the tiny town. On November 8 , at 9:43 PM the snow began to fall. An hour later, the snow was blinding, violent, unstoppable, a storm force moving in unlike anything they had ever seen. East coast winters can be unpredictable so they would take Mother Nature's punishment as it came. Riko Nanami's punishment might be different.

Charlie West and his favorite two sidekicks were camped at Charlie's place watching a bad movie on TV, drinking and eating day old pizza. The wind outside was banging against the siding of the house. The movie was just getting to a part where a nice young lady had pulled out her "big titties" to the cat calls and cheers of Charlie and his buddies when the lights in the house zapped out. The men groaned and boo'd and one of them threw his beer can. "Hey, don't waste that, ya shit," Charlie yelled.

He got up and banged his knee on the table, cursed loudly, and made his way to the back of the house. "Fuse box is in the back hall," he called out. He made his way through his small kitchen where, in the dark, dishes were piled in the sink unwashed in over a week. He shuffled carefully into the back hall and reached for the fuse box, finding it relatively easily. He pulled it open and flipped the breaker once but nothing happened. He cursed under his breath. He flipped the breaker again and there was another zapping noise and the lights came back on. He heard his buddies cheering from the other room. He smiled and closed the fuse box, turning to walk back through the kitchen.

She was there and moved on him faster than anything human ever could. She was beautiful with pale skin, black eyes, and a long flowing white dress. She also had brutal inhuman strength as she gripped Charlie West by the throat and forced him against the far wall where the fuse box was. "What the hell?" he screamed. Her face suddenly contorted into a hideous monstrosity and she dropped him to the floor. He tried to struggle to his feet but she wouldn't let him. Her hands shot out but they had changed into what looked like long, thin, sharp bolts of steel. Charlie begged for mercy. He could sense this thing was pissed.

She ignored his pathetic pleading. The sharp instruments shot out towards Charlie. They caught his palms and pinned them back, the sharp edges crucifying him against the wall. He screamed in torturous pain, blood running down his arms. She hovered over him, keeping him pinned precariously. Her twisted, disfigured, pale face moved where she was only inches from Charlie. He expected to feel her breath on his face but there was nothing. He unclenched his eyes and looked into her black, empty eyes. She only looked the slightest bit human and yet it finally dawned on Charlie West who this thing was. "You bitch," he sputtered. He was delirious and felt very little at this point. "I know you!" He couldn't move and any flinch he made only caused thicker red blood to stream down his wrists and onto the wall where he was pinned. She stared at him and through him. Neither of them moved for what felt like minutes. Finally Charlie tried to speak but his mouth was dry and parched.

"Whaddayou want?" he whispered, his voice hoarse and barely audible. "It wasn't my idea."

She sniffed. It was like she smelled something but exhaled at the same time. Charlie flinched as cold, icy frost came from her face. He couldn't tell if it came from her nose or mouth, or a combination of both. The frost spat across Charlie's face, freezing into his stubble and making his lips numb. "Why are you doing this?" Charlie cried out.

The steel swords slipped out of his palms and transformed back to normal. Charlie dropped to the laundry room floor. Blood poured from the wounds, as he tried to wrap them in the ripped Metallica T-shirt he was wearing. The woman looked down at him and her head tilted. She said nothing. "What the hell, Charlie," said his buddy Nick, rounding the corner in the kitchen. He froze in his place as the woman turned to him and roared a blood curdling, ear splitting screech. Nick covered his ears and he dropped to his knees. This creature meant a far worse fate for both of them and the rest of the occupants of this house and beyond.

Charlie's third friend, Joseph, rushed into the kitchen. Charlie and Nick were on their knees weeping. A pool of blood was forming around Charlie's knees. He was losing too much blood from his wounds. "Geez," Joseph began to yell. The woman turned on him, throwing an open palm in his direction. A blast of cold air shot forward and lifted him off the ground, throwing him violently backwards to the far wall. Nick would have been thrown backwards by the blast as well had he not been on his knees holding his head. She turned her attention back to

Charlie who was cowered in the corner begging for his life.

"This wasn't my idea," he repeated. "It was the guy in the diner...John Smith...he said we should do it...it wasn't me damn it! Please, please, please..." he begged, a trail of snot running down his face.

"*Anta wa honto no aku dayo*," she responded. Charlie looked up at her. He understood nothing she said but what he understood was that she meant to kill him. She reached out for him, slowly and methodically. He knelt in place, terrified, unable to move. Nick also did not move. He was still on his knees on the kitchen floor staring through the transparent ghost. Joseph had recovered from her violent outburst towards him and had retreated to the living room. Charlie West kept his "lucky" shotgun on a wall mount above a bookshelf. Don't let that fool you; Charlie had very little use for books. The shelf was mostly filled with old magazines and mechanics guides that he hadn't read. Joseph grabbed the shotgun, grunted, and cocked the gun angrily. He was pissed off and felt far more powerful with the shotgun in his possession. He turned back to the kitchen and marched in there like a cowboy.

She was reaching for Charlie's chest. He could only watch as she seemed to reach through him. He didn't feel the physicality of her touching him and yet when he was face to face with her, he felt his insides began to freeze. His entire body felt like it was numb and he went from being frozen in fear to literally being unable to move. Nick could see Charlie's terror and finally stood up. "Hey!" he yelled. He took two steps towards them as Joseph flew into the kitchen. He had anticipated Nick still being on the floor and the woman towering over Charlie. He was wrong on both accounts. He blindly fired and the gun exploding was deafening in the little kitchen. Nick's chest exploded outward as the shotgun shells tore through him from behind. His body dropped to the linoleum, pieces of him on the walls and appliances. Joseph's rage and determination to save his "buddies" made him completely oblivious to the fact that he had just blown his "buddy" away. Joseph fired again, closer this time, and she turned. Her hands were deep inside Charlie's chest up to the wrists, but her head turned seemingly independent of her neck.

She took out one hand, leaving the other one buried in Charlie. She turned towards Joseph and held it out. She waited several seconds and then twisted her wrist. The gun flew away from Joseph's grasp and at the same time his entire body twisted. He was lifted off the ground and his torso and neck turned to his right, and his waist and legs to the left. When he dropped in a heap to the floor he was dead, and his joints in several places were severed. The shotgun clattered to the ground behind him.

Now her attention was back on Charlie. Charlie had absolutely no feeling from his chest down and his head was buzzing. He looked up at her and her eyes were completely black. She truly was beautiful. Her hair fell over her perfectly angled face and he thought she was becoming more transparent. She looked down at him and he swore she actually smiled. Unfortunately, it was not a smile of remorse or mercy or even pity. He thought perhaps it was a smile of pleasure. She sunk her second hand back into him and the pain shot through him. His teeth grinded and he groaned unable to open his mouth. It seemed like several minutes before she released him and floated back several feet. Charlie shivered, his entire body was like ice. He forced his mouth open to speak and instead a blast of condensation came from his mouth. It was at that moment Charlie West's heart stopped. It probably would have exploded under the pressure but his organs were frozen, as was his entire body. He did not fall over. He stayed there in a kneeling position looking up at his killer. She was gone seconds later, as quickly as she had come.

26

"We tracked her from Wolf's Head hundreds of miles to this very spot where I could finally trap her here," Raines explained.

"My God," Mark whispered. He had sat down behind Raines. Camp and Father Patrick were still standing. Patrick was pacing now as he listened to the story.

"I've studied her for months since she massacred 22 people in Wolf's Head, New Jersey, starting with Charlie West and his friends."

"I never heard anything about any massacre," Mark replied, running his hands over his face.

"No sir. And you won't likely ever hear anything about it. It was covered up, buried. The people of Wolf's Head buried all of this and cut themselves off as best as they could. Nobody wants a story of mass hysteria over a ghost plastered all over the news. It's bad for tourism," Raines explained.

"You're telling me an entire town buried a mass murder without anything leaking out?" Patrick asked.

"She leaked out," Camp replied, speaking up.

"But why? Her vengeance should have ended with Charlie West," Patrick asked.

"Onryo's enraged spirit does not go for justified revenge. In fact, there are tales of Onryo wiping out people and leaving the person who wronged them alive. Riko, however, started with Charlie West and cannot be stopped. However, I believed Onryo to be territorial. If there is one question left in my mind it would be why she left Wolf's Head without wiping out every last one of them. I was preparing to use my alternate reality on Wolf's Head and trap her there and anyone else who would come through. Instead I had to track her here," Raines replied. His leg was throbbing but for the most part was fine now.

"She followed him," Mark said quietly. "Dear God, she was following him." Raines and Camp both looked at Mark and then at each other. "The man...the man who killed Riko, the way you described him, the way he operates...it was Peter Oswald. She's out here, on this highway, in this storm because she was hunting Peter Oswald."

Raines smiled and then winced from his leg wound. "Well done officer, you've made the connection. She hunted him across several hundred miles!"

"And now we're all being hunted you asshole," Mark screamed.

Raines turned and faced Mark Harrison and Father Patrick. "Dr. Camp and I are leaving now. All the best to you, Mr. Harrison."

Mark pulled his weapon once again and aimed it at Dr. Raines' head. "You must be out of your mind. You're not going anywhere until you get us out of here."

"I told you before Mr. Harrison, I don't even know if any of you could go back to...the real world so to speak. Coming through one way is one thing, going back is another."

"If you and Camp can go back so can we."

"Dr. Camp and I have gone back and forth several times, we seem to have the right...genes let's say. I went through three different assistants before I found one like Dr. Camp that could pass back and forth effortlessly." Raines smiled and seemed to brace himself on his good leg. "Ready Dr. Camp?" Mark turned around to see where Dr. Camp was. He saw Father Patrick but no Dr. Camp, at first anyways. Patrick's face was drawn and worried. As he shuffled from the shadows he could see Dr. Camp had Patrick in front of him with a gun pressed into his back.

"You son of a bitch. You had a weapon this whole time?"

"Everything was part of the experiment. I was biding my time," Camp replied.

Mark stared at Camp who was peering over Patrick's shoulder. He was a quick judge of an armed man and he knew that, despite Camp's demeanor, he would use the weapon if he had to. "The priest stays here," Mark replied. Raines nodded. "Give me your gun." "And the magic bag," Camp added.

It was several moments before Mark gave up. He lowered his gun and passed it to Raines who took it gladly. Then Mark removed the small tightly wound bundle and tossed it to Camp who caught it and shoved Patrick aside. Both doctors trained their guns on the two men as they backed towards the door. "One more question," Mark spoke up. Raines did not stop his retreat out the door. "What's the magic bag for?"

"It's dark magic. A collection of herbs and ingredients that keeps evil spirits at bay. We were fairly certain it would work and it does. Too bad you didn't have one...you'll need it," Camp replied across the room. Moments later Camp and Raines had disappeared out into the storm. The temperature in the rest stop was frigid now. The lights seemed to have given up trying to come back on and it was completely dark.

"What do we do now?" Patrick whispered to Mark.

"We leave here, right now. We find the edge of this thing he's got us in and drive right out. Get Andrea and Hannah and take them to their car. I think they're safer there than in here. I'll try to prepare Ethan."

Patrick looked at him warily. Mark nodded encouragingly and held out Andrea Green's keys that he had taken from Josh Barton. Patrick went to collect Andrea and her little girl. Heather held Ethan's head in her hands. He was still sweating profusely but there was no doubt he seemed better than before. Father Patrick bundled up Andrea and

Hannah and escorted them outside to the van. This left only her and Ethan and Mark in the rest stop. Josh Barton's body was covered with an emergency blanket that Heather had gotten from the back room.

Ethan moaned and Heather looked down. His eyes were open, he was actually coming around. "Oh Ethan!" she exclaimed. She set his head down gingerly on the makeshift pillow and moved around to his side. He winced slightly and, against all odds, tried to sit up.

Heather immediately discouraged him and gently pushed him back down.

"It's freezing in here," he whispered hoarsely.

"Don't get up, Ethan. You're still in the rest stop."

"That thing...the monster," he whispered. Heather's eyes filled with tears and he noticed immediately. She had only caught half of the conversation between the two doctors and the two men but it was enough to be completely petrified. "Are we...okay."

She should have reassured him but instead shook her head. Ethan pushed to sit up again but grunted in pain and lay back down. "Josh is dead," Heather said.

Ethan seemed to think about this. "Who?" he replied despondently. Heather wiped the tears from her eyes and cleared her throat.

"Josh...Barton..., never mind."

"Peter Oswald attacked me, he shot me."

"He's gone...missing and so is Big Mike. That thing you mentioned, she attacked the stop, came right through the doors and killed Josh," Heather explained.

"Where's Father Patrick?" Ethan asked.

"Mark wants to leave the stop, all of us. Father Patrick went to get Andrea Green's van so we can put you in the back."

"Where is Mark?" Ethan asked.

"Gathering whatever supplies he can find. Ethan, things are really... they're really screwed up right now. Dr. Camp...he controlled that thing...and he's got us trapped here."

"What in the hell is going on?" Ethan said and pushed his way to a sitting position. This time he was successful and Heather helped brace him. He reached over and touched the wound that had been mostly well covered and wrapped. A small spot of blood showed on the bandage but it was holding solidly.

"Dr. Camp knows something about that thing out there. Camp... well...he controlled her after it killed Josh. He made it go away." She looked at Ethan apologetically. "It's complicated," she explained.

"Man, the things that happen after you get shot."

"He did save you...Dr. Camp, I mean. He removed the bullet and bandaged you," she said, motioning towards the gauze on his shoulder.

"Water?" Ethan asked and Heather provided him with a half drank bottle, which he swallowed greedily from. "Can you tell Mark...tell him I'm awake, I need to speak with him."

Heather nodded and walked to where Mark was rooting through the kitchen. She spoke to him and together they walked back to Ethan. Ethan nodded at Mark but he did not respond. Ethan thought Mark looked worse than he did. "Heather, do you know of any large bags, canvas sacks or back packs around here?" Mark asked.

"Officer...I don't know if..." Heather stuttered.

"Heather, we're gonna be okay. But we need take these supplies with us. Whatever you can find would be great." Heather nodded understandingly.

"I think there are some canvas bags in the kitchen."

"That'd be perfect." Heather nodded again and went to retrieve them. She spent more time going back and forth to the kitchen tonight then helping anyone with any one project.

"Mark...," Ethan forced out. Mark sat down beside him in a chair. "Peter Oswald is a killer."

"I know. You have no idea how much I know," Mark replied in a curious tone. He noticed Ethan looking at him in confusion. "Before I stopped here," Mark began to explain, "I was in Philadelphia at a convention seeking advice on a case. The case was regarding a serial killer in King City County."

"The King City Killer," Ethan replied.

If Mark was surprised that Ethan knew of it, he didn't let it show. He only nodded. "A very long story short, Peter Oswald appears to be that killer." There was a long bout of silence between the two men.

"What are the odds," Ethan said, finally.

"Unfortunately, very good and, worse yet, I let him get away. I underestimated him. It didn't sink in until it was too late and he ran outside."

"What happened with Dr. Camp?" Ethan asked. "Heather seemed very upset." Mark took a long pause and looked into the shadows around the rest stop.

"You were out when that ghost attacked us, twice. The second time, after it broke every bone in Josh Barton's body, our very own Dr. Camp controlled her. He used some sort of black magic bull shit to send her back out there." Mark looked at Ethan. "He knew something about all of this."

"What is all this?" Ethan asked. His voice was clearer now, stronger. He was waking up and recovering as much as could be expected. Mark had no idea where to begin and wasn't about to explain everything he had gotten from Raines and Camp but it didn't matter because Mark did not get the chance to answer. There was a sobbing yell from behind them. Ethan made an attempt to turn towards the voice and Mark stood.

Heather was walking or shuffling back towards where they were. The shadows around her hid the fact at first that she wasn't alone.

Mark noticed the arm wrapped around her neck first and then, as she neared them, he saw that snarling, nasty smirk of Peter Oswald. Somehow he had circled around to the back of the stop and ended up back in the diner. The hand that was wrapped around Heather's neck was holding a long silver cooking blade. The serrated edge was pushing against her pulsing neck artery. If she moved wrong the blade would slit her wide open.

Mark moved towards them aimlessly. He had no weapon and no reason to think he could disarm Oswald from where he was. Ethan couldn't see exactly what was happening from where he was laying and he doubted he was ready to get up. "Let her go, Oswald," Mark demanded, and Ethan's stomach sank. He didn't need to get up or turn to look, Oswald was back and he had Heather. Mark noticed Oswald's face was red and raw from the ice and snow outside. He probably couldn't feel anything on the parts of him that had been exposed out there. "Just let her go. Take my keys, take my car, and leave this stop. I'm giving you an out."

Peter laughed a forced laugh that barely sounded human. "I don't need an out," he said, emphasizing his words. "I'm in control. I was never not in control." Mark circled them, moving to the left and keeping them in his sights as best he could in the dark. "Ya gonna risk little hottie here? Huh?!" Oswald demanded, pressing the blade harder against her throat. The veins in her neck were surfaced and exposed to the knife's edge. Mark locked eyes with Heather. He didn't know what was going to happen but he was trying to read her face and see where her head was at. She was terrified clearly but she was not panicking either. The storm seemed to come to the rescue at an opportune time. There was a loud thumping noise that sounded like a large mass of snow had fallen from the roof onto the ground outside. Oswald was already high strung and the loud noise took him by surprise. He looked in the direction of the window and Mark's hopes were fulfilled. Heather took the opportunity to push back against him. He had loosened his grip on the knife so that it wasn't as tight against her throat. Her maneuver worked and he stumbled back. The knife he was holding dropped to the ground, making a distinctive noise against the floor. She bolted towards Mark who had grabbed the nearest thing to him, a chair.

She didn't run fast enough. Oswald regrouped and grabbed her again with his good hand. Heather screamed. There was enough distance between them now and even in the shadows and poor light Mark took his chances and tossed the chair towards them. Oswald grunted and Heather screamed again. She fell forward and the chair caught Oswald broadside in the head and he fell. Peter Oswald sprawled onto his back. Heather was crying now and she rushed over to Mark, cowering behind him quickly. Oswald was not moving. "What in the hell is going on?" Ethan called out. He had tried to swing himself around but the pain was just too much.

"Go to Ethan," Mark instructed. Heather seemed hesitant to leave Mark but he looked at her demandingly. Once she was gone Mark stepped slowly towards Oswald's form on the ground. The dark was beginning to swallow everything. Oswald looked incredibly still. He had no idea where the chair had hit him but doubted it was enough to render him unconscious. He would not underestimate Peter Oswald ever again. This was the last thing Mark Harrison thought before Peter Oswald sat straight up. The knife he had dropped but recovered in his pratfall was in his good hand again and was quickly and cleanly plunged to the hilt into Mark's stomach.

Mark didn't even holler because he simply didn't have time. All he could do was look down at that familiar smarmy face sneering at him as he pushed the knife deeper. Mark fought as hard as he could not to let himself fall to the ground. The knife was deep inside him but even in the situation he suspected it wasn't fatal as long as Oswald didn't pull the knife out right now. Unfortunately, this was all speculation and Mark found himself on his knees. Oswald was climbing to his feet. The chair had hit him in the head and sent him spiraling backwards but after the pain of his arm being snapped, it felt like nothing. Whatever happened for the rest of this night, Peter Oswald's arm was permanently screwed.

Oswald now stood over Mark Harrison. He still had his hand on the hilt of the knife but he let it go and just admired it sticking from Mark's gut. He laughed again and Mark felt sick. "Pig," Oswald said and spit on his face. Where was Patrick with that van, Mark wondered pointlessly?

27

It took only a minute for the three of them to find Andrea Green's van. Andrea held Hannah tight in her arms and Father Patrick took up the rear behind them. The snow was downright angry, discouraging their every movement across the parking lot. Patrick hit the car remote when he thought they were almost there but they could see nothing. "There!" Andrea Green said pointing to their right slightly.

They hurried through the blizzard and finally came to what had been her van.

Saying it was buried doesn't give the proper conception. The van was completely gone. It was a hill in the middle of the parking lot with side view mirrors poking out of the white mound. It would take an hour just to dig this car out before it was even remotely usable for their escape pod. Patrick wanted to curse but he had done enough of that for one night. He thought about what Mark had said before he took Andrea and Hannah outside in this. Don't come back, not for anything. Straight to the car, get in the car, bring the car back to the front doors...or what was left of the front doors. Without another thought Patrick dove into the side of the snow bank. He began digging with both hands into the side of the van until he could actually make out the window. It was so dark inside the van. It looked like peering inside a coffin.

Even his gloves couldn't ward off the frigid feeling in his hands as he clawed his way through the snow to the van. He managed to essentially clear a four foot section around the driver's side door and the sliding passenger door. He stepped back and hit the unlock button again. This time they could see the glow of the headlights as they blinked approvingly. He reached down and pulled on the door handle. Nothing. There might have been some slight movement but not enough to even register. He pulled again without success. Andrea and Hannah were standing behind him and they had to be freezing already. Even with Hannah's face buried in her mother's shoulder she had to be feeling the cold.

Would there be any possible way of driving in this? It had not let up for hours. The snow they had walked through was three feet deep in some places. If not for the brutally violent wind spreading the snow around, Patrick thought, the rest stop itself would be buried underneath a forty foot snow bank. He braced himself in the snow as best as he could and hauled on the door. It groaned with the wind and then opened slowly. He pulled it, and then pushed it, and pulled it again so that it was open a couple of feet. "Get in!" he yelled, getting treated to a face full of snow when he turned to instruct Andrea. She obeyed immediately and dove into the car still holding little Hannah tightly. She climbed into the frigid box and across the center console into the passenger seat. Patrick followed her and got into the driver's seat. Closing the door was almost as hard as opening it had been. He pulled on it violently until it nearly closed, or close enough.

Their breath fogged out in front of them in thick white clouds. Patrick fumbled with his gloves and then got the keys into the ignition.

"How's your car start in this sort of weather?" Patrick asked, trying to smile.

"We just got a check up," Andrea replied, quite seriously. Patrick turned the key. The ignition sputtered to life immediately. Both of them sighed out loud. The unfortunate thing was, Patrick knew he would have to get out again and clear off the car. Even if he could gun his way through this spot they were frozen in, the windshield would never clear itself of the three feet piled onto it. He gunned the engine a few times to make sure it was truly running.

"I have to go out and clear the windshield," he said, looking at Andrea secretly hoping for an alternative. She had none to give. "Do you have a snow brush?"

Andrea was gently stroking her daughter's hair. Hannah seemed to be quiet again, which was stunning considering the circumstances. She nodded and reached into the back seat and grabbed a plastic snow brush that looked like it had hardly been used. Yet again, Patrick pushed on the driver's side door and pulled himself out into the weather. He stomped through the snow to the front of the van. It was more like shoveling mounds of snow off the caked windshield with the brush. After several passes he looked in and saw Andrea's face. She had reached into the backseat and placed the sleepy Hannah into her car seat. Andrea looked worn out, Patrick thought. He smiled at her and she smiled back but it was less than half heartedly. Patrick motioned that he would only be another moment. He passed the brush over the windshield again. The snow was covering it as fast as he could clear it. He knocked on the glass and when he had

Andrea's attention he pointed to the wipers.

It took her a moment to realize what he wanted but then reached across and hit the wipers to the one position. The headlights on the van came on at the same time and spat out two cones of light as far as they could manage. Patrick shielded his eyes from the light and when his vision adjusted he could see Andrea's face peering out of the windshield. Her eyes were wide and she did not look tired anymore. Instead she looked completely terrified. He looked at her quizzically and realized she wasn't looking at him but rather beyond him. His stomach sank. The woman...the ghost...Patrick turned but never actually got the chance to see her behind him.

The woman scooped him up in the same way she had tossed Josh Barton and threw Patrick into the air. He rolled through the air for more than thirty feet and fell into the snow like he had fallen from the sky. The snow had created such a thick blanket on the ground that it saved Patrick's life...for now. His body tumbled carelessly through the snow sending sprays of powder into the air. He slid to a halt only feet from the busted front door. He could hardly breathe and he was face down in the snow. Andrea and Hannah were his only thought. He scrambled to his feet and winced. The bitter cold slammed into his bare face. He was also certain he may have broken a rib. He forced himself to push forward and his feet caught a solid bank of snow and he went down again on his front.

When he regained his composure and went to stand up, his hand brushed the solid snow he had tripped over. He was face to face staring into the frozen solid, naked body of Big Mike Otterman. Big Mike's eyes were gaping open in terror. His face was swollen and blue and like a block of ice. Patrick clenched his eyes and sobbed. He had never seen anything like this. "Think of what is above, not of what is earth. For you have died, and your life is hidden with Christ in God. When Christ your life appears, then you too will appear with him in glory. In the name of the Father, the Son, and the Holy Spirit." Patrick uttered these words mostly to himself. His throat was clogged with ice and he couldn't breathe. A scream cut through the air. Patrick pulled himself up and pushed himself back towards where he had been.

He could see the headlights now and he could see the beast. She was hovering over the car. Andrea had opened the driver's side door, stepped out and was screaming at the woman to leave them alone. The apparition was staring down at the car. The snow was swirling around her like a cyclone. Andrea was in danger and Patrick knew it. He cleared his throat as he bounded through the snow towards them. He had one chance to save them and this was it. "Hey!" he screamed. The wind carried his cries away. It was gone before it left his lips. He screamed again. "Hey, hey over here!" He was less than twenty feet away now and could see everything.

"Hey...you didn't kill me...hey!" Patrick screamed, waving his hands. Andrea heard him. She was turning to look.

He felt his stomach sink in both relief and fear as the ghost turned her head and looked at him. Only her head turned seemingly independent of her body. She really was beautiful to look at, hypnotizing in fact. "Hey!" he screamed yet again, but it wasn't necessary.

She had turned her entire body and was now floating towards him. He had accomplished his truly horrible plan. His only thought was Dr. Stephen Camp had managed somehow to make her leave the rest stop earlier and perhaps he could do the same. She moved towards him slowly and gracefully. "Our Father who art in Heaven," Patrick began reciting. He took a few steps backwards and she continued to come towards him. Her head tilted ever so slightly. "Hallowed be thy name," Patrick continued. His lips were chapped and frozen.

The ghost was not fazed by his recitation. If it bothered her in any way he couldn't tell. She continued towards him but lifted her right hand in the air, her palms turned upwards. Patrick hardly noticed. He continued backing away from her slowly. Andrea was still standing beside the open driver's side door. Hannah was still inside and thankfully the heat was kicking in now so the van was warming up. The windshield wipers pumped quickly trying to keep up with the buildup of snow. The van lurched only an inch and no one even noticed at first. Andrea was watching the stare down between Patrick and the woman and hardly noticed her car slide ever so slightly. The ghost raised her hand higher and the van lurched forward again. This time Andrea saw it move. She looked at her van as though she was imagining things. It was in park, it couldn't roll, and the snow would probably prevent it from rolling anyway. This time the van shuddered and slid a foot nearly pushing

Andrea out of the way. She screamed and dove into the open driver's side door.

No sooner had she gotten inside then the car slid three more feet pushing the snow aside as it slid. The tires were not moving. The entire car was sliding across the snow like a sled seemingly involuntarily. Andrea looked around frantically as it moved jerkishly another two feet. She instinctively reached down and threw the van into reverse. Her foot pumped the gas and the car groaned and revved angrily. The tires spun hopelessly against the slick ice and snow. The ghost raised her upturned hand even higher and the van began to effortlessly move across the parking lot towards her and towards Patrick. Patrick could see now that Andrea had gotten back in the van and he could hear the engine, just barely, revving and the tires spinning. Was she driving towards him? He thought it looked like she was slowly moving forward. He made no connection between the ghost raising her hand and the moving vehicle.

The ghost was emotionless. Patrick took a moment, still backing away, to look at her face. She looked completely calm and void of any expression. The snow did not fall on her. She was bare foot and her eyes interchanged colors while he watched.

He wondered what was behind her eyes, what this was all about. Maybe it was a matter of asking her...he thought. Suddenly he was jolted when his back thumped against something. Maybe it was the wall of the rest stop. He could hardly see anything now that his eyes were practically frozen closed. He looked behind him and almost felt like laughing. He had backed himself into his very own car which was closer to the stop than the van had been. His car was practically buried, though its location to the building had sheltered it from some of the snow.

Patrick was literally backed into a corner. She still moved towards him as did Andrea Green in their van. What he didn't know is that Andrea was fighting to reverse the car. The tires were scraping against the ice and the snow as it slid closer to the ghost woman. Andrea hollered in frustration and Hannah woke up. "Where we going Mommy?" she asked nonchalantly. Andrea eased up on the gas and looked behind her into her daughter's face. What an exhausting night for her, Andrea thought.

"It's alright baby," she whispered. "We're going to go find Daddy and Dane." Hannah seemed pleased with that idea. The ghost woman lifted her hand and then thrust it forward. It almost seemed to take effort on her part to push her hand towards Patrick. The van slid faster, lurched, and then jumped across the parking lot skidding through the snow at an alarming pace. Andrea screamed. The vehicle was completely out of control as it slid straight across the lot past the woman and towards Patrick. Patrick saw Andrea coming. His thought was that she was going to bring the van around, pick him up and outrun this bitch. He thought wrong. The speeding car was not under any human control. It slid slightly to the side and the ghost woman's face began to instantly change from the calm demeanor to a snarling, angry sneer. She roared and it deafened Patrick and drowned out the sound of the storm.

Patrick was lifting his hands to his head when Andrea Green's van piled into the side of his own car, crushing him horrifically between the two vehicles. He felt nothing. It was too quick, although he thought he remembered hearing the unfathomable sound of metal on metal and the crunching sound of the steel between the two cars. Andrea was screaming still, Hannah was wailing. Thank God, she had strapped her daughter in. The two of them jostled around the van as it slammed into the other car. Andrea had no idea where Patrick was but she never once suspected he was between the two vehicles. At the last minute, the van had slid to its side so that the driver's side door was what hit the car first and then it finally fell silent. There was only the wind again.

Andrea lifted her head. Blood trickled from above her eyebrow where she had banged her head against something...she would never know what. She took deep breaths. The van's engine remarkably was still running. The heat was still blowing through the van which felt good. She looked into the back seat and was stunned to see Hannah was completely silent, looking around at the wasteland around them. Andrea smiled in sheer relief. "Father Pat!" Hannah said, smiling and pointing towards Andrea's window.

Andrea turned to her window to look and let out a blood boiling scream. His face was only inches from her window. Blood spewed from his mouth and even what looked like a trickle from his right eye. His mouth gaped open and his eyes looked at hers lifelessly. His face was right outside her window but so was the other car. He was crushed hopelessly between the vehicles. She could never open her door; she would have to climb around. Against her better judgment, she hit the automatic window button and the window protested but then lowered.

"Oh no," she moaned. His face was blue and swollen. Blood seemed to come from every possible place it could on his face.

"Go...," came the stuttered voice. He had spoken. My God, he was still alive.

"Patrick, oh no Patrick," she cried, reaching out for him.

"Go," he repeated. Blood splattered from his mouth when he tried to cough. It almost hit Andrea in the face but fell short. "Go now, don't come back," he said.

"We can get help," she begged. Patrick literally looked angry now, his last bit of emotion ripping from his body.

"GO!" he screamed. It echoed through the van and Hannah began to cry. "Go now, we're all finished," he hollered. The last of his breath came out with "finished" and Father Patrick John died. His body below his waist was severed nearly clean through when the cars collided against each other, though he would never know that.

Andrea kicked the van into gear and stepped on the gas, the window went up faster than it had gone down. The tires spun pointlessly on the ground. Now, she only had the snow to contend with but the fact that the van was entwined to another vehicle like two lustful lovers losing themselves in each other made it more difficult. "Come on, damn it!" Andrea cried. Hannah screamed louder. "Shuttup!" Andrea screamed. Her foot was literally to the floor now and the van suddenly disengaged itself and shot furiously away from the wreckage. It shocked her of course and instinctively she tried to brake. The van slid in circles around and around the lot. She was certain it would pile into something else, whether another car or a lamp post. It didn't. A minute later, she had controlled the skidding and was actually facing the south bound exit. Could she do this? Could she leave all of this behind? She looked into the back seat at her daughter's tear stained face. She had no choice. Andrea Green pressed on the gas and the van headed for the exit ramp. In moments, she would be gone from this place, forever.

28

Oswald had no idea what tackled him at that moment. Neither did Mark. Before he had time to finish the job and end Mark Harrison's life, someone hit Oswald broadside and they went to the floor in a heap. The knife was left inside Mark's gut. Ethan Datsun had finally gotten himself up and turned around in time to see Oswald get the better of Mark. With all of his strength he rushed Oswald and toppled into him bringing them both to the floor. Heather watched in horror as the two men wrestled with each other. Ethan was in no condition to be fighting anyone. Oswald quickly pushed him off before getting up again.

The lights in the stop flicked and buzzed threatening to almost come back on. Mark looked at Oswald who was now standing over

Ethan looking at him. All he had to do was finish the job he had started on both men. He turned to face Mark who was still on his knees. Weakly Mark looked up at him. "Just go," Mark begged. Heather was standing to the side looking at Oswald wondering what she should do or could do. Oswald smirked.

"I'm not going anywhere," he spat angrily in Mark's face and reached down for the knife still inside Mark. He intended on pulling it out and maybe relocating it to a new spot, more fatal this time. Heather screamed and all three men looked in her direction. The apparition was back again. She had slipped in the front of the rest stop with the snow and wind and was now standing watching them all. Peter turned towards the ghostly figure yet again and his jaw dropped. It was her. He would recognize the china doll face anywhere. This crazy bitch, he thought to himself. He all but forgot Mark Harrison and began to walk towards her. Heather rounded the table where she stood and rushed towards Mark and Ethan who were sprawled on the floor close to each other.

Peter walked defiantly towards the ghost. This would be their showdown, a long overdue showdown. Peter Oswald was gonna finish her...again. He probably should have thought about how he planned on doing that. A battle of wits would leave Oswald broken and shattered in some corner of this God forsaken rest stop. "You bitch," he hissed under his breath. He couldn't even feel his shattered arm anymore. It could have been lopped off and he wouldn't have even noticed. He had one good arm and even that was less than stellar after using it frequently in the last couple of hours.

The woman tilted her head, looking toward Oswald. She seemed to be analyzing him. She knew this man. She hated this man. The hatred for him burned inside her dead spirit and was the fuel to the fire that kept her going. He was walking towards her determinedly.

She lifted her hand and held it out towards him in a "stop moving" gesture. Peter stopped. Not because he was obeying her but only long enough to laugh loudly and throw his head back. "Anata wa, watashi no riyuudesu," she said. It was perhaps the clearest thing any of them had heard her say since this began. None of them knew what she had said, but heard her speak the words clearly and concisely. Oswald moved to laugh again but if it was the last laugh he wanted, he got that much. She lifted her hand and Oswald slipped into the air effortlessly as though he were being pulled by ropes to the ceiling. She lifted him up and moved her hand to the side sending him crashing into a support pillar. Pieces of the pillar shattered as Oswald's body thumped against it and then swayed back out towards her. Again, she moved her hand and sent him cascading into the pillar a second time. She was controlling him telekinetically with seemingly no effort at all. Oswald moaned and screamed as he hit the pillar again sending pieces of tile shattering to the floor.

She lowered her hand thus releasing her grip on him and he fell to the floor with a thud and a crack. Something had broken, probably his leg. He was panting and sobbing as she moved closer to him. She wasn't hovering so much anymore as she was simply walking across the floor. She was also less transparent than she had been before. Peter had lost his cavalier attitude. He pulled himself up on that one good arm. His face was bloodied and broken. Pieces of the support beam covered his side that had bashed against it. He desperately tried to push away from her as she came towards him but too much of him was broken to even move.

That awful controlling hand came forward again and Peter immediately felt her power grip him. She turned her hand and his body flipped violently so that he was on his back nearly looking straight up at her. She pushed him back effortlessly and he began to slide across the linoleum floor. Heather, Mark and Ethan looked at this beating in terror. She was not trying to kill the man but rather she wanted to torture him and meant to make him feel each step of the process. He hit chairs that went skidding to the side as she slid him across the floor effortlessly without ever touching him. Finally his back thudded against the bakery counter. She was still coming toward him. Her eyes were wide now and her head was cocked to the side. Her face had no expression and yet Mark felt like she was getting some sort of redemption from this torture. He could relate to that after hearing her story from Dr. Raines.

Suddenly Peter Oswald was launched into the air again. He hung suspended above the floor, his arms outstretched, his face was covered in blood and his tears were streaming through the blood. "*Anta niwa Jigoku nimo heiwa nannte naiyo*," she hissed at him and for the first time lifted her other hand, as though she were going to conduct an orchestra. This was not her intention at all. Her left hand seemed to take control of Oswald's head while her other hand kept him hanging in suspended animation. Her next roar was deafening.

Glass shattered from somewhere in the stop and Ethan, Mark and Heather clamped their hands over their ears as she screamed angrily. Her left hand twisted and Peter Oswald's neck snapped. His scream of terror was cut short. She did not stop twisting his head until he was observing the bakery behind him while still facing the front of the rest stop.

Mark had seen enough. His King City Killer, Peter Oswald, was as dead as he could possibly be and now it was the three of them left to survive. "We need to leave right now," he whispered. Heather looked at him. She was crying relentlessly. Her lovely face looked haggard and worn in the shadows and darkness. "Ethan, can you walk?" he asked. Ethan nodded hesitantly. His wound had reopened enough that blood was seeping through.

"You can't go anywhere with that...," Ethan motioned at the knife still protruding from Mark's stomach.

"I can and I will." Mark wasn't so sure but he was going to stick with that until he could get something to put pressure on the wound when the knife was pulled out. With that, Mark moved forward, staying low to the ground as though they were caught in a shootout.

Heather followed him and Ethan was close behind. The knife wound felt like the world's worst paper cut and that thought almost made Mark laugh. As they passed the table where Ethan had been laid up for the latter half of the night, Mark grabbed a few of the makeshift towels from the seats around it. The three of them ducked towards the front doors. The wind burnt their faces. There was a sickening and definitive thump behind them and Mark guessed that she had dropped Peter Oswald to the floor. His assumption was correct. Riko Nanami's vengeful spirit had snapped Oswald's neck into pieces and dropped his very dead body down across the diner counter. Then she stopped. She stopped and she stared at his body. If she could feel the emotion of relief, she would have, but she could not. Onryo was pure vengeance whether the subject of that vengeance was eliminated or not.

However, if there was a clear sign of her satisfaction in the death of Peter Oswald it came in the most concise and obvious way.

Instantly, suddenly, unequivocally the storm, the brutal, lashing, angry, unrelenting snow...stopped.

The wind died down instantaneously. The snow and ice stopped pushing in towards them. Mark paused in relief. It was still cold. The temperature couldn't possibly change that much given how much snow had fallen. There was a good foot inside the rest stop front doors now. Mark turned to face Heather in the darkness. "The snow stopped," he said stating the obvious. She had noticed it as well. Ethan joined them, huddled beside the soda machines near the entrance.

"Is she still here?" Ethan asked. He winced and put his hand to his shoulder wound which was really bleeding now.

Mark stood slowly and looked over the tables. The stop was so eerily dark. The only things behind them were shadows and glints of chrome from the appliances behind the counters. There was no sign of the ghost. "Ethan, are you alright?" Heather asked. She was bracing herself against him.

"Dammit, I have to get this knife out," Mark cursed. There was a significant amount of blood around the knife handle which was grotesquely protruding from his stomach. Mark sat down with his back against the soda machine. Ethan was glad to take the break and sat as well with Heather's help. "Heather, are you squeamish?" Mark asked.

"Mark, you can't pull that out!" Heather exclaimed.

"Ethan is hurting, and I will be no good to him or you like this."

Heather and Ethan looked at him with fear and doubt. "It could be keeping an artery closed, but I've been stabbed and shot before, and I think the wound is a clean cut. I can take the knife out and pressurize it with towels. We just need to get to a vehicle."

"The knife would be clean. Dr. Camp took it from the kitchen and Big Mike insists on the best sterilization," Heather said.

"Can you help me?" Mark asked. Heather seemed hesitant but nodded. Mark waved her over and she knelt beside him. "I'm going to lie on my back. I'm going to try to help you pull this out, straight up and out. As soon as it comes out you need to put towels on the wound and press hard. I don't care how much it hurts me...do you understand?" Heather was looking at the knife and she had tears in her eyes. "Heather, do you understand?" Mark asked again. She nodded.

"Mark...," Ethan began to protest but Mark was already using a coat under his head to lay on his back. Heather was on her knees beside him and Mark tried to crane his neck down to see what was happening.

"Heather, when I say pull, you pull. Straight up. The blade has a serrated edge and if you don't pull it out the way it went in it'll split me open, do you understand?" She nodded again. Mark took deep breaths. His blood pressure seemed normal and his heart beat was strong. "Do you need a count?" Heather shook her head.

"No, let's do this." She gathered the towels that Mark had grabbed from the table. "Some of these have Ethan's blood on them," Heather said. Mark smiled half heartedly.

"I'm going to go politically incorrect and say that I trust Ethan has nothing I need to worry about catching," he said, both stating and asking.

"Alright. Ready?" Before Heather could respond this time, Mark yelled, "now!" Heather did exactly as she was told. She pulled on the knife that she had made countless sandwiches with. The knife came out of Mark's stomach with shocking ease. It had missed any vital organs but it had punctured his stomach cavity. The knife slipped from his belly and blood spurted out. Mark hollered and Heather grabbed two towels and placed them over the wound and put all her weight on them. She was shuddering and crying but never hesitated. She held the towels down as the bottom one soaked through quickly.

Mark's head was spinning. He would not allow himself to pass out, not now. The second towel did not seep through. It seemed as though the first towel had managed to clot the wound, at least for now. "Keep him awake," Ethan instructed. Heather looked down at Mark whose eyes were drooping quickly.

"Mark," she said. His eyes closed briefly. "Mark," she said louder and with confidence. His eyes shot open. "Don't close your eyes," she demanded.

"Screw this, I'm going to get a car," Ethan said. He used the soda machine to push himself up and onto his feet. "I'm going to get my truck, it'll push through this." Heather was concentrating on Mark's wound and keeping him awake. Neither of them could protest Ethan leaving them. He pushed himself towards the front door and outside. The air was crisp and clean and the sight of no snow falling was such a welcome relief. Ethan paused and looked up into the sky. There was not a single star in the sky. Ethan was still unconscious when Raines had explained the alternate reality so he had no idea the sky he was looking at was not the one he had always known.

He looked across the parking lot at various snow banks and snow buried vehicles. To his right was the priests' small two door coupe. Even from where he stood he could tell the car was completely crumpled on the driver's side. In front of the crumpled car was a large splattering of deep red. Ethan immediately began pushing himself towards that car. All of that mess on the snow could only be someone's blood. Andrea, Hannah, Patrick...it could be any of them. When he finally got to the car his stomach lurched and he would have vomited had he had anything to vomit. He braced himself on the hood of the car which was damaged as well. Pieces of someone were on the side of the car, on the ground, in the dents in the car, and all over the snow.

"Jeezus," Ethan muttered. There was a screeching noise that had Ethan moaning out loud and dropping to his knees beside the car. When he knelt down he could see the face of Father Patrick staring back at him from just under the car. His abdomen was covered in snow and so was part of his face but it was him. There was another screeching noise. It sounded like metal on metal but also had an animalistic sound to it. He tried to stand again and looked in the direction of the sound. The apparition was back again and she was hovering nearly thirty feet above him on the roof of the rest stop.

She was already contorted into a nasty sneering beast. Her face looked more dog-like than human and she was shrieking that horrible and terrifying screech. Ethan stood and stared at the beast. He had no answers. He hadn't been awake for the truth behind Riko and her passionate tirade of vengeance. Ethan knew he had to run but his wound ached and he was so exhausted. He took several steps back, keeping his eyes on her. He didn't even know if she knew he was there. As it turned out she did know. She shrieked again and the roof of the rest stopped seemed to reverberate. Snow began to slide off the roof top falling to the ground in large clumps. Underneath that snow was solid ice. Ethan took another few steps back. Her next shriek rocked the whole area. Even the damaged car seemed to shudder from the sound waves of her shriek. More windows shattered and Ethan suspected it was the roof top windows. Ethan was ready to get the hell out of here. He turned just as several sheets of ice slid flawlessly off the roof. Most of them shattered to the ground but others pieces of the ice slid off the roof and fell dangerously close to where Ethan was standing.

A long, thin piece of ice slid through the shingled grooves in the roof. This piece was over a foot thick and aiming for trouble. It came down and slid onto the roof of the damaged car. It didn't stop as it slid across the roof of the car and was launched several feet forward. Ethan was running as fast as he could when the piece of ice slid effortlessly through his back and exploded from his chest. He was dead before the piece of ice even finished its slide through him but his body instinctively went three more steps before collapsing facedown into the snow. The ice broke off in his body when he hit the ground.

29

The darkness was swallowing everything around Heather and Mark. Tears were rolling down her face as she held the towel against Mark's wound. Mark was still not conscious or at least fading in and out. There was a roaring noise and scraping of ice and snow falling off the roof and Heather jumped and cried out at the sounds. She was nearly shaking both from the cold and just from straight up fear. She felt like this was the end. Everyone in this rest stop was missing or dead. Prior to tonight Heather Morton had poured thousands of cups of coffee, made hundreds of sandwiches, greeted thousands of travelers, and now in one night she had seen a ghost, people shot, people stabbed, people beaten up and a man practically mangled when he was thrown through the rest stop. The boy she had flirted with for months had disappeared...probably dead, she thought, and now she had just pulled one of the very knives she had made sandwiches with from the stomach of a cop. All these thoughts raced through her mind and she did the only logical thing she could do. She screamed. It was an angry, air piercing scream that rivaled the monstrous roar of Riko Nanami. Heather was terrified and pissed off.

Nearly a minute passed when she stopped and just listened. The wind had died down, the snow outside had stopped and there was very little noise in the rest stop. She knelt over Mark sobbing. "What a friend we have in Jesus, all our sins and griefs to bear...what a friend..," she whispered and sang. She really only knew what she had head Patrick singing to Hannah earlier.

"Stop singing," said the weak, raspy voice.

Heather looked down at Mark and, in her exuberance, released the pressure on his wound. He winced and coughed and she apologized and pressed on his wound. "Sorry...about the singing, I'm pretty awful."

Mark was breathing heavy. "Nothing...nothing to do with that. Every time someone sings that song...things get worse." He reached up and put his frigid hands over Heather's. "Get me a jacket," he whispered.

Heather let Mark hold down the towel on his wound while she rushed around to find a jacket. She found someone's discarded coat nearby and brought it back to him. She had no idea whose jacket it was and didn't really care. She didn't want to think about who was missing or dead and whose stuff was scattered around the stop. Mark took the coat and slid it under him wrapping the arms around the towel covering his wound making the most impromptu but successful bandage job she had ever seen. He braced himself and shouted as he yanked the knotted arms tight. It might have been a rush job but it served the purpose by holding the towel securely in place.

"You can't move," she said.

"Like hell. We're leaving here, where's Ethan?"

"He left. He just ran outside."

"Oh no, no, no," Mark said. He sat up and Heather watched him cautiously for any signs of trauma. "Help me up," he instructed and she did. He braced himself against the soda machines and took deep breaths. When he looked at Heather, his heart felt for her. She looked completely drained. She had been absolutely incredible during all this from keeping them fed to helping save his life and Ethan's. Mark actually managed to smile at her and offered his hand to her. Heather took his hand and squeezed it. "We're leaving here, and never coming back."

"Where are we?" she asked. It seemed like such a stupid question.

She could look around her, she could scour every inch of this place that she knew so well and she knew she was in Big Mike's Rest Stop. In a few hours when the morning light pierced the darkness the coffee shop and the bakery would be bustling with people and everything would be back to normal, or so it seemed. Only she knew, she knew beyond a shadow of a doubt, that this was not Big Mike's Rest Stop. She knew even before Dr. Camp and Dr. Raines' had told their extravagant tale of the angry spirit, and their alternate dimension they had trapped them all in, that they weren't in the normal world.

"I have no idea," Mark replied honestly. "But I do think we will drive out of here and not look back and we will find our way back to reality."

"Do you think everyone else is okay?"

"Everyone else?"

"Big Mike...Paul...Ethan...Andrea Green's family..."

It was a loaded question. Technically Mark had no idea about Paul or Ethan, though he suspected Paul was dead. "Raines told me the others were fine," he said, thinking about the statement as he said it. He noticed Heather was looking at him, looking for answers. "Heather, Big Mike...he's dead, I'm really sorry. Peter Oswald told me he killed him." Heather's eyes saddened but she did not cry. She had done enough of that for one night and besides she had suspected Mike was dead, along with Paul Janson. "But when I was interrogating Raines...he told me the others...the ones that were missing were fine. He said Andrea's husband and Father Patrick's partner and Ethan's boss were all fine. I wonder where they are." Mark spoke mostly to himself at this point. He reached into his pockets. He fully expected his keys to not be there with the way this night was going but he felt the hard plastic of his SUV key chain. "Let's go," he said authoritatively. Heather nodded and the two of them made their way towards the exit of the stop. Mark limped slowly and Heather walked only a step behind him to make sure he did not fall.

He stopped only feet from the exit. He was looking at the hatch on the wall where the fire hose was lodged. It was a see through glass window with the familiar "fire logo" on it. Inside the window was forty feet of fire hose connected to the rest stop water supply line. In the center of the hose hanging on a hook looking polished and shiny was a stereotypical fire axe. It was right out of the movies. The ax was bright red with a silver blade and a sharp edge on the back end of it. The handle had BIG MIKE'S marked on it in press-on black letters.

Mark looked at Heather and nodded at it. "Get that," he instructed.

"The hose?"

"The axe," he replied.

"You think that would stop her?" Heather asked doubtfully. The look Mark shot her made her realize he was done answering questions and simply wanted to be obeyed and get the hell out of here. She was not offended by this; in fact she was more than happy to oblige him. She opened the glass door and took the axe from its hook. Before they continued Heather looked back into the stop. It was full of darkness and shadows. It was the last time she would ever see Big Mike's Rest Stop. It was the last time anyone would ever set foot in one of the busiest spots on this interstate. She held the axe down to her side and Mark put his hand on her shoulder.

"It's over," he said. It was meant to be words of encouragement. Somehow it worked. Heather allowed Mark to wrap his arm around her shoulder and the two of them made their way outside.

30

Aftermath

"Mr. Green?"

Eric Green had his head in his hands and was staring at the cold metal tabletop under his elbows. His head was pounding; he wanted to scream and cry but could do neither.

"Mr. Green?" said the voice again. Oh, he was insistent and completely irritating, Eric thought.

Reluctantly, Eric looked up at the man who was in his late forties and was wearing a very expensive designer suit. His tie probably cost more than Eric's entire wardrobe. The man had a thick, dark Tom Selleck-like moustache that didn't really suit him. He was staring at Eric with his piercing inquisitive eyes.

"I've told you everything I know," Eric insisted, speaking slowly and concisely.

The man sighed. "Mr. Green, you have to appreciate my situation here. Your wife and a handful of other people in the area went missing. On top of that, an extremely busy rest stop explodes into flames in the middle of a snow storm only an hour after you left there."

"Appreciate your situation Agent?" Eric said sarcastically. "I don't think you even comprehend my situation. I was out on that road helping that kid and his girlfriend."

"Sheila...Watson?" the agent confirmed on his sheet. Eric nodded.

"Yes, Sheila and her boyfriend. I turned around and her boyfriend is gone and so is my wife and kids." "But you claim your son...Dan..."

"Dane," Eric corrected him.

"Dane...was in the middle of the road all by himself, just laying there."

"He was. He was in his car seat, but in the middle of the road. My wife would have never left him like that," Eric insisted. His tears were building again and he had to swallow the lump in his throat.

"And then?" the agent questioned.

"I took Dane and Sheila and I walked to the rest stop." The agent clearly wanted more than this so Eric continued. "There was no one at the rest stop except a Priest and a trucker."

"A Priest?"

"Yes that's right. Noah White was his name. The rest stop was open but there was no one working there. It was like they had all vanished. Noah and the trucker both said they were with people but they both stepped outside for one reason or another and when they came back in, their companions were gone."

"So you called the police?"

"Of course I did. People were missing, including my wife and daughter. We called the police and they sent a cruiser to get all of us.

They were supposed to send back units to investigate the rest stop."

The agent nodded. "And they did. But when they returned, the entire stop was engulfed in flames. According to the fire Marshall's report the cause of the fire was a leak in the propane lines." The agent closed the folder that was open in front of him. "Where's your wife Mr. Green?"

Eric stood up, shoving back the plastic chair he was sitting in. It scraped on the bare cement floors. "Dammit, I have no clue. Don't you understand? I didn't just come to this hospital by my own volition. You all called me...you all called me and told me you found my daughter,

30

Hannah, and now you won't let me see her. Where is my daughter dammit!" he screamed.

The agent, who was an agent of the FBI, cleared his throat and began to gather his things. "Your daughter, Mr. Green, was found by the team that went to investigate the stop. She was found nearly frozen on the side of the highway walking completely alone."

"Oh, dear God, Hannah. Is she alright?" Eric asked.

"That would be a question for her doctors and I think I have all I need for now so I will let them take you from here. The specialist that has been tending to her is in the hall." He stood and opened the door, stepping aside for Eric to leave. "Mr. Green," the agent said before he left. Eric turned to face the man. "This isn't over. I will need to speak with you again." Eric nodded and left the room. There was an older gentleman waiting for him in the hallway of the hospital. This was a children's hospital in downtown Pittsburgh. They were in a lock down ward for specific types of cases though Eric could not understand what this was all about. He only knew that they had found Hannah. Andrea had not been with her and she had not spoken a single word since they found her. It had taken them nearly two days to identify Hannah and find Eric. His little girl had been without her family for two days.

"Mr. Green?" the doctor said. He smiled and offered his hand. Eric shook the man's hand reluctantly. He didn't feel much like being cordial. The man was using a dark colored mahogany cane to support himself on. Eric wondered if it was just an injury or something more permanent. The truth is the doctor walked with a distinctive limp having been shot in the foot less than three days ago. He told people it was during a botched mugging attempt and that "they should see the other guy," which always elicited some laughter.

"Doctor, may I please see my little girl."

"Of course, this way." The doctor led Eric down a long, very bland, white hallway with overhead lights that seemed piercing. Eric had to slow his pace so he could stay in step with the limping doctor. He used a key on a large set of double wide metal blue doors. It was marked "Pediatric Psychiatric Care." The doctor noticed Eric frowning when he saw that. "We are just taking precautions. We didn't want your daughter to wander off. You understand, she hasn't spoken, not a word." Eric did not reply. They continued up the hallway. It seemed brutally silent in this wing of the hospital. "Your son Dane, is he alright?"

Eric nodded. "He is. He had some minor frostbite from our walk to the rest stop but otherwise he's fine. He's with his grandparents today. I dropped him off when I got the call...about Hannah." The two men walked several more feet before Eric spoke again. "She hasn't said a single word?"

"Nothing. She is completely catatonic; she is currently being fed via syringe and IV. I must warn you, Mr Green, it may be hard for you to see. She's been here nearly 48 hours and she just sits there, eyes open, no response whatsoever."

"Was there damage from the cold? Is she healthy?"

"We ran a battery of tests and everything came back fine. She had a touch of hypothermia but nothing that isn't easily treated. She simply refuses to connect with us. We are hoping that she will respond to you."

The two men approached a door with a long window in it. Beside the window was marked room number 943. Hanging from the side of the door was a clipboard with Hannah's medical chart on it. They stopped and the doctor turned to face Eric. "I want you to understand Mr. Green that even if your daughter does speak to you, she may not be coherent. Some of what she says is likely to be...confused and created in her own mind. She has been through something very traumatic." Eric nodded and looked to the door anxiously. The doctor smiled. "Of course, go on in and see your daughter."

"Thank you doctor...," Eric replied. The doctor shifted his cane to his other hand.

"Raines. Thomas Raines," he replied offering his hand again. Eric shook it. Dr. Raines opened the hospital room door and stepped aside so Eric could enter. The door closed behind him and Raines stayed in the window looking in at them.

Eric walked into the room and looked around. It was a small room but not cramped. It had bright yellow walls with stencils of various zoo animals on them. It was at least an attempt at making the room child friendly. Hannah Green sat at a small desk, much like an old school desk, with coloring pages in front of her that were left uncolored. She sat straight up and stared at the wall. She was wearing a pink T-shirt with a kitten on the front and navy blue corduroy shorts. This must have been something that the hospital had found for her to wear. Eric looked at her curiously. She did not move. Eric sat down on the small bed with the crisp blue hospital sheets tightly pulled across them. He was right behind where Hannah was sitting and staring. Eric did not see Raines glaring at them in the window. Hannah did nothing when Eric sat down.

"Hi Hannah, its Daddy," Eric said quietly. The little girl did not turn her head. There was no response. "Do you want to talk about what happened?" he asked her. Still nothing. "Hannah, where is Mommy?"

Finally her head turned but only slightly. Her back remained to her father but her head turned and looked at the door of the hospital room. Raines was still looking through the long window. His eyes locked with Hannah's for the first time. She had not given any indication that she recognized Raines up to this point. She stared at him blankly. Eric followed her gaze to where Raines was standing.

Raines smiled at her and nodded.

"I needed fodder. I needed prey to see how she hunts. I needed to know how she eliminates and kills.

We tracked her from Wolf's Head hundreds of miles to this very spot....she massacred 22 people in Wolf's Head, New Jersey."

Hannah's piercing eyes widened, her pupils dilated and Dr. Raines felt a knot in his stomach. She recognized him. She wasn't catatonic, not truly anyways. Seeing him clearly got a response from her and now she was looking right at him, not through him or even in his direction but at him. Raines opened the door and stepped into the room. He cleared his throat and smiled at her. "Hannah, sweetheart, do you know who I am?" he whispered to the little girl. Hannah only stared. Her hand rose very slowly from her lap. She was turned now and facing him completely and her hand lifted and her index finger extended until she was pointing directly at Thomas Raines. She continued to point at him. "Stop that," he demanded forcefully. She did not.

"Dr. Raines, please don't speak to my daughter in that tone," Eric said, getting off the bed and kneeling next to Hannah. She still made no indication that she recognized her own father. She continued to stare at Raines with her finger pointing at him.

"She's gonna find you," Hannah whispered. The first words she had spoken since they found her.

Raines turned to the door and fumbled with the handle before getting it right and quickly leaving the room. He turned and walked towards the exit of the south wing. Eric looked at his daughter and tried to put his arm around her. "Hannah, sweetheart?" She continued to ignore him and stood up. When a nurse peered into the room to see why Dr. Raines had left so quickly Hannah was standing in the center of the room, hands at her side, staring at the door. Her father knelt behind her calling her name.

It was at that moment Hannah Green began to sing. It wasn't loud at first but before long the nurses at the desk could just faintly hear her lovely voice. Although impossible Thomas Raines would swear he could hear her singing as well even as he hurried to the hospital parking lot.

"What a friend we have in Jesus, all our sins and griefs to bear! What a privilege to carry, everything to God in prayer. Oh, what peace we often forfeit, Oh, what needless pain we bear,

All because we do not carry, everything to God in prayer!"

The story continues in Isolation